THANÁTOU

THE BLOOD WITCH SAGA
BOOK 1

NATALIE J. CASE

This book is dedicated to my family, both blood and chosen. You inspire me every day.

And to my beta readers/editors for the incredible feedback.

CHAPTER 1
OF UNKNOWN ORIGIN

My earliest memories are of blood, the hot, sticky taste of it on my tongue, the strange, copper scent of it suffocating me. I had no context for these things. I knew that I was small, and I knew that the stain of it was on my soul, but like so much of my life before I was ten, I could only guess.

That was where my life began, on my tenth birthday.

It began on a bench outside a police station one early Saturday morning. I was found in a semi-catatonic state, sitting with an old beat-up suitcase containing a few changes of clothing, and a backpack with a note inside giving my name, Thána Augusta Celene Alizon Archer, and age, along with a few books and a stuffed dog named Rusty.

I was found during shift change, and my next hours and days were filled with fear and disorientation as I was taken from the police station to the hospital, and from there to a group home. I spent the better part of a year there before they found me a place in foster care. All searches for my parents came up empty. All attempts to figure out where I'd come from came to nothing.

At times, nightmares would soak my dreams with terror, taking me back to that memory. I would wake gasping and rubbing at my skin, trying to clean the blood from it. I was

1

always off-kilter for days when it happened, and it took me until I was nearly seventeen to realize that it always happened on the same night every year. I guessed it was some kind of anniversary.

I was luckier than some, my tour through foster care only saw three homes, and I only left the first one when my foster mother got a job transfer to Texas and the second one because the couple was divorcing. I arrived at my final foster home one week before the start of school my junior year of high school. I graduated near the top of my class, which wasn't hard considering the number of stoners in the class, and I managed to scrape up a few scholarships and grants to apply toward my state college degree. I worked at a bookstore just off campus to supplement my education and allow me to eat. It also served to keep me in books, and even allowed me to indulge my passion for "ye Old English" and the study of the surviving literature from the time. I was wise enough to know that the job prospects were small in such a rarified field, so I graduated with a business degree just generic enough to afford me a chance at almost any kind of job in the corporate world I decided to chase, though I continued to take elective classes to feed my love.

I entered the adult workforce a month after graduation, starting in a mid-sized company that produced small gadgets, at the time it was largely calculators and the like. I started in the quality control group. By the time I was nearing thirty, I had worked my way into middle management. The next year, our company got absorbed into a bigger company, and eventually, I was relocated to El Paso, Texas to work in one of their plants.

I was in a small rental apartment, most of my belongings still in storage back in New York, making do with a bed, armchair, and a bistro table. It wasn't like the place mattered all that much. I knew going in that it was temporary. I was going to be there a year tops before I was sent to Silicon Valley to manage a new product line. I was running late to work one morning in late October, thumbing through a file folder of employee reviews on my way to the car when I heard a man clear his throat. I glanced up and involuntarily took a step back.

The man was disheveled and out of place, his black, dust-covered clothes looking like something from an earlier century, or a black and white movie from the fifties. He had a hat atop his mop of black curls, which hung well below his shoulders, with a ridiculous feather tucked in the band. It alone seemed untouched by dust, or maybe it was sand, its blue and green ruffled by the light breeze. He cleared his throat again and stepped closer. "Thána Alizon?"

I wasn't sure who this man was or why he knew my name, even if he was pronouncing it as if the h wasn't there, but I found myself nodding slowly. "Thána, actually. Like thick. And my last name is Archer. And you are?" Alizon was a part of my name according to the note in my backpack all those years ago, but it had given my last name as Archer. It spooked me a little bit that he knew that part of my name.

"No one of consequence. I came to warn you."

My eyebrow arched of its own accord. "Warn me?"

He nodded urgently, stepping toward me again. "You are in danger here."

"Right." I dismissed him and moved to my car, unlocking the door, and tossing my briefcase and the review file onto the passenger seat. "Look, buddy, Halloween is next week."

"I know, that's what I'm here to warn you about. You must be vigilant."

"Right," I said again, getting into the car. "Go try your line on someone else. Halloween's a pain in the ass, but it isn't anything more. I'm late for work."

"Yes, very late," he said, his eyes lifting to the sky.

"Whatever." I started the car and pulled the door shut, shutting out the weird man and his weird warnings. If I broke the speed limit down Railroad Avenue, I might get to the office in time for the morning stand-up meeting. My assistant met me at the door of the conference room with a cup of coffee and my day started. It was much like any other day. I handled time off requests and sat in on meetings about circuit board quality and RMAs. By the time I left to go home, the strange man and his strange warning were all but forgotten, at least until I saw him again.

I stopped at a grocery store to grab a few things because I was sick of takeout in a town where takeout consisted of pizza and Tex-Mex burritos. I had a few things in my cart, and I was rounding the corner onto the cereal aisle when I saw him. He had his hat in his hands and he seemed nervous, more so than he had been that morning.

"Thána Alizon, you must hear me."

"Dude, are you following me?" I asked, fishing in my pocket for my cell phone. "I could call the cops."

He shook his head almost violently and held out one hand. "The police cannot help you. Let me."

"Look, I don't know what you think is going to happen to me, but I'm a big girl and I can take care of myself. So, get lost."

"You can't handle **this**, not without help."

"I've had enough of your crap. Leave me alone." I pushed past him in a fit of anger, grabbing a box of store-brand granola and throwing it in my cart on my way to the checkout. The man had put me in a foul mood, and I still had to finish employee reviews.

I purchased my meager supplies which mostly consisted of food I could microwave, the granola, and two bottles of wine. Fortunately, my apartment complex was only a few blocks away and I could get home, put away the food and open a bottle of wine. A nice pinot noir would be a good companion to reviews. It wasn't like I'd known any of these people for more than eight months, so my evaluation of them wasn't going to be at full value.

With a bag of microwave popcorn and a glass of pinot, I dropped into the comfort of the plush recliner. Taking a sip of wine, I tucked the popcorn between my thigh and the arm of the chair and reached for the folder. I'd groused that the process wasn't automated and digitized, but I'm fairly sure it fell on deaf ears. Our plant manager was the kind of guy that wanted everything in hard copy, even to the point of making his secretary print out all of his emails.

I worked my way diligently through the folder, and the bottle of wine, until I got to the last few reviews. I'd saved the hardest two for last. Juan Cordova and his buddy Rodrigo Alvaro, the two troublemakers on the line. With a sigh I got up to pour the last of the bottle into my glass, shaking my head as I considered how rough to be on them in the review. They were always the last two to come in for their shift, maybe not late every day, but cutting it close. More than once they'd come back from lunch break with the smell of beer or tequila on their breath. They did good work, most of the time, and Juan's soldering technique was among the best in the plant.

Deciding to come down closer to the middle, I wrote praise for what they both did well and marked them down for attitude and attendance, and called the whole thing done. I was ahead of schedule, which was how I liked it. I could start the one-on-one conversations with them the following week and have them all turned in to my boss before the November first deadline.

I downed the last of the wine, threw the popcorn bag in the trash, and decided to head to bed. It was early, but so was my alarm. I double-checked the door lock, changed into my pajamas, which basically meant a T-shirt and shorts, and climbed into bed. It was a warm night, and I pushed the comforter to the end of the bed and fell into the warm fuzziness of the slight buzz from the wine.

Pounding on my door woke me some hours later, pulling me up from dreams about blood and ash. I stumbled to the door, disoriented. Strong hands pulled me out of the door when I opened it, and that scared me into wakefulness. Sirens swirled in the air around me and the strong arms belonged to the building manager who was shaking even as he let go of me. The building was aflame, residents staring and standing sullen in puddles of water from the hoses trying to quench the flames.

I joined them, watching wordlessly as firefighters tried valiantly to save the building. I blinked and tried to climb out of my wine-soaked brain failure, my vision temporarily obscured by that frustrating and frightening memory. It wasn't coherent, and it changed from time to time, but there was always blood, a lot of it, and sometimes maybe fire. Someone died. Of that I was sure. I pinched the bridge of my nose and pushed the whole thing away. I hadn't figured the dream out in the twenty-two years since waking up on that bench, I wasn't going to figure it out standing there in a puddle of water in my bare feet in the early hours of the morning.

By the time the sun was up, the fire was out, and water dripped from what was left of the building. My apartment still had walls, but the ceiling had been burned away and everything inside was smoke and water logged. One of the firemen brought me some stuff from my dresser, including Rusty the stuffed dog, and my briefcase that had been near the door, and they rescued the folder from the kitchen counter, though that too had been soaked. Everything was dripping wet and stunk of smoke.

There was talk about where we would stay and how it would be arranged, followed by most of us breaking up into small groups. For once I was grateful to have left my cell phone in the car and for the fact that I kept a spare key in a magnetic box hidden under the back bumper. I called into work to let them know I wouldn't be in. My boss was sympathetic and told me to let her know if I needed anything. I sort of laughed and told her I needed just about everything.

That was when I saw him again, the strange man. His suit was clean and unwrinkled, his hair practically shined in the morning sun. His green eyes were watching me as I got out of the car and started toward the property manager. I detoured toward the man. "Did you do this?" I asked when I got close enough, my voice pitched a bit higher than normal.

"Of course not. I warned you."

"No, you were a cryptic creep. Is this what you were warning me about?"

"I told you it isn't safe. They know where you are."

"Who?" I asked, crossing my arms. It probably looked ridiculous in my shorts, T-shirt, and bare feet, but I knew that when properly suited for work, it had a withering effect on anyone I leveled the look at.

"I could explain it all if you would just come with me."

I shook my head. "I'm not going anywhere with you. Explain now or I'll tell the fire marshal that you were acting strange and following me."

He shook his head and tried to take my hand to lead me away. "Please, it isn't safe. They weren't sure which apartment you were in, but now you're exposed. They are probably watching us right now."

"Wait, are you saying that whoever started this fire was looking for me?"

"It fits their way. They would kill an entire building of people just to flush you out so that they could get to you."

I don't know if it was the fire, the old memory dancing in the back of my mind or what, but somehow his words chilled me. "Who would want me dead?" I asked, glancing around us. "I'm nobody special."

"It isn't so much you specifically, and they're trying to kidnap you…so that they can kill you later. Come with me, I will keep you safe."

"I'm not going anywhere with you. I don't even know your name."

He took a step back and removed his hat, sort of bowing toward me. "Forgive my manners. I am Finneas Connor. I was a friend of your father's."

That brought me up short. "My father?" I shook my head. "I've never had a father. Or a mother. You clearly have the wrong person."

7

"How many Thána Alizons do you think exist in this world? I am not mistaken. Neither are they."

"Who are they?" I asked, frustrated now that I'd let him draw me in this far. "You keep saying 'they' but you're not explaining."

"It is a long story, one better told by a warm fire with a glass of brandy. Come."

"I've had enough fire for one day, thanks." I turned away and started back toward my car. I needed to try to get the smell of smoke out of my clothes and find a pair of shoes and sort out what else I needed. I didn't have time for fairy tales.

"Who is that?"

I looked up to find the woman who lived in the apartment beside mine. "Some whack job," I responded. "He says he knew my father." I snorted and looked back at him. "I didn't even know my father, so…" I let the thought trail off before looking back up at her. "Sheila, right? So, what are we doing?"

"Chuck's getting us set up at that motel across the street, at least short-term. Bill has been through this before." She pointed at a man I didn't know. "He lost a house about five years ago. He said he'd help with getting through the Red Cross stuff and whatever. He's collecting information for them."

I nodded, locking my car with its reeking pile of clothes and my briefcase. At least I had that which meant I had my wallet, so I could get money. I followed Sheila to where Chuck, the building manager, was on the phone. All in all, there were about ten of us out of a home, all of us in our thirties and early forties. All of us without spouses or families. We were a sad lot.

By noon, we were checked into the motel and able to shower. Bill had scrounged up clothes for us with the help of the Red Cross. I pulled the track pants on without bothering with the underwear of unknown origin and tugged on the T-shirt over the sports bra they'd given me. The bra barely covered my larger than average breasts but held me in tight. Everything was very clearly secondhand, especially the broken-in sneakers, but I was dressed. That meant I could get food and clothes for work in the morning.

I returned to the bathroom to pull a comb through my hair once the mirror had defogged. My black hair was super curly, except that I visited a salon once a month to get it chemically straightened. Left to its own devices, it would become a mop of frizz. I seldom bothered with makeup, my vaguely olive skin was naturally smooth and evenly colored, and I'd always thought that eye shadow and mascara and the like were just too much work for every day.

My dark-green eyes looked dull and tired, which I suppose was a pretty fair assessment of my state of being at that moment. I wasn't sure how much sleep I'd gotten between the end of that bottle of wine and the fire.

Satisfied that I was presentable enough for hitting the mall, I grabbed my car keys and headed out, though I admit to glancing furtively around me as I went, vaguely afraid some boogeyman was going to jump out to grab me.

CHAPTER 2
WORDS ON A PAGE

My assistant, Jessica Flores, met me at the door with coffee and a frown the next morning. "Why are you here?"

I took the coffee and drank nearly half of it in one go. The motel had miserable coffee. "I work here, last I checked."

"No one expects you to be here."

"You did," I countered, lifting the coffee cup.

"Well, I know you better than the rest. Here are the notes from yesterday, I figured you'd want to see them before the stand-up."

"Thanks." In return, I handed her the now mostly dry file folder with the employee reviews. "I think I saved them. Mostly. Can you go through them and make sure everything is legible?" I took the notes, glancing over the page. "Have we figured out what is causing the excessive solder problem on the wave line?"

She shook her head. "John Padilla is going over the boards from yesterday. He thinks it's a board design issue."

I nodded and turned toward the conference room. "Make sure I get results from him by close of business." We parted ways, and I took a moment to take a big breath and steady myself before facing the assembled line supervisors and product managers. I waded through all of the platitudes and attempts at offering me comfort without actually throwing any punches, which I figured was something I didn't get enough credit for on a day-to-day basis.

By the time the end of the day rolled around, my shoulders were tight, and my head was throbbing, and I wanted to go back to the crappy motel and crawl into its crappy bed and try to sleep more than I had the night before. However, Jessica reminded me that we were supposed to be meeting at the Iron Horse for drinks for one of my inspectors' birthday.

I pulled into the local watering hole, which doubled as a biker bar, and promised myself a single drink and the minimal amount of socializing before I got out of the car. I half expected Finneas whatever his name was to be lurking in the shadows, or maybe his mysterious bad guys. I put him out of my mind and headed inside the Iron Horse Saloon, where I could see a group of my product line was already in full swing. Lupe, who was the birthday girl, was laughing, bent over the table as I came in and approached the bar.

I held up two fingers to the bartender, then indicated Lupe and dropped a twenty on the bar. Best to get my birthday drink out of the way early so I could skip out. Debbie poured two shots of tequila and hung a lime wedge on each glass. I took it to the table as Lupe sat up, wiping her eyes.

"Boss, you made it!" Lupe stood, her smile wide. "You didn't have to, you know?"

I smiled and handed her the shot. "Wouldn't miss it." One of the guys passed the saltshaker and I dutifully mirrored Lupe's movements to down the shot. They all moved seats so I could sit and my lead, Arturo, leaned close enough that I could hear him over the general din. "Hey, don't feel like you need to stay. We all know what you're going through."

I nodded at him. "I got nothing to go home to but an empty motel room with a crappy bed, worse coffee, and a broken hot tub."

He crinkled his nose, then lifted his hand to signal Debbie, then a circle to indicate he was buying a round. "I don't need another," I said.

He chuckled. "Everybody needs another."

"I have to drive home." Nevertheless, I did the shot with the rest of them. Which meant I had to stay and buy a round for the whole group.

Before I knew it, I was four shots in and starting to regret my decision to come in the first place. I got up to go to the bathroom and stopped at the bar on the way through. "One for everyone but me, I need caffeine and food. Peter still in the kitchen?"

Debbie nodded. "Nachos, fries, and some wings?"

"Am I that predictable?"

"Only when you're drinking tequila," Debbie answered. "You should stick to whiskey."

"Tell me about it." I was a little unsteady on my feet as I made my way into the tiny bathroom with two stalls that seemed to shrink every time I came in the place. My head was buzzy, and my stomach reminded me that I hadn't stopped for lunch that day, making that greasy roach-coach breakfast burrito at morning break my only food. I relieved myself and washed up, stopping back at the bar to give Debbie my credit card to run for the round and the food.

I hung around another hour, keeping to my diet coke, and eating until I felt like I was sober enough to walk the three blocks to the motel because I had no delusions about being sober enough to drive. I wished Lupe a happy birthday one last time and made my exit, tucking my keys between my fingers like they'd taught me in my sixth grade PE self-defense class because I had three blocks to walk, and it was close to midnight in a city that had a lot of violence. Not that I had a lot of illusions about fighting off thieves and rapists, but I wasn't afraid to slash and run.

I could walk back and get the car in the morning. Most of the walk was through a residential area, but the last of it was on well-lit and busy streets. I was cutting through the parking lot of the nearly defunct shopping center and could see the door of my motel room when I heard tires squealing and looked behind me to see a car barreling right toward me. I ran toward what I thought was the safety of the building, but it kept coming, picking up speed.

I jumped to the side, falling and rolling on the broken concrete as the car crashed into the brick wall of what had once been a Dillard's department store. Climbing to my feet, I was already cursing, and obviously not thinking clearly as I yanked open the driver's side door. I only had a second to look before hands were grabbing me and pulling me away.

"Are you crazy?"

I blinked into Finneas's eyes, confused as he pressed me into the wall around the corner from the car. "I'm not the one driving like a fucking lunatic." I pushed him away and moved back to the corner. I could have sworn there was no one behind the wheel. Now there was no car, just the impression it had made in the wall. "What the actual fuck is going on?"

"Like I've been trying to tell you, someone is after you. They would prefer to take you alive, but dead works too."

I rounded on him, shoving him against the wall. "For all I know that someone is you. None of this started happening until you showed up here."

He held up both hands in surrender. "No, not me. As I said, I am a friend of your father's. We heard rumors that someone caught your scent, so I came to try to find you before they did." He chewed his lower lip and bobbled his head a little. "I probably led them to you, now that I think on it, so maybe you're not wrong."

"Tell me why I'm not dragging you up the street to the police?"

"They can't protect you," Finneas said.

"And you can?" I asked, less than amused by the turn my whole existence had taken since this man had come into my life.

"Gods, no. I can only help you find help. My gifts are largely passive, tracking and the like."

"So, help me, you had better start making some sense or I'm going to start throwing punches," I growled the words, getting more irritated with the man as the seconds crawled by.

"May I suggest we get off the streets? No telling where your would-be assassins have gotten themselves off to." He gestured toward the motel, shrugging me off, and ducking around me before straightening his suit coat and adjusting his hat. He set off at a brisk pace, leaving me no real choice but to follow.

I unlocked the door and opened it, my eyes searching around the gloomy room. I half expected someone to jump out of the shadows at me.

"Not to worry, I warded the place before I came to find you," Finneas said, as he held a hand to the door and then murmured something I didn't catch. The whole door seemed to shimmer and then he was pushing me in and following. There was a wooden box on the bed, a trunk really, beautifully carved with ornate scrollwork, and a silver clasp. "I've been holding that for you since…well for quite some time."

"Who **are** you?" I asked, half certain that the answer to that question would only raise ten more.

"Just a family friend."

"I have no family," I responded, though the bite in my words was dulled by my distraction with the box.

"You may find you are wrong," Finneas responded, bowing slightly.

I inhaled, tearing my gaze from the trunk to look at him. I was tired, half-drunk, and ready to be done with all of it. "Get out."

"I'll leave you to your business, but I will be near enough to protect you until you are safe." He tipped his hat toward the trunk. "I think you'll find that your transfer to San Francisco will come sooner than you expect. You need to get there soon. You'll be safer there."

I turned to the trunk, fingering the clasp. "What do you mean I'll be safe…" I turned to look, but Finneas was gone, just like the car.

"Fucking tequila," I muttered. I rubbed my head and stared at the trunk, not entirely sure I wanted to know what was inside. For the moment I decided it could wait and I went to the bathroom to get a glass of water. My head was not going to be a fan of me come morning.

Still rubbing at my head as if that could stop the impending headache once I was sober, I sat on the bed, turning the trunk to face me. It was only slightly smaller than my old steamer trunk had been, but much more beautiful. The bulk of the trunk was a pale wood, nearly white, but the scrollwork and accents were in a rich mahogany. The lock was unlike anything I had seen before, and I wasn't sure exactly how I was supposed to open it. There was something that looked like a button, so I pressed it. For a moment nothing happened.

"Right thumb, please," a voice said.

I looked around, half expecting that Finneas had returned from wherever he had gone, but when the strange man didn't appear, I lifted my right hand to the box and touched my thumb to the lock. There was a whirring sound and then a pop, and the lock opened. For a long moment, I just stared at it, trying to decide if I was drunker than I had thought I was, but really? I had seen a car ram into a brick wall and then just vanish, and a man had disappeared between one word and the next and a strange box had spoken to me.

So, yeah, I decided that it was the tequila and vowed to never let them make me drink it again.

Still, curiosity won me over and I eased open the trunk's lid, shifting closer slowly, half-convinced something was going to jump out of it and eat my face. Instead, I found a neatly ordered trunk filled with what seemed to be family memorabilia from a family I didn't even know. There were baby clothes and a silver rattle, an envelope of baby teeth and as I shifted some of it, my hand found something heavier.

I lifted it slowly. The binding was old leather with an unusual coat of arms etched into the front and it was bigger than a phone book. I sat back against the headboard and let one hand caress the leather reverently. Whoever had crafted this book had been skilled.

I opened the cover, my breath short and escaping from behind my teeth which had clamped down over my lower lip as my heart raced. I don't know exactly what I was expecting, but the first page deflated those expectations.

The words appeared to be in some foreign language that might have been an approximation of Greek or maybe some Cyrillic language, or something like it, but I was only guessing based on some tickling in the back of my brain that I couldn't identify. I couldn't read it, and that was the important bit. With a little less trepidation, I turned a few pages until I came across something I did understand, pictures.

They were old, ancient even, faded and yellowed, the sepia tones bleeding into one another as wizened old faces grinned out of them. Clothing from a century ago or more hung from gaunt frames while toothy grins beamed at the camera. Women wore furs and had hair swept up off graceful necks while men wore suits and hats, not unlike what Finneas wore.

The quality of images improved a few pages in, and I was starting to notice which faces went with which faces, and as I turned another page, I saw a face so similar to mine, I had to look up at the mirror across the room from me to confirm what I was seeing.

She was younger than me, and the picture was sixty or more years old, but those dark eyes that gleamed in a bright afternoon sun were my eyes, and the thick, unruly black hair that hung in curly sheets, all puffed up in the humidity was the image of my own, or mine before I had chopped it to shoulder length and paid a fortune to have it straightened every month.

Her skin was far fairer than mine, however. I baked in the sun like a Thanksgiving Day turkey does in the oven, my skin going from pale olive to a roasted tan that let me blend in with the locals enough that everyone was surprised I didn't actually speak Spanish, other than the little bit I remembered from Ms. Lorenzo's Spanish class in high school.

My finger caressed over her young face, then as I turned a page, an envelope fell from the book, sliding to the floor under my leg. I set the book aside and retrieved the envelope, turning it over to find my name in a beautiful script. It was just my first name, and it was only plain blue ballpoint ink, but it struck me hard. I don't know why, but suddenly it was real…or something.

This trunk had belonged to someone before me, someone who knew me. Someone who was family.

I put the envelope down and stood, pacing to the door, then around the bed, and into the bathroom, round and round while I pulled my hands through my hair and shook my head and tried to deny that any of the last week had happened.

My family was gone. I had accepted that fact a long time ago. I had no family. I had filled those empty holes with my work. I didn't need old wounds ripped open by some fucking magical box from some family who had abandoned me on a park bench when I didn't even know who the hell I was.

I wasn't doing this. I shoved the envelope back into the book, put the book in the trunk, and put the trunk on the wobbly table by the window. I slammed down another glass of water and brushed my teeth, double-checked the lock on the door, and turned off the lights.

I was going to forget the whole damn thing.

CHAPTER 3
MERRY MEET

MY PLAN WORKED, TO FORGET THE ENTIRE WEEK, TO FORGET Finneas, and not look at the trunk. I got through the weekend, got Rusty and my smoked-out clothes to the laundromat to rid them of the final remnants of that mess, and I even went to a Halloween party that a coworker was hosting at her new McMansion in the new subdivision and stayed for nearly a half-hour before I claimed a headache and took off for the motel.

By the time Monday rolled around I was able to put it behind me, as long as I didn't look at the wooden trunk. To solve that problem, I put it in the trunk of my car. Out of sight, and all of that.

Monday, I was juggling my coffee and briefcase to get my badge out of my pocket, when my boss opened the door for me, grinning like she had a secret. "Either you let your husband back in the bedroom, or you got Jaime to actually study for a test," I joked.

She followed me to my desk. "Remember when you told me you couldn't wait to get out of here?"

I raised an eyebrow. "You mean, the day I landed here? It grows on you." The city would never be home, it was too dry, dusty, and stifling for that, but I had started to get used to the place.

She nodded knowingly. "Yeah, but you're not going to say no to a transfer."

That got my attention. "What?"

She held up a hand. "It's not exactly what was promised, but they have a product line that's struggling, and their manager just walked out. Corporate office wants to send you out early, see if you can get it on its feet again."

"Isn't that what I was supposed to be doing here?" I asked, turning on the computer.

"You have. Your line has improved tremendously. I'm giving it to Alex. It's a step up for him. They want you in San Francisco by the end of the week."

I blinked at her, trying to catch up. At least I didn't have a house to sell, or much in the way of belongings. "Okay…so what's the incentive for me?"

"Pay increase now, and another when you get the move to the new product line, plus a housing benefit for the first three months to give you time to get settled. They have corporate housing. There's a furnished apartment waiting on you."

I sipped my coffee and nodded slowly. "I guess I better get Alex in here and start getting him up to speed." Alex was a good guy, and he had the chops to be a good manager. He'd started out on the lines, moved up to line lead, then to inspector, and from there he had been working under a senior product manager for more than a year while he finished his BA. This would be his first position with the title manager, but he had the skills.

I spent the time from then to the morning meeting getting my things together for him, which was fairly easy, considering I always knew the job there was short-term. I'd expected another six months, in reality, but I wasn't going to argue with the change. I wanted out of El Paso after the week I'd had.

We told the product line later that day and had a brief going away party at lunch on Tuesday. Before the sun was up on

Wednesday, I was on the road, headed west. It was October 31st, Halloween. I wasn't a big holiday person. Holidays always made me feel like the interloper I was, lurking in the background of my foster family's happiness.

Halloween was worse than Christmas at times. My costumes were always hand-me-downs from years past, worn by other foster kids before me and trick-or-treating always felt far too close to begging for me to be comfortable. It was just as good to be on the road then. I wouldn't have to deal with trick or treaters or anything.

I got as far as Los Angeles and got a hotel room. I left the mysterious trunk with its mysterious contents in the trunk of the car, but pulled in my suitcase, and grabbed Rusty off the dashboard. Maybe it was silly, a grown woman hauling around a stuffed animal that was so threadbare and worn, patched in multiple places, and goofy looking, but it was the only thing I had left of the time before, and I'd gotten accustomed to always having him near.

I planned on ordering pizza and getting a good night's sleep so I could head out fresh in the morning. It was six and a half hours to the corporate housing place, and I wanted to get there with enough time to check in with my new boss.

Two bites in, there was a knock on my door. I muted the TV, which I'd set to a news station, and went to the door. I looked through the peephole, squinting at the old woman on the other side. "Girl, stop eyeballing me and open this door," the woman demanded, making me step back.

"I don't know you," I responded, frowning at the door.

"Of course you don't, but I aim to fix that. Now, open this door."

I will probably never understand the impulse at that moment to do as she said, but I unlocked the door and opened it. There in the hotel hallway was the most unlikely woman I had ever seen. She was old, in her eighties or nineties maybe; I'm a terrible judge of age. Her hair was an array of white with blue, purple, red, and yellow braids that were arranged in a mess of swoops and loops spilling out from under a precariously perched green top hat with yellow tulle exploding out one side.

The wrinkles around her eyes seemed to make them sharp somehow, and her nose showed signs that it had been broken at some point in her life. Her emerald green dress was like something from a Victorian painting and yet didn't seem out of place in the least. She tut-tutted at me and waved her intricately carved cane in my direction before bustling herself over the threshold and into my room. "Not even a beginner's warding. Really, this simply won't do!" She dropped an old-fashioned handbag onto the bed and turned to look me over. "Close the door, dear. You're letting in the bugs."

I was staring. I knew I was staring. I shook my head and closed the door, confused about what exactly was happening. "Who are you?"

"Ah, yes. Good. You have at least some common sense then. I am Merry Ander-Wheather. Your—" she squinted at me like she was trying to remember something, "Your great-aunt."

"What?" I was still stuck on the sight of her and the way she barged into the room. I looked at her again and realized. "Finneas." I pinched the bridge of my nose and held my breath, wishing the whole mess away.

"The dear boy did say he was having trouble getting through to you. That's why I'm here instead. We felt maybe family would be more—"

Cold rage dumped into my stomach, and I threw the piece of pizza in my hand in the general direction of the box. "I have no family." I ground the words from between my teeth and stepped toward her menacingly. I had nearly a foot of height on her, but she was clearly not intimidated.

She drew herself up to her full height, planting her cane between us like some kind of boundary. "You may not know it yet, Thána Augusta Celene Alizon, but you do indeed have a vast and varied family who have spent **years** looking for you."

I took a step back. "I'm not that hard to find." I had never heard my full name pronounced that way. Like Finneas, she said Thána with that odd inflection, the h nearly silent. I'd only ever seen the full name written, on that note in my backpack that day. Everyone ignored my middle names. I was just Thána Archer most of the time, though I did have a couple of foster sisters that called me Arch. I turned away from her, hiding the tears that had welled up unexpectedly. "I lived in the same town for years."

She was staring at me; I could feel her. "I mean, the same place where I was left. Twenty-two years ago." The anger stirred again, and I turned back. "You should have started there."

Her black eyes softened, and she nodded sadly. She pulled the only chair in the room closer to her and climbed up on it. She was so short her feet didn't reach the floor. "Oh, mi paidí, I know." Her voice took on an accent of some sort, but I couldn't place it. Maybe Greek, but not really. "If we had known where she took you...but everything was so—" she waved her hands and shook her head. "There is time for that when we are all safe."

"Safe?" I asked. "Safe from what? Disappearing cars?"

"Finneas told us, of course. Their methods are crude." She shook her head. "There is much for you to learn, dearest Thána. So much. For now, let us just call them 'those that wish you dead'."

I closed my eyes and pinched the bridge of my nose again, as if the action could magic me back to before Finneas. It was all too much. My stomach churned with rage, mixed with an age-old desperation for family, and I thought for a moment I might be sick from it all.

"I should have come myself to begin with, but then, I am no tracker like Finneas."

I turned to look at her, and for a moment I was reminded of a woman's face I had seen in that book that was in the trunk Finneas had given me. It was the eyes. Her face was set round with wrinkles and her hair had lost the shiny black of youth, but her picture was in the book. "So, Great-Aunt then?" I asked. "And you're here to...what, exactly? Tell me I'm a fairy princess and whisk me away to a magical land to ride unicorns and drink dewdrop tea?"

She snorted. "Heavens no, child." She shook her head vigorously and laughed so that the entire chair shook. "No royal blood in either of your family lines...well, except that Lord... whatshisname five generations back on your father's side, but his family was disgraced long before we rejected the monarchy as a governing system." Her eyes swept the room. "Where's the trunk?"

I was frowning so hard my face hurt and I tried to force myself to relax the muscles, at least a little. "What?"

"The trunk. Finneas did give you the trunk?"

Right, the one with the magic lock on it. "It's in my car."

"Oh, no, that won't do." She stood up and bustled to the door. "It's not safe out there."

"It's fine," I answered. "It's locked in the trunk."

"Oh, child, you have much to learn. We must bring it inside."

"I don't want it inside," I said abruptly, moving so I was between her and the door. "I don't want it at all, honestly."

Her face clouded over, and she stared at me for a long time like she couldn't believe I had said such a thing. "You can throw away your heritage, Thána, if that is what you desire, but it will not protect you one little bit from those who mean to end you before you've begun. Now, go and get the trunk, and be quick about it."

I grabbed my keys from the dresser, shaking my head as I went out the door and down the stairs to my car. I popped open the trunk and took the ornate box out, setting it on the ground so I could close the trunk again. I had no idea why I was humoring the crazy old woman. If I'd had to guess it was that little girl inside who ached with not knowing her family, latching on to the first semblance of family that presented itself.

When I got back to the room, Merry was busy emptying her

handbag on my bed. I shut the door and crossed the room to put the trunk on the table. "What are you doing?" I asked.

Merry didn't answer, just started humming and she took a bag of rocks to the door. I watched her stack them in sets of two. The rocks were nearly perfect cubes and they seemed to catch the light as she moved. When she had four sets of rocks spaced evenly across the front of the door, she sat back, her mouth moving, though I heard no sound.

There was a flash, and something seemed to extend up from the rocks to cover the door. It was see-through, but it shimmered in the light from the nearby lamp. "There now, that's better."

I squinted at the door and moved closer. "What is it?"

"Wards," Merry answered, moving back toward the bed. "A simple sort of wards to guard a door or window."

I ghosted my hand over the shimmering surface. Static electricity filled the gap between my hand and the barrier, prickling my palm with energy. When I turned around, Merry had retaken the chair and was happily munching on a piece of my pizza.

"I'm starting to think this whole thing is just some crazy tequila-fueled nightmare," I muttered, shaking my head. "Maybe if I go to sleep now, I'll wake up back in my apartment and none of this will have been real."

Merry apparently found that funny, her eyes twinkling at me as she chuckled. "Come, Thána, you know in your heart what is real." She tapped the box with her cane. "Open."

"You're awfully bossy for a woman I just met," I muttered, but I dutifully pressed my thumb to the lock and the lock opened. I reached into the box and pulled out the book, opening it where the envelope had been stuck into it.

"You haven't read it yet?" Merry asked, jabbing a finger at the envelope.

"No." I still didn't want to read it. Instead, I pointed to a picture. "Is this you?"

She leaned in, her eyes crinkling as one finger traced over the much younger face. "Ah yes. The woman beside me is your grandmother, my sister. Her name was Celene Edith. Now she was a powerful woman."

I looked back at the picture. Celene Edith stood inches taller than Merry in the image, a rich-looking fur coat drawn around her. She was well-coiffed, her dark hair smoothed and shaped and swept up into a tidy knot while Merry beside her looked like she had crawled out of bed for the picture, her hair a wild mass of black curls.

"You should read the letter."

Merry's voice pulled me back from the picture and her finger poked the envelope closer to me.

"Maybe I don't want to," I responded. "What good could it do? It doesn't change the fact that I was left abandoned with no memory of who I was." The words sounded overly bitter, even in my ears. I was behaving like an adolescent.

I snatched the envelope and paced the room with it. Unopened, it was nothing significant, just some artifact of a long-forgotten past. Once it was opened, everything changed.

"I can tell you only that you were loved, child," Merry said, her words softly hanging in the air between us. "Your mother saw no other recourse to keep you safe."

"My mother?" I had long ago come to grips with the notion that either my parents were dead, victims of some horrific death that was so great I blocked it, and them, from my mind completely, or that they were heinous people who couldn't be bothered with me.

Neither of them gave me great comfort, but it seemed easier than what Merry was saying, what secret this envelope held. "I can't take you the next step on this journey until you've read the words your mother left for you," Merry said.

I sighed and turned the envelope over. I was being silly. Just open it. I slipped a finger under the flap and broke the seal. A folded piece of paper was all the envelope contained. I pulled it out and unfolded it, turning to the light from the window to read it.

CHAPTER 4
REMEMBER ME

My dearest Thána,

My beautiful child, forgive me for what I have done. I was desperate to keep you safe from the men who killed your father. I hoped that by blocking your gifts and hiding us from your memory you might escape their grasp.

The spell I used was powerful magic but has already begun to erode. If you are reading this, a blood tracker was able to find you, and the time has come for the spell to be undone.

The words below will pull the string and allow your gift and memory to unspool. Everything you need is here in this trunk. The house awaits you; the key and deed are here.

If I can, I will come to you there and we can be a family once more. Until then, be safe.

Love,

Alana Alizon, your mother

I WANTED TO CRUMBLE THE PAPER UP AND THROW IT AWAY, BUT MY eyes were drawn to the tidy script over and over. At the bottom of the page, there was a series of strange words, foreign and weird. My mouth moved, sounding out the words in a hushed rush. *"Me aftés tis léxeis, anatrépste ti échei gínei."*

"Ginei, the G should sound like a Y…" Merry said as she watched me. "And soften the x in *léxeis.*"

I repeated the words with her corrections and held my breath. I don't know what I was expecting, but nothing obvious happened.

Merry, on the other hand, looked thrilled. "Good, good. You should probably sleep now. That spell will take its toll."

"And what about you?" I asked.

"I'll be right here, keeping watch. No matter how open the veil is, no one will find you tonight."

I was certain I wouldn't sleep, not with a strange woman in the room, not with so much happening that seemed impossible. I pulled back the blankets and slid into the bed while Merry moved around the room turning off lights. She hummed softly to herself and settled back into the chair. My mind churned around the words of the letter. My mother and father had once been a part of my life. I had no idea what either of them looked like, what their voices sounded like. No matter how I strained for the memory, all I had was static and blood.

I don't know how long I spun around and around with questions and doubts and that nagging question about my sanity, but eventually, it spun me down and unconscious.

I woke to the smell of coffee and the sweet, yeasty scent of donuts. Merry was sitting in the same chair, feet tucked up under her, a pair of glasses perched at the end of her nose, a powdered donut in one hand, a tattered paperback in the other. On the table in front of her were two steaming cups of coffee and from the smell of it, not the usual motel swill.

I stretched slowly, feeling each joint pull and realign and come back together before I slid out from between the sheets to get to my feet. I eased into the bathroom and shut the door, thinking about the drive ahead and wondering if my newfound relative was planning on riding with me. I did my business and washed my hands before emerging back out into the main room.

Merry looked up from her book and nodded at me. "Better. I got breakfast." She nudged a white paper bag toward me as I came closer. "Chocolate frosted with sprinkles."

I blinked at her, but it was too early for the likely answer to my question about how she knew, so I just accepted it and took the donut and my cup of coffee back toward the bed. I drank half the coffee gone before I went after the donut, and when that was half gone as well, I cleared my throat. "Is it safe to assume that you will be joining me for the ride north?"

"Someone's got to keep you alive," Merry responded. "How's your head?"

I frowned at her. "My head?"

She shrugged. "Figured you might be a bit tender. You did just rip off a twenty-year-old Band-Aid last night."

"I'm fine." I frowned at my donut, trying to figure out what she meant. "A hot shower, then I'm ready to go." I finished my donut, then the coffee, and headed back into the bathroom. A part of me still believed I was going to wake up to find it all a dream.

I showered efficiently, scrubbing my fingers through my hair, and tilting my head back to rinse the shampoo out. I kept my thoughts centered on the drive and what to expect when I got there. I froze as I reached to turn the water off, suddenly remembering words from my mother's note. *"The house awaits you; the key and deed are here."*

I climbed out of the shower and started to towel off, then wrapped a towel around myself, though it was too small to cover me completely, and opened the bathroom door. Merry still sat in the chair, donut, and book in her hands.

"What house?" I asked, pulling my suitcase up onto the bed.

"Your house, of course," Merry said, as if the answer was obvious.

"I have a house?" I was frowning again. I forced myself to

stop. An image floated up from the dark recesses of my mind, a blue cottage-style house, with a big, grassy backyard. It felt familiar, though I would have sworn I'd never seen it.

I pulled on pants and a shirt from my suitcase and crossed to the wooden trunk, opening it and looking through the various papers and mementos until I found the deed. It was old, the paper yellowed, and it seemed to be written in Spanish, but the dialect was unlike any I had ever seen. I translated what I could before I looked through the attached pages.

Essentially, the land had been granted to my mother's ancestor, back when California had still been held by Spain. It had included five acres, which eventually was whittled down to one acre as the family sold off lots over the years. On that acre sat a house, and behind it stretched a wilderness area and garden.

I set aside the deed and looked in the box for the key. I found a small velvet bag and opened it to find a set of keys, and stones like Merry had put at the door. I dumped them into my hand and rolled them around. They felt familiar, but the thought was fleeting, and I couldn't hold on to it.

"We should get moving," Merry said. "The blood tracker could already know where you are."

Putting everything back into the trunk, I had another image bubbling in the back of my brain, a woman with dark hair and dark eyes, tears on her face telling me I would be okay, and it was for the best.

I shook my head to clear it. Was it my mother? I had no memory of her to compare the image to. I blinked away tears I didn't want to shed. I had put my thoughts about family away a long time ago. I didn't need them creeping up to cripple me.

"Let's go." I nearly growled the words, though my frustration was only with myself. Merry didn't deserve that. I sat on the bed and pulled on my boots before zipping up my suitcase and closing the trunk.

Merry mumbled some words and picked up her stones, secreting them away into a pocket. She picked up the trunk and nodded. Together, we left the room and went down the stairs to my car. She stood behind it for a long time, her eyes closed.

"They haven't caught up yet, but they can't be too far behind. And who knows how many of them got through while the veil was at its thinnest," Merry declared as I opened the car trunk and put the suitcase in.

I took the trunk from Merry and tucked it in beside the suitcase. "Are you ever going to tell me who 'they' are?" I asked as we climbed in, and I started the engine. "And why they want to kill me?"

She didn't respond until I had us on the freeway headed north. "They are a...religious order, for lack of a better term. Very old-fashioned notions about your kind. They are the reason there are so few of your kind left. They believe you are the kin of Hathus."

"My kind? Hathus?" I asked, sparing a glance at her. She was staring out the windshield, her face unreadable.

"Hathus is the god of the dead. These people call your kind *thánatou*, the death bringer."

"Excuse me?" I managed not to drive us off the road but earned a few angry horns from drivers beside and behind us. "Death bringer?"

She shook her head. "You are a blood witch, Thána. You eat disease and flush it out through your menses. Sometimes that heals the sick. Sometimes it eases them into the next life."

What? What I was hearing simply couldn't be real. That was Hollywood stuff. It was ludicrous. "I don't understand anything you're saying."

"I speak the truth. You will know it soon enough. In the meantime, we need to beat these fanatics to a place that is safer, strongly warded against their trackers."

I shook my head, but the words kept rolling around inside me. Blood Witch. Death Bringer. Sparks of knowledge flared in my mind, but none of them brought any clarity. Splatters of memory, unconnected and unexplained followed words that sounded like a made-up language, maybe. At least they weren't Spanish, German, or Hindi. I was familiar enough with those sounds.

Some part of me kept telling myself that they had the wrong person. I was no witch. I didn't believe in witches or magic or whatever god this woman was talking about. Hell, I didn't even believe in the gods I was familiar with.

I would explain that to the next would-be assassin, I decided. Once they knew that I was just a middle-management corporate lackey, they would leave me alone.

Right. I managed to believe that until we were nearing the turn-off for Los Baños. It was almost one in the afternoon, and I pulled us off to find lunch. Merry stirred from her spot, yawning, and looking around us before nodding.

The truck stop was busy. I pulled up to the pumps and got out to fill the tank while Merry fussed with her shoes and her hair, which had all sort of shifted to one side while she slept in the passenger seat beside me. She shuffled off in the direction of the bathrooms while I pumped.

I was alone then when it happened. Out of nowhere, hands grabbed me and pulled me backward between the pumps and I could feel the sharp edge of a bladed weapon against the skin on my neck. I held up both hands in surrender and stilled my instinct to try to run.

"My wallet is in the car," I said, though part of me was quite sure no thief was brazen enough to strike in broad daylight in full view of the security cameras like that.

"We don't want your money, *Thanátou*." The voice was gruff and even without seeing my assailant, I could tell he was angry.

"Okay, what do you want?"

"To bleed you dry and end your blasphemous life."

That escalated quickly. "Here?" I have no idea why that was my response. He pulled me back, one hand fisting in my hair. We turned, and I could see where he was taking me. This wasn't happening. The corral that hid the station's trash was in front of us. Sure, I thought, that seems a much more likely place to be stabbed.

"Hey!"

Two men were coming toward us, and they started running when my assailant flashed the knife in their direction. "Stay out of this."

"Not today, pal." The first of them was within striking distance and I was whirled to the side, into the fencing of the corral. His hand was firm, pressing my face into the fencing while he brandished his weapon at my would-be saviors. I squirmed, but all it accomplished was the fencing embedding itself in my skin. I heard sirens in the distance and wondered if someone had called the cops.

I would hope so. It was the middle of the day after all. The sound of a punch landing intruded on my thought and the man holding me fell back against me.

"Knife."

"Yeah, I see it."

I tried to turn to see, but all it showed me was the back of the man's head. Then he shuddered, and the knife clattered to the ground. His hand left my head and I pushed off the fence and away from him. I could see police cars now, at least two of them closing on us. My assailant growled and shoved my rescuers off of him before he fled. Several of the arriving officers gave chase. I got a good look as he dodged around a car. He was my age maybe, with a shaved head and dark skin, wearing a black suit.

Somehow, I wasn't surprised when he vanished.

I was trying to catch my breath when the taller of the two men who came to my aid touched my arm. "Are you okay, ma'am?"

"Thanks to you, yes."

He was at least six feet tall and built like a linebacker. His friend was a few inches shorter and wiry, but he was the one who had apparently knocked the knife away. "That's some kind of knife." He squatted next to the blade, keeping his hands away, but giving it a good once over. "You see this, Jerry?"

Jerry was clearly the taller guy who leaned over to see. Before I could learn the name of my second rescuer, police officers were approaching, and we were sectioned off to answer their questions.

The woman who guided me back to my car had a nice face, her red hair pulled into a neat bun at the back of her head. She introduced herself as Officer Simmons and asked me to tell her what happened.

My heart was still racing as I told her the story, my eyes skipping to the spot where I'd been standing when he grabbed me. She stopped me a few times and asked me questions. My hands were mostly done shaking when I was finished. I gave her my cell phone number and thanked her for the quick response.

Merry was coming back to the car now, her eyes wide as she registered the scene. I shook my head at her and went to thank Jerry and his friend once more before I took my turn to go inside and use the bathroom, then grab a couple of sandwiches for us to eat on the road.

As I paid at the register, my eyes swept the faces around me. My heart skipped when I spotted a bald head, but that man's skin was much lighter, and he had a bottle of water in his hands, not a knife. I tried to tell myself to settle down, but when his eyes met mine, I *knew* that he was one of them. Chills ran down my back as I took my sandwiches and burst through the door, all but running for the car. My eye skipped to the rearview mirror as I tossed the sandwiches in Merry's lap and started the car, pulling out quickly as I spotted the man moving toward us, even if he didn't seem like he was in a hurry.

"You okay?" she asked when I pulled us out of the truck stop.

"Yeah, just a little shook up," I responded, still glancing behind us. "It was close. And I think there was another one of them in the store."

"They're getting desperate. They know their window is closing."

"Window?" I got us back out on the freeway, wanting to put as much distance as I could between me and the men who wanted me dead.

"By tomorrow, they have to cross back through whatever portal they forced open or be stuck here until they can capture a permanent portal or until the next time the veil thins. Their next opportunity to cross with a temporary portal will be six months away. A lot can happen in six months."

I shook my head, still not understanding half of what the woman said. She unwrapped my sandwich and handed it to me. I took a bite and firmly determined that once we got to the other end of this drive, I was going to make her sit down and explain everything or tell her to get out and leave me alone.

CHAPTER 5
HOME IS WHERE THE
MEMORIES LIVE

IT WAS EARLY EVENING WHEN WE ARRIVED AT THE ADDRESS ON THE deed. The house stood at the end of a cul-de-sac, and while it looked like it could use a paint job and some other work, it mirrored the image in my mind's eye.

On one side of the house was a hulking McMansion that had to have at least five bedrooms. On the other was a more moderate house, with a 1967 Mustang in the driveway. A knee-high, white picket fence ran around the front yard, and cultivated flower beds lined the inside of the fence. Climbing roses filled trellis walls up the front of the porch.

In my mind I could see a woman standing on that porch, calling us in for supper. I turned and saw two girls racing up the street, dressed for summer and gleeful as they fought to be the first one to touch the gate. I shook my head. I couldn't have been but seven or eight in the memory.

I pushed open the gate, holding the keys in my hand. I half expected her to step out of the door, the woman I was assuming was my mother. There was something familiar about walking up that path. The steps creaked a little as I stepped on them, and I could see that some of the wood was sagging in the planks of the porch.

No one had lived in the house since whenever we left, and I still had no idea how old I was when that happened. Still, someone had been taking care of the yard and the flowers. I looked at the keys in my hand, trying to figure out which one of them fit into the lock. It was obviously not the big one. That was an old-fashioned kind of key, and this was a modern lock. I picked wrong the first time but got it right the second and swung open the door.

The door opened on a hallway with a hardwood floor and walls painted bright sunshine yellow. As I stepped through the door, my nerves stilled. I could almost hear the sound of children playing, smell dinner cooking.

I shook it off as Merry joined me. To my right was a staircase and to my left, a large archway opened into a living room. Slipping the keys into my pocket, I followed the hall to find a bathroom, a dining room, and finally a kitchen. Everything was spotless, as if whoever lived here had only just left.

Off the kitchen was a greenhouse of sorts, a porch covered and surrounded by glass and filled with all manner of herbs and other plants. Here too it seemed no time had passed since someone had tended the garden.

As I came back into the kitchen, I found Merry making herself to home. She had found pans and dishes and was busy preparing a meal.

I frowned. "How is the stove working?" There shouldn't have been any gas or electricity functioning. No one had lived in the house in at least twenty years.

"Magic," she said, chuckling lightly. "Go on, explore. Maybe it will help shake those memories loose."

I wasn't sure where she had found food but decided that any answer I got would only lead to more questions. I left her to it and circled back around to the stairs. I ascended slowly, my hand on the rail. There were pictures on the wall, stopping me in my tracks. The largest was a wedding photo, in the middle of the staircase. I recognized the bride as the woman in my slowly returning memory, my mother.

The man who stood beside her was handsome. He was dressed in a dark suit with shiny black shoes. His hair was the lightest shade of red I'd ever seen, with streaks of blond weaved through. I stepped closer, lifting a hand to touch his arm. I had no memory of this man.

Then the memory slammed into me: *Yelling, someone shoving me away, the acrid stink of burning skin, fear flooding me as a familiar voice told me it would be okay, strange words and suddenly everything was quiet…the heat of blood on my skin, metal on my tongue, sirens, then more blood, swallowed down with fear and fury.*

I sat down hard on the step, my hands shaking. I had been small, maybe five. It was the day my father had died. Protecting me.

The blood on my face was his. The man who had come for me, the man who had killed my father…it was his blood in my mouth. I had taken his life. My father had hurt him badly, but I had put my mouth to his and pulled the life out of him.

My stomach heaved, and I ran for the bathroom, dropping to my knees to vomit into the toilet. I dry heaved after emptying the contents of my stomach, until my sides hurt, and the memory blurred some.

I flushed without thinking and got up, wiping my mouth. The memory had never been so visceral, nor as complete. I had watched my father die. Still a little shaky, I left the bathroom and tried the stairs again, keeping my eyes away from the image of my father.

At the top of the stairs, a hall led me first to a child's bedroom. Toddler toys were overflowing an old-looking toy chest, and a basket of dolls and stuffed animals filled one corner. The walls were purple and there was a mural over the twin bed of a unicorn with a rainbow arched over it.

Across the hall was another bedroom and somehow, I knew it

had been mine. The walls were a deep crimson, accented with white stars and the bed was covered in a soft blue comforter. There was a desk on one side and there was an open book on it. Math, I knew instinctively. We had fled in the middle of the school year.

There was another bathroom next to my room, and what I knew was my parents' room, but it was the final door that I stopped beside. When we had lived here the room had been off-limits, though I had no recollection why. I lifted my hand to the door hesitantly. My heart raced as I turned the knob, though I don't know what I was expecting, I only know that what was behind that door didn't meet those expectations.

The door opened into a walk-in closet, one side filled with what looked like old pickle jars, empty mason jars, and boxes. The other side was filled with clothes on hangers, winter coats, and formal gowns, plus several garment bags I didn't bother to open. The closet seemed longer and wider than could be possible, the back end of the closet lost in the dark. I stepped into the closet, reaching for the light switch, but not expecting the light to come on.

Nor was I disappointed. There was an urge to know what was back there in the dark. I pressed my lips together pensively, then glanced behind me, half expecting someone to come along and yell at me. Shaking my head at myself, I stepped deeper into the closet, one hand in front of me until I found a wooden door. My eyes slowly adjusted to the lack of light as my hand skimmed over the door in search of a door handle. I eventually found it, and I felt over it before trying to turn the knob.

I wasn't surprised to find it locked. My fingers felt down under the knob to find the keyhole. It was larger than a standard lock, and it reminded me of the big key on the ring I'd found in the wooden trunk. I fished the keys from my pocket and fumbled my way to the lock with the key.

The door opened outward, and I expected to find myself on a balcony or something over the backyard, possibly on top of the greenhouse porch. The space beyond that door was darker than it should be if it were a balcony, after all, it was still daylight outside.

I noticed too that off in the distance I could see signs of the sun rising, which made no sense at all.

"Oh, my. Hello."

To say I jumped backward would be an understatement, tripping over the door jamb and falling on my ass with a thud and a sudden exhalation of breath.

"I'm so sorry," the voice said, making me look up.

Through the door, I could see...well, I didn't know what I was seeing. It couldn't be real though, that much I was sure of. Because seven-foot-tall men with horns and black skin, dressed in leather and boots just were not a thing that was real. And, let me be clear: when I say black skin, I mean the kind of black that devours light, and when I say horns, I mean **horns**, thick, black horns rising up from his ample head of black hair somewhere above where I expected his ears were and curling back around and down around toward his face.

I crab-walked back further as he reached out a hand to help me up. "What the actual hell..."

He smiled and stepped through the open door. To my shock, as he did so, he transformed. The horns melted away and his skin took on a rich mocha color. Only his eyes remained the same, a startling amber shade that I couldn't take my eyes away from. "I didn't mean to startle you. I wasn't expecting anyone to open the door today."

At least ten questions rushed through my brain in a race to be the first thing out of my mouth, but they were all beaten by, "I'm sorry." I continued staring long after I was sure I should look away. "I...you..." I closed my eyes and shook my head. "Who are you?" I finally managed to sputter as I got back to my feet.

He performed a flourished bow and as he lifted his head, he smiled at me. My knees went a little weak, which had never happened to me before that moment, except that one time I had the flu and a temperature of a hundred and four.

"I am Cambious of Abagh, my friend. Guardian of this Gate."

Like everything about my life since the first time Finneas had shown up in it, I didn't understand what was happening. "Cambious...of...Abagh?" I made the mistake of looking into his eyes again. The pit of my stomach dropped, and I had a sudden need to kiss him, to offer myself to him.

Cambious cleared his throat and stepped away from me. "I'm sorry, it's been a while since I've been in the presence of humans who aren't inoculated for my particular pheromones."

"Your particular what now?" My head buzzed, and my thoughts were fuzzy. I was more sure than I had been before that I had suffered some terrible catastrophe and was lying in some hospital bed, still in El Paso, dreaming up this whole crazy trip.

"Pheromones. I'm an incubus. Well, half incubus. Half succubus. You can call me Cam."

"Right." I was hallucinating, like I did that time with the hundred-and-four-degree fever. Then it was dancing toads and flying mice, but my hallucinations had taken a turn for the decidedly grown-up, if the urge to touch myself was any indication. "I think I should go check on Merry."

"Oh, is she here?" Cambious followed me out of the closet and down the stairs. "I hope everything is okay. I've been keeping an eye on this place while you were gone."

I kept hoping that if I walked fast enough, I would leave the hallucination behind, but he talked about the gardens and the plants on the porch until we reached the kitchen. Merry turned at the sound of our voices and Cambious rushed past me to sweep her into a hug.

My knees were rubbery, so I sat at the small table in the breakfast nook. It seemed obvious that Merry and Cambious had history, though I found their conversation impossible to follow as it slipped from English into something that sounded vaguely Celtic, then dropped back to English.

Of course, my two hallucinations knew one another. I rubbed a hand over my face and tried to tune them out. That was harder to do when Merry put a plate in front of me, filled with a grilled cheese sandwich and a bowl of tomato soup and the two of them sat at the table.

"I knew you were coming, of course," Cambious said. "I just didn't realize it would be today. I thought Finneas was going to keep you safe while the veil was thin."

"Oh, he wanted to," Merry replied. "But this one wouldn't listen to him. Which is why I'm here." I looked from him to her and back again. "Eat, girl. You need your strength."

I blinked and picked up the sandwich, taking a bite tentatively. I chewed and swallowed, then put the sandwich down and looked at her. "Where did the food come from?" I asked, pinning Merry with my eyes. "And how did you cook this when there isn't any electricity or gas? Who is this guy and why was he in that closet?"

It seemed once I started letting questions out, they just kept coming. "How did you find me in Los Angeles? And what is this veil? And how did those men just disappear an entire car?"

Cambious set a hand on my arm, and it brought my demanding questions to an abrupt halt as all of my attention focused directly on the warmth of his skin against mine and how it made me want to melt. He pulled his hand back and I almost reached out for it, wanting to keep touching him, wanting him to keep touching me.

"I filled the pantry and a cooler yesterday," Cam said. "Merry probably used a spell for the cooking, her specialty is kitchen magic. I introduced myself upstairs. I am the Guardian of this gate. I wasn't so much in your closet as I was outside of it...on the other side of it?" He looked to Merry who shrugged. "Technically speaking I was in Spítia."

I didn't know what to say to that. "I'm going crazy. That's the only explanation." I picked up my spoon and pointedly ignored both of them. Maybe if I ignored them long enough, I would wake up and go back to my normal life.

"I should be getting back to the gate. Not that I expect trouble, but it is my job." Cambious stood. "It was lovely to meet you again, Thána. Welcome home."

He was gone before I realized I had never told him my name. I turned to look toward the staircase, but there wasn't even a shadow of him.

"You must be exhausted," Merry said, pulling my attention back. "You finish eating and I'll bring our things inside."

I put my spoon down and stood. "No, I'll do it." There was no way I was letting a ninety-year-old woman haul in my suitcase. I emptied the car, which didn't take long. There was only my suitcase, the trunk, and a couple of other odds and ends. By the time I was done, I was yawning and even though it was early, I was starting to think that sleep sounded good.

I carried my suitcase upstairs where I waffled between my old room and my parent's room. I eventually went into my room and set my suitcase by the dresser. I stripped down into my shorts and T-shirt and crossed to the bed. The sheets were clean and smelled of jasmine as I pulled back the comforter and top sheet. Cambious must have done more than gardening and grocery shopping.

Rubbing a hand over my face, I sat, yawning again. I was just about to turn out the light when Merry appeared at the door. She smiled at me. "I trust you'll be alright now. The veil is closing, and Cambious will guard this gate. I should be heading back. It's a long trip for me."

"Wait, what? I have so many questions."

She nodded, her braids bobbing along. "Read the book, it will help. I'm sure your mother left more information in the trunk too. Get some sleep. We will meet again."

She left me sitting there. I heard Cambious's voice as he welcomed her and talk about transportation, then the door closed, and the house fell silent.

CHAPTER 6
UP FROM THE PAST

I was disoriented when I woke the next morning, the unfamiliar room making me panic a little until it all came back to me. I pulled myself out of bed and down to the bathroom for my morning constitutional.

After flushing, and realizing I was going to need to call utilities and such to make the house livable, I paused at the sink, which had no water, and wondered where my wet wipes had ended up. My reflection in the mirror over the sink stopped me.

My hair was a mess, the once neat braid that I'd worn to keep it out of my face for the drive was nearly nonexistent among the strands that had fought their way free. I pulled the hair tie loose, finger-combing through it until I gave up and went looking for my bag with my toiletries and such.

I found it on the bottom stair, behind the wooden trunk that sat on the floor and supposedly held all the answers to all of the questions swirling around in my head. I reached into the bag for my brush and came out with my cell phone instead. I hadn't even thought about my phone since arriving.

At some point, I had turned it off and stuck it in the bag. I thumbed the button to turn it on and set it on the stair as I sat and went back into the bag for my brush. The sound of my voicemail notification sounded, and I picked the phone back up. The number was a San Francisco number. I set the voicemail to play on speaker and started brushing through the mass of knots in my hair.

"Hello, Thána. Bonnie Farva here. I wanted to be the first to welcome you to the San Francisco area. I know you were driving in, so take your time and get settled in, then give me a call. I'd like to see you start on Monday if that's possible."

Monday, so I had a few days. I finished brushing my hair and called Bonnie back, confirming that I would be there on Monday morning. She warned me about the traffic and told me what public transportation options were.

The better part of the morning was spent on the phone, getting the gas and electric and water turned on. With my battery nearly dead, I found a box of cereal in the pantry and a quart of milk in the cooler, so I could eat something. I was still going to need to do something about internet, but that was not as urgent a need.

I figured I would eat, and then I could plug the phone into the car charger while I waited for the water and PG&E guys to show up. I sat on the front porch with my bowl of cereal, my eyes scanning the other yards and houses. It was nearly noon on a Friday, so the street was pretty quiet.

Finishing my cereal, I set the bowl on the rail and stretched. I had a weekend to sort out the insanity that had befallen my life before I would return to something resembling normal.

Not that I knew how to even begin doing that.

I decided that I need to start with the trunk and the book inside. With a heavy sigh, I grabbed the bowl and headed into the house, hefting the trunk up off the floor after putting the bowl on top. I deposited it on the kitchen table and put the bowl in the sink, grabbing a bottle of water from the cooler before I returned to the table.

Trepidation filled me as I pressed my thumb to the locking mechanism and opened the trunk. Since Finneas had given me the damn thing, everything I knew about myself had turned upside down and traumatic memories I had repressed for twenty years were creeping back into my head.

What else would I remember if I dug deeper?

Easing the lid back, I reached in, pulling out the book and the deed to the house and setting them aside. I went back in, pulling out the stacks of papers, the silver rattle, and a small jewelry box.

I sank into the chair holding the jewelry box. There was something vaguely familiar about it. Small, barely four inches by three inches, it was silver and heavy. I opened it before setting it on the table. The inside was lined with red velvet and held a necklace on a silver chain, plus a couple of rings.

The pendant was weighty as I lifted it by the chain, which was long. Antiqued pewter surrounded a large ruby, or what looked like a ruby to me. Around the ruby, there were words etched in that same, strange language that was in the book. I rubbed my thumb over it, my eyes closing as memory bubbled up. I had worn a similar pendant when I was found on that bench, but it had been stolen from me, and I had never known its significance.

I slipped the chain over my head and let the pendant fall against me, it landed below my breasts and lay heavy against my stomach. Somehow it felt...right. I turned my attention to the two rings. One was clearly meant to match the pendant, its heavy silver etched with symbols and holding another ruby. I slipped it onto the middle finger of my left hand.

It fit perfectly and after only a moment, it felt as if I had always worn it. The last ring in the box was black with age, but it had been silver at one time. The stone was faceted like a gemstone but was blacker than any gemstone I had ever seen. I set it back into the jewelry box and made a mental note to pick up some jewelry cleaner when I went out next.

I shifted my attention then to the pile of papers, sifting through them. I found my birth certificate, issued there in California. The name Archer was nowhere to be seen. My mother was listed as Alana Celene Alizon. My father was listed as Patrick Marvin Alizon.

I sat back in the chair, holding the paper, staring at the words. I had turned thirty-two years old a little over a month before, and it was the first time I had ever seen the names of my parents.

For a long moment, I couldn't breathe. I had spent a lot of sad and angry years as a teenager wishing for and hating the parents I couldn't remember. It had taken a lot of counseling and self-determination to come to terms with the fact that, whoever they were, they didn't want me.

Blinking away tears, I set the paper aside. I also found a birth certificate for one Daria Alexis Thea Alizon. She was born three years after I was, in the same hospital. I had a sister. The little girl in that memory of running for the gate.

She would be twenty-nine, somewhere out there. Wondering if my mother would have left any clues to where to start looking, I dug into the rest of the pile.

I had to relinquish my quest when PG&E arrived to check the gas lines, so they could turn everything on, and the same when the man from the water company arrived.

By four o'clock in the afternoon, I had a working house, which meant I could cook myself some dinner. I plugged my phone in and set about getting to know my new kitchen, and what food Cambious had stocked.

I emptied the cooler into the fridge, leaving out the half dozen eggs and pulling some potatoes and a loaf of bread out of the pantry. A few minutes later I had some home-fries cooking and was scrambling a couple of eggs when I heard footsteps.

I froze for a second, then turned toward the sound. I don't know what I was expecting, but I felt let down a little when I realized that Cambious was standing in the archway.

"I hope I'm not intruding," he said softly.

"No. I...wasn't expecting to see you so soon," I replied, turning back to my cooking.

"It's Friday. I tend the greenhouse on Friday," Cambious said, inching toward me. "Unless you would rather do it."

My mouth opened and closed of its own accord. I knew nothing about gardening. I gestured toward the porch greenhouse. "Be my guest."

He smiled, his white teeth gleaming, and my knees got weak. As he got closer, I made myself look away. Something about him made me want to do things I hadn't even thought of in a while. He slipped past me and out onto the porch and I forced myself to focus on my cooking. I poured the eggs into the potatoes and stirred.

I could hear him out there puttering around, humming and singing as he moved through the collection of plants. Curiosity got the better of me, and I moved so I could see him. He had a watering can that looked as old as me, and he was making his way down the long counter, giving each plant attention, watering and singing to them. I found myself drifting toward him, but when he looked up, I pulled myself back to my dinner, which was starting to burn.

I turned off the stove, then plated half of what I'd cooked and took it to the table. I ate while looking through more of the papers, trying to ignore the thoughts in my head about Cambious. I hadn't had such libidinous thoughts since my crush on Muriel Hart in college. She had been a year ahead of me, my roommate's cousin. I had it bad for Muriel and it led to some less than stellar moments in my life, including my first sexual experience, though that wasn't with Muriel.

In fact, it had been with Joseph Myers, which confused me beyond belief. We'd both had a little too much to drink, and I had been desperate to find a way to sate the desire after spending two hours at a party watching Muriel dance with nearly everyone but me. Joseph was happy to oblige my lust.

We dated off and on for a while, despite my confusion. I had been convinced up until that point that I was gay because the only people I seemed attracted to were women, but I discovered that I liked sex with men, so maybe I was wrong about the whole gay thing.

It didn't occur to me then that I was actually bisexual, that took me a few years. But that didn't help me figure out why my head was full of thoughts of Cambious and sex. Distractingly so. I'd just read the page in my hand for the third time when he reappeared.

"I left some food for you, if you're hungry," I offered without looking up and hoping it sounded casual and not like I was begging him to stay.

"Thank you."

I heard him pick up the plate I'd left on the counter and serve up what I'd left behind before he came to join me at the table.

"I see you're settling in."

I nodded and set the page down. I had no idea what it said. I swallowed hard and turned to look at him. "You smell good." I said the words spontaneously, surprising myself.

"Pheromones," he responded, smirking. "We really should get you inoculated if we're going to continue spending time together."

"Are we?" I asked breathlessly. "Spending time together, I mean."

"That's up to you." He took a bite and chewed for a minute. I licked my lips, wanting to follow his fork and press my lips to his.

"The garden…" I managed, trying, and failing to pull my eyes away from his face. "I don't know how."

He frowned at me, as if my words didn't make sense. "To garden?" he asked after a moment.

I nodded. "Do you taste as good as you smell?" What? What the actual hell was wrong with me?

"I think that's my cue to exit." He stood, his chair scraping backward. "I'll see about sourcing some inxbane for you."

"Inxbane?"

"The key ingredient in the inoculation you need." He started for the stairs, but paused, nodding to the papers spread out around the table. "I'm glad you're getting to know your past."

He disappeared, and I turned my attention back to the disjointed story the contents of the trunk told. Everything in the box spoke of my mother, and only the birth certificates told anything of my father.

I pulled the book to me, clearing a space for it in front of me and opening it. The pictures seemed to mean more, now that I knew they were ancestors, family. I examined each face hoping for some flicker of memory. The writing changed languages, the people in the pictures seemed more modern.

Near the middle of the book, I found a page written in English, with pictures of a small house, set back among trees, with a woman who reminded me of Merry standing on the steps with two children.

The note under the picture read: *Celene Edith Abernon with her children Alana and Beauford.*

I looked at the children again, squinting at the girl, trying to decide if this Alana was the same person as my mother, if this woman was my grandmother. I flicked my eyes back to the top of the page.

If it is then the wish of the witch to hide herself from those who would bring her harm, gather these herbs in the dark moon: Wolf's bane, holy thistle, bloodroot, and candlewick and crush them together.

The instructions continued from there, but I was fairly sure that I didn't believe in spells, so I turned the page. The next page was a spell to expel demons, and the next one to hide bad memories. It seemed that the book was not just a family photo album, but the family spellbook as well, and, cookbook, as I came across a recipe for "Stewed Venison Pot Pie, as told to me by Nana Forsight." There was a note in another hand that said that beef could be substituted and taste as good.

The next few pages were back to the strange original language that seemed like so much gibberish, at least to my untrained eyes. There were more pictures, one looking down at a small city from a hill. It seemed it could be nearly any European city, with cramped roadways surrounded by buildings built in varying styles with red clay roofs. It was no place I recognized, however.

Under the picture were the words, "Into *Mágisa*, from the *Vóreion*."

I flipped a few more pages before I found a picture of my mother. She was young, maybe fifteen or sixteen, her dark hair tamed into twin braids that came almost to her waist. She wore a pair of faded jeans and a tank top with a shawl around her shoulders as she stood beside a boy who was taller, but clearly younger. Both of them beamed at the camera as they leaned back against a car. Under it was another picture of her at the same age, sitting with a small child of maybe two in her lap and surrounded by five other small children. The caption was "Alana with her baby sister Anna and brothers Adrian and Christophe, cousins Damen and Josephine, and Astra Linga, daughter of Lissa."

My mother had brothers and sisters…which meant I had aunts and uncles. That was more family than I had ever imagined. I wondered where they were now if they too were being hunted like I was.

A cold chill slithered up my spine as I realized that they might not even be alive anymore. I turned the page, putting that thought behind me. I wasn't ready to mourn family I had never even known, even if I was starting to remember the love my mother had held for me.

Stuck between the next pages was a small cloth bag tied with a ribbon. I lifted the bag, running my fingers over it. Whatever was inside was small, rounded. I held it in my hand and my eyes traced the words written in that strange, nonsensical language on the page. *"Epistrépse se méana aftó pou eíni dikó mou."* I mouthed the words before moving to the English underneath. "Caraway and mustard seed, to be carried by day and put beneath the pillow at night to return lost memory. Recite the words often. Translation: Return to me that which is mine."

I still didn't believe in spells, but I tucked the cloth bag into the pocket of my jeans. It couldn't hurt, I figured.

The room had gotten dim, and I got up to turn on a light, glancing at the screen of my phone. Somehow it had gone past eight in the evening. I had learned a lot, but nothing to indicate where my sister or my mother might be. I left everything where it was and headed up the stairs. I had meant to shower, but a bath was starting to sound better.

I set the tub to filling and went looking for towels. I had some in the car but didn't want to go back downstairs. I had a vague memory of watching my mother put laundry away and let it lead me to the closet in the hall. Sure enough, there were clean, fluffy towels stacked there. I had to remember to thank Cambius when I saw him again. I didn't know how long he'd cared for the house, but he'd done a great job.

I put the towel on the rack near the tub and stripped down, before stepping into the hot water and sinking down. I hadn't had a proper bath in years. The hot water surrounded me, and steam rose up from the surface. I closed my eyes, leaning back against the back of the tub. The only thing that would have made it better was a glass of wine.

CHAPTER 7
INXBANE

IT WAS THERE, IN THE BATH, THAT MEMORY CAME FLOODING INTO ME. We were small, Daria and I, playing in the bathtub as our mother watched, laughing. Daria was barely old enough to sit upright on her own and she splashed in the water, giggling as if it were the funniest thing she'd ever done. Daria's skin was pale compared to my olive tones, and the little tuft of hair on her head was a shade of red like our father's.

Mom knelt by the tub, one hand in the water beside Daria in case she needed help. Our father came into the room, leaning down to kiss the top of Mom's head, his eyes sparkling.

The memory was a happy one, happier than I could remember being since. Tears stung my eyes as I sat up, half expecting I could reach through to touch those happy people... but I was alone.

I pulled the plug on the tub and stood, reaching to grab the towel. I dried my legs and wrapped the towel around me, grabbing my clothes as I left the bathroom.

My childhood bedroom seemed to be hung with memories as I sat on the bed. The closet was the magical doorway to some faraway land when I was small. I would go in and close the door and put on my dress-up shoes and dress and emerge a princess.

Or sometimes I chose what must have been a cowboy costume that I transformed into a dragon tamer outfit.

I fished the sachet out of my jeans pocket and slipped it under my pillow. So far, all the magic stuff had seemed real, so maybe it wasn't all make-believe.

I dropped the towel and pulled on the T-shirt and shorts I had adopted as my pajamas and turned off the light. Sliding into the bed, my hand reached under the pillow to hold the sachet and I whispered the words again, "Return to me that which is mine."

Sleep was elusive. I tossed and turned, vague snippets of memory chasing me, but nothing solid, nothing I could hold on to. I finally dozed off somewhere after midnight, only to be dropped into my recurring nightmare. It was clearer than before and started earlier in the memory.

A big, warm hand held mine and his voice was telling me we needed to hurry. It was Daria's birthday, and we were bringing her cake. The sun was warm on my skin, and I was wearing my favorite blue dress with white flowers on it.

Daddy suddenly pulled me to the side, behind a car. Our house wasn't far away, I could see it. Daddy was telling me to run for the gate, but I was scared. I could hear my heart in my ears. A man was yelling, magic crackling in the air around him.

"Stay down, Thána. Stay down." He pushed me down and I sat on the pavement, moving under the bumper of the car as Daddy stepped out to face the man. The sound of fighting made me cover my ears, but I could still hear the words the man hurled at my father, telling him that the thánatou child must die.

The smell of smoke and burning flesh, screams as my father took the brunt of the spell, and countered with one of his own. I knew I should run to the safety of my mother, but I couldn't move, not until it was quiet and then I crawled out from under the car. My father lay still on the ground, his face turned toward home.

I crawled to him, tears stinging my eyes. "Daddy?" I turned his face to me, patting his cheek to rouse him. "Daddy?" I leaned in to try to feel his breath on my cheek, my lips brushing his. The air tasted like pennies, flat and ugly and it made me nearly ill.

Daddy's lips opened with my touch, and I opened mine as well. Blood coated his mouth and I sucked in without thought, swallowing as a great breath left him. "Daddy!" I was screaming now, hitting him, begging him to come back. Inside me, a warm feeling was stirring in my tummy, fingers of pain clenching around my small body. My father's eyes were dull, and I somehow knew he was no longer there.

Behind me, the man who attacked us groaned and I turned to him, power burning through me as I grabbed his face in my tiny hands and pulled his mouth open, sucking in until he too was still beneath me.

Blood covered my face and hands, my favorite dress, even my shoes as people began appearing around me. Daria's cake was broken on the ground, pink frosting coating the pavement, my father's hands, and even the side of the car. I curled up with my head on my father's chest, my little hands holding to him, even as my mother came and tried to pull me away.

I woke breathlessly, jumping from the bed and looking around. The dream had been so real, I half expected to be covered in blood. I gulped in air and tried to calm the raging beat of my heart, realizing as I pulled my thoughts back into the here and now that the warm feeling between my thighs was the start of my monthly cycle.

It was early by nearly a week, but then, the only predictable thing about my cycles was that they had never been predictable. I found my toiletries and took care of that situation, dropping my shorts into the pile of clothes I needed to wash and pulling on my backup pair. I was going to need to pick up some new clothes. I had even fewer than I'd had when I'd gotten to El Paso.

I was awake enough that I wasn't going back to sleep, so even though it was only five in the morning, I headed downstairs to make coffee.

That was another thing I was going to need to get out to buy. Cambious had put some in the pantry, but I could tell he wasn't a coffee drinker just by his choice of coffee. I figured I could get out later in the day, find the closest grocery store, and stock up. The clothes would wait until I got an idea of the average dress in the new shop. No point spending money on a bunch of dresses and suits to find out I could get away with jeans and T-shirts.

I sat at the table as the coffee brewed, the dream playing through my mind. That man had been alive before I touched him. His face filled with fear as I leaned over him and he murmured that word...*thánatou.* I was a child, but he feared me. In my dream, he was a dark-skinned bald man, dressed in a black suit, but I couldn't tell whether that was the truth or my subconscious adding the description based on my attacker at the truck stop.

The coffee pot beeped, and I got up to pour myself a cup, thinking about what I had done. I had wanted that man to pay for taking my father from me, and after I kissed him, he died. I had killed him. I wasn't exactly sure how I knew that, or how I did it, but I knew it was true.

I had killed him, and I had taken my father's pain, releasing him to die peacefully. The proof was the way my body reacted. I had become hot in the next hour and my mother had taken me into the forbidden closet, sitting me down on a chair that had a hole like a toilet seat, with a bucket underneath.

I bled. My body cramped as my tiny uterus shed blood like I was a grown woman. Through her tears, my mother tended to me, wrapping me in a makeshift diaper when my exhaustion had me falling out of the chair. We both slept in her bed that night, and for many nights thereafter.

We didn't leave the safety of our property, which was well warded, though at the time I didn't know what that meant. Sometimes we hid in the secret closet. At least once we even went through the door to the other side.

Other men came, their dark suits populating the town around us, searching us out as we tried to live our daily lives. Each time one found us, Mom would do something to change the wards around us and even expanded them to include the whole cul-de-sac. There were spells for us too. Amulets we each wore that were meant to hide us, words we had to say whenever we left the wards.

Eventually, there were too many men, constantly finding us, and we finally ran. I was seven when we left the house.

I sipped at my coffee and considered that memory. It was the day after a man yelled those words at us in a grocery store. Mom piled as many of our things as she could into the car, and we left. She promised we'd come back someday, and that we should see this as an adventure.

The memory ended there. Whatever came after that was still hidden in the dark recesses of my mind. Sitting there, staring back at that moment though, I found myself reexamining my known life.

My menstrual cycle had never been what could be called normal, and it began when I was barely eleven. Of course, this memory made me realize that wasn't entirely true. It was a light flow when I was young, but there were times in my life when it was more like a river pouring out of me.

When I was thirteen, I had a good friend in school who had cancer. I didn't know much about cancer, but I was watching her wither away. My foster mother took me to see her in the hospital. They were saying this was the end, that she wouldn't survive.

I remember crawling up into her bed with her and cradling her close and kissing her to say goodbye. A jolt passed through me, and I jumped from the bed, terrified that I'd somehow caught her disease.

I ran from the room and out to the car. By the time my foster mother got us home, I was cramping and what followed was seven long days of bleeding that was debilitating. I almost ended up in the hospital myself, but when I could finally stand on my own, they were saying that a miracle had happened, and Kate was coming home from the hospital.

My coffee had grown cold as I sat there contemplating what it all meant, so I got up and poured it down the sink and poured a new cup. They called me Death Bringer, but if my memory wasn't lying to me, it wasn't death I'd given Kate. I reached for the book from the wooden trunk and wondered if the answers were somewhere in there.

I had seen the words blood witch under various photos, several of my ancestors had been blood witches, according to the book. I flipped back to the page where my grandmother's face stared out at me, my finger tracing the side of her face. She looked tired. In her hand was a small bunch of leaves of some kind. From there, I moved backward, finding the last noted blood witch before me. She was my great-great-grandmother, Alexis Anagnos. There was only one picture of her, and little more than her name and the notation that she had been a blood witch.

I sat back, sipping at my coffee, looking at her face, and wondering about her life.

I flipped pages, my eyes scanning the words and images, though I wasn't sure what I was looking for. I stopped as my gaze caught on the word "inxbane", and I dragged my eyes up to the top of the page. *"For those who wish to socialize with one of the various creatures who dull the senses, mix a general serum and to it add a drop of blood from the said creature and the proper plant or plants as given below."*

Scanning back to where I'd seen the word inxbane, I found it listed under Incubi, Succubi, and other related lust-inducing creatures. "Yeah, so how do I mix a general serum?" I muttered.

The more I seemed to learn, the more I realized I was in way over my head. With a sigh, I turned the page, skimming through pages of pictures, recipes, and as I found the back of the book, a family tree.

Like the rest of the book, it was focused on my mother's side of the family, going back generations. My name was beside my sister's name, leading to our mother, her mother, and back. Every two or three generations there was an asterisk beside a name, which a note in the bottom right corner indicated meant they were a blood witch.

The page folded out to nearly half the length of the kitchen table. Other markings told of family that were exiled, presumably through a portal like the one upstairs if what I'd learned so far was true. Those who lacked magic ability, certain kinds of criminals, and some blood witches were exiled. Some of the names had titles under their names: Musta Hargrove, Mayor of Cra; Celene Everton, Mistress of Keys for Her Grace, Ella Nore; and others that made little more sense to me.

I finished my cup of coffee and stood up to refill it. The sun was just starting to come up, filling the greenhouse with a gorgeous golden light. I wandered into it with my cup of coffee, glancing over the assembled plants. Some I thought I recognized, but most looked more or less like every other plant to my untrained eye.

I wandered down to the end where there were some miniature trees planted in barrels, the last of the season's fruit on their branches. One was lemon, while the other was orange. I breathed in deep of the scent. It was a mix of rich earth and sun-warmed air, as well as a deep herbal smell that was less any one plant and more the combination of them all.

As I stood there, I could almost see the porch as it had been when I was small, when my mother was tending to the plants. Everything had been lush then, the air scented with mint and jasmine. Like Cambious, my mother had hummed and sang as she worked, and I remembered loving to listen to her.

It was hard to believe so much had changed in the last week. I had been alone in the world until Finneas had found me. Now, if the book was to be believed, I had a family full of aunts and uncles, a sister I was only starting to remember, and a house haunted with memories of a time before I was alone, if only I could remember them.

I drank the last of the coffee in my cup, turning to go back into the house, when my eyes found a row of books along the back of the workbench. They were old, the covers faded. Setting my coffee cup down on the bench, I reached for the first. It was small, the cover a dull red that was worn near to white in places. The writing on the cover and spine had once been gold but was unreadable now with only slivers of gold clinging to the edges of the letters. I opened it, turning past the first few pages.

It seemed to be a recipe book of some sort, though I didn't recognize any of the ingredients, and the instructions were in that strange language I was getting used to seeing, handwritten in an elegant script. I reached for the second, with its blue cover in a similar shape to the red one. Inside the words were English, old English, but readable. Like the red book, it contained recipes with ingredients like mugwort and roots of dandelions and rose thorns. Notes were scribbled in pencil alongside some of them saying things like "substitute thistle pricks to keep depression at bay" and "carry in a pouch to protect from evil eye" and other such odd things. The handwriting was crisp and neat, block letters in black ink.

As I progressed through the books, it seemed I moved through the years, finding near the end a journal that was in a familiar hand I thought was my mother's and filled with her own recipes and notes about plants and spells. The last book was the newest, and it fell open in my hand to the last page with writing on it. I recognized the writing, even if it had yet to develop into the scrawl I knew best.

It was a child's hand, and I had copied from my mother's book, and from the others, small spells to improve memory, to protect from bullies and other similar ones. It wasn't even a quarter filled, but as I paged through, I found a picture, taken on the front porch. We smiled out of the past, my sister and I, our knees and faces dirty, our clothes disheveled, but it was easy to see we were happy.

Under the picture my mother had written, "Thána and Daria, ages 6 and almost 3." My thoughts shifted to the day my father died. This picture had to have come before that, so I was a little older than I had first assumed.

Gathering the books to examine more completely, I headed back into the kitchen, stopping when I found Cambious standing there. In his large hands, there was a small jar. He smiled and my knees got a little weak. Thoughts flashed through my head, thoughts about sex. I pushed them away and deposited my books on the counter.

"I brought you some inxbane," Cambious said, lifting his hands a little.

"That's great," I responded, sighing. "It would be even better if I knew what to do with it."

He chuckled and gestured toward the books with his chin. "To start with, you need to make a simple serum. The instructions should be in the brown book there. Once it's ready, bring it to a boil and drop in a pinch of this and I'll add a drop of my blood. Let it cool and drink it down."

I nodded. "You say that like this is just normal." I reached for the blue book and started paging through it.

"Well, for me it is." Cambious put the jar on the counter. "I'll gather what you need from the greenhouse. You get started in here. You'll find a saucepan in that cupboard by the stove."

"What, no cauldron?" I asked as I squatted down to look in the cupboard. He peeked back from the doorway out into the greenhouse.

"Well, we could, but it's a bit big for what you need."

I closed my eyes and shook my head. "Of course there's a cauldron." With a deep sigh, I banished my thoughts about Cambious and sex, then the ones about how crazy this whole thing was and the wondering when I'd wake up to find myself still in El Paso. I pulled out a saucepan that looked big enough and set it on the stove, pulling the book closer and searching through it until I found a page titled, "Simple Serum, for use in various spells, incantations, and inoculations" and let my eyes scan the page. It seemed simple enough.

I rummaged through cupboards until I found a Pyrex measuring cup and put two cups of water in the pan. I turned the heat up to medium and turned my attention back to the book.

The recipe was written in a neat hand, but the notes in the margins were little more than a scribble and hard to decipher. "There should be jars in the pantry with the liquid ingredients." Cambious's voice floated in from the greenhouse.

I raised an eyebrow at the door before picking up the book and taking it into the spacious pantry beside the refrigerator. Everything in there was neat and tidy, canned goods all lined up with their labels facing outward, boxes lined up along the top shelf. In the back, next to what appeared to be canning jars filled with assorted vegetables, there were old-looking glass bottles that looked like they were made for keeping spices, or maybe lab specimens.

Consulting the book, I needed rose quartz and obsidian waters. I had no idea what that meant, but I read the labels, all lined up in alphabetical order. I located the two I needed and went back to the stove where Cambious was shredding something green and herb-like into my pan of water. He looked up and stepped back, gesturing to the stove. "You look like you're doing just fine," I said, setting my two bottles down.

"Ah, but then you wouldn't learn." His deep voice rumbled through me. I could feel it in my chest, and it sank through me into my groin. My insides trembled with unbidden desire. "I've done the first step. I'll move away until you're ready for my blood."

I nodded absently, shutting my eyes, and breathing in slowly until I felt the urges settle a little. When I opened them, Cambious was not in my line of sight, so I moved back to set the book on the counter.

The water was just starting to boil, the shredded greenery churning in circles and diving down, only to rise again and circle around until the current sucked it back down. It was nearly mesmerizing. I tore my eyes away from it and read through the next step.

I needed to add three drops of each of the two waters, then boil for two minutes before adding the chamomile, which I was at least familiar with. I rummaged in the drawer nearest the stove, somehow knowing that I would find an eyedropper there. First the obsidian. Something tickled the back of my brain about obsidian being protective, a barrier of sorts.

Carefully, I let three drops of the vaguely darkened water drip into the pan, then moved to the rose quartz. That done, I turned to the pile of small flowers on the counter. I'd never seen chamomile fresh like that, only dried for tea. The book said to crush the flowers before adding them to the water, so I set about doing that. I almost forgot Cambious was behind me as I worked until I heard him murmur, "Good, stir it now and take it off the heat."

I was a little startled but grabbed the wooden spoon that looked older than I was and gave the concoction a stir before lifting the pan off the burner and setting it on a cold one. "That's it?" I asked, glancing back at Cambious,

I regretted it almost immediately as my stomach lilted and heat flushed through me. I turned back to the stove to try to control myself.

"Sprinkle a pinch of inxbane over the surface while it is still hot," Cambious instructed.

I could feel him coming toward me and tried to narrow my focus down to my own hands and what I was doing so his close-ness wouldn't affect me. It didn't really work, but I pretended that it did. The inxbane was in a frosted glass apothecary jar, the kind that my foster mother kept potpourri in when I was in high school. It was larger than it had looked in Cambious's s giant hands.

With him behind me now, I opened the jar and took a pinch of the dark brown powder. The smell was a bit like cut grass that had been allowed to dry, got rained on, and dried again...not quite moldy, but unpleasant. I sprinkled it into the water and suddenly Cambious reached around me, holding his thumb over the pot. He had already pricked it with something, and he let a drop of blood fall into the liquid in the pan.

The smell that lifted off the potion was a potent mix of that grassy scent of the inxbane and a strange metallic scent that I assumed had come from the blood. "There, now just let it cool before you drink it. Best to swallow as much as you can at once, the taste is awful."

He turned to leave, and I almost reached for him. "You don't have to go," I said, my heart thumping almost painfully against my chest. I licked my lips as my eyes traveled over his leather-clad legs, stopping at his groin for a long time.

He cleared his throat and pulled my attention back up to his face. "If I stay, I fear we may lose control of ourselves. I will come back tomorrow, and we can talk all afternoon if you like."

I was fairly sure he was in no danger of losing control. In fact, he seemed to be the picture of control as he left me standing there in the kitchen. A sudden release of pressure dropped on me when he was no longer within sight and my knees even wobbled a bit.

I reached for the stove and breathed in deep, then realized the dampness in my underwear was probably more than just my arousal. I had somehow managed to forget that I had started my period.

CHAPTER 8
INCUBUS

I STARED INTO THE COFFEE CUP, TRYING TO WORK UP THE COURAGE to drink my anti-incubus potion. Which was a ridiculous notion if I thought too much about it. Like so much in my life since I first laid eyes on Finneas, I was trying really hard not to think about it too much.

Being me, that meant an endless loop of my brain cycling through thinking about all the ways that this was insane, and I was having a nervous breakdown, to thinking it was some sort of fever dream I was having while lying comatose in some hospital somewhere, to shoving it all down into a dark hole under a manhole cover in my head so that I could function as if it was all perfectly normal.

Finally, after waffling for at least a half-hour, I picked up the mug, took a deep breath, and filled my mouth. Cambious was not wrong about the taste. I almost spit it out and after I'd swallowed, I wasn't sure I wasn't going to just throw it all back up, but a couple of deep breaths seemed to do the trick. At least until I dumped the last swallow into my mouth.

I gagged after getting it down, leaning over the sink just in case. I could taste moldy grass and something musty and oddly dry. I rinsed the cup and filled it with water, chasing the potion down, and hoping it shut the door to regurgitation behind it.

I had books covering most of the surface of the kitchen table, the book from the trunk, the books from the greenhouse porch, and books that I'd found hidden in among more traditional volumes in my parents' old room. There were straight-up spell books, history books that resembled no history I had ever learned in school, and several that were in a language that was not the same language I was becoming used to seeing. If I had to guess I would have said Welsh or Gaelic.

Pushing down the feeling of my stomach attempting to heave itself up through my throat, I went back to the table and my efforts to make sense of the memories that kept bubbling up inside me and the assorted "magic" that was apparently my heritage.

I pulled the black book that had clearly been mine closer and opened it to the beginning. On the first page I had written, *"This book belongs to Thána Augusta Celene Alizon, of the Houses Alizon and Anagnos, Blood Witch."*

The next page was dated September 10, 1990. My seventh birthday. There was a poem of sorts on the page, rhyming couplets that was labeled "A Spell for Patience" and I found myself speaking it out loud.

Patience is a virtue,
This I know is true
Let patience grow inside me
Make me still like a tree

I wasn't sure it made any sense, but then what about my life did at that point? Each page was dated and contained either a poem or a recipe of some kind. There were more blank pages than filled, and the last was dated April 4, 1991.

There was no recipe or spell, only the words, *"Símero, févgoum. Mia méra, tha epistrépsoum."*

Sighing, I reached for one of those that I took for history books, only it bore little resemblance to the history books I'd read in school. It told the early history of when people began migrating from the world on the other side of the door hidden in my closet.

There were portals in many countries around this world, and presumably, they connected to the world that was my parents' homeworld, though I was starting to feel some prickle of knowledge lurking just out of reach about many portals and many worlds. I was giving myself a headache attempting to remember so I relinquished the thought

Families from Spítia, my mother's home country, and others on that world, sent those born with no magic through those portals, at first to protect them from those who believed that the handicap should not be allowed to propagate. Eventually not having magic was outlawed for a while and banishment was the only option to prison or death.

A side note on that chapter said that blood witches were sometimes banished as well, due to the stigma attached to the gifts usually granted to a blood witch. I wondered if that was why I had been born here, on this side of the portal.

From what I could tell skimming through the book, the world on the other side of that door upstairs was divided into eleven countries, who, much like the world I lived in, fought long bloody wars over points of theological and philosophical beliefs, imagined slights against their leaders, border disputes, as well as points of magical contention.

It seemed the more I learned about the past, the more I saw I needed to learn. Setting aside world history, I went back to my family book, turning the pages until I found the picture of my mother when she was younger. I turned several pages without really looking at them, stopping when a feeling of ice creeping up my hand drew my attention down to an image of a fortress of sorts with a caption under it, "Mauno Kourt, home of the *Adelfótit tou Día.*" My eyes scanned up the page. The lettering

was neat and clean, each stroke even and lined up. "The Brotherhood of God formed first among priests of Jeus who broke off
over the belief that "*Aíma mágissa*" or blood witches, sometimes
called *thanátou*, were abominations from the god Hathus. This is
believed to have itself been a bastardization of the prophecy of
Aímatos, the gathering of all bloods to fill the river Spítia and
purchase another ten thousand years of our lands from Hathus,
to whom it belongs."

Under that paragraph was a list of names, ages, and dates. A
chill seeped into my bones as I scanned them, all women with
the last name Anagnos, which must have been my mother's
family name seeing that I had claimed it in my own book. There
were twenty or so, the dates separated by everything from
fifteen years to nearly one hundred and fifty.

I didn't need words to tell me that these women had died for
little more than the fact that they had been born, blood witches
all of them. Like me. Had I been born in the same times and
places, it might have been me. The youngest had been merely
nine years old.

There was nothing to tell me how they were killed, but I
knew it was gruesome and painful. Closing the book, I left the
room, turning off the light as I headed upstairs. It was early, but I
felt as though I had just finished that kickboxing class my
assistant had thought would be a fun form of stress relief. I made
a stop in the upstairs bathroom to deal with the confirmation of
my womanhood and the lack of zygote implanted in my womb,
then stripped out of my clothes, dropping them on the floor and
crawling into bed.

I was dropped almost instantly into dreams of the past. I saw
the day we left that house, running past a car attempting to
block us into the dead-end street. I saw a tiny cottage house
covered in ivy and climbing roses where my mother's smile was
sad and my sister played in a sandbox with someone's forgotten
army men, calling them her bo-bos.

There were flashes of men with bald heads, or maybe the

same man over and over, I couldn't be sure, but I knew each time I saw him or them, we would pick up and leave, usually in the dead of night.

Toward morning the feeling of the dreams shifted, and that same cold burning sensation shook me as I fell down a hill, running madly, bare feet pounding against barren land, stumbling over broken earth.

"Althea Anagnos, you have been convicted of being thánatou. Your punishment is death by Aimorragía." The woman screamed around the leather gag and thrashed in her captor's hands, fighting desperately to break free of the heavy chains around her wrists. She was dragged forward, up some scaffolding to a platform. The shift she wore was ripped from her bruised and bloodied body and a rope was tied around her ankles. The men that surrounded her wore deep red robes and hoods and gloves, the only flesh showing was around their eyes. An order was given, and Althea was lifted feet first from the platform, struggling even then to get free.

Three men stepped up to her, blades in their hands. Silently they stabbed her skin, careful to avoid major arteries until they had opened fifteen wounds. Then they carefully cut open each thigh and her neck to expose the pulsing arteries. Each was carefully pricked with the sharp, curved point of their blades, ensuring her death would be slow and no doubt excruciating.

I could hear the chanting then and that fortress filled my vision, almost as if I were flying toward it. A woman was curled up in the corner of a cold, stone cell, surrounded by men in the same dark red robes, chanting something I couldn't quite understand.

I woke to the sun streaming in the window, shaking a little as the dreams shifted into memories that were my own and those that could never be mine. Something made me wonder if that was part of being a blood witch…something about shared blood, connection, which could transcend the limitations of time.

It was Sunday, and I still hadn't gone to get groceries, so I decided that would be my first course of action. After a quick shower, I threw on the last of my clean clothes and reminded myself I needed to do laundry. I hadn't seen a washing machine in the house, so I bundled all of my dirty clothes into my duffle bag and headed out to find a laundromat as well as the grocery store.

In all, it took nearly three hours, but when I came back to the house, I had clean clothes for a couple of days, and food that would get me through the week.

As I was unloading the car, I had the feeling that someone was watching me, but looking around I couldn't see anyone. It was a little disconcerting, especially knowing that there were people out there who wanted to kill me. The image from my dream sprang to mind, Althea Anagnos hanging from her ankles as her life's blood drained from her body.

I shook it off and juggled my grocery bags and duffle to get the front door open. Hands reached through the door, taking my groceries before it had even registered that someone was there. Cambious grinned and headed to the kitchen with the bags while I closed the front door. I followed behind him, feeling like something was different.

It took a minute for it to dawn on me that the potion must have worked. I could look at him without the overwhelming lust. The feeling, or the lack of feeling, was odd. "Thanks," I muttered when I caught up to him.

"How are you feeling today?" Cambious asked, emptying my bags, and starting to put things away.

"A little anxious about work tomorrow," I said honestly.

He nodded. "First days can be hard." He moved around the kitchen easily, like he owned the place. In some ways it was more his house than mine.

"Can I ask you some questions?" I asked, sitting at the table with all of my spread-out books, most of which only filled me with more questions and very few answers.

"Of course."

I wasn't sure where to start though. I pulled my mother's big book to me and opened it to the page with the fortress. "What can you tell me about this place?" I asked, turning the book toward him. My fingers tingled where they touched the picture.

He raised an eyebrow. "That is the Mauno Kourt. Why do you ask?"

"I saw it in my dreams last night," I said. I scanned the words above the picture. "I saw her too." I pointed to Althea's name. She had died nearly a century before at the age of twenty-six. "I watched her die."

His eyes were filled with concern as he sank into a chair beside me. "Your gifts are awakening."

"I'm not sure nightmares count as a gift," I said. I shook off the apprehension that the dream brought with it. "I saw someone else too. Here." I touched the picture again, the same cold tingle rising up my fingers and into my palm. I pulled my hand away. "She was in a cell. These men were chanting…I don't know what they were saying."

Cambious made a face, like he smelled something rotten. "The Brotherhood."

"Are they the men trying to kill me?"

He nodded. "Most likely. There are a few other sects, but they stick primarily to preaching and trying to legislate their hate. It's only been the last seventy years or so that the laws banishing blood witches have been lifted. There are precious few of you left. The Brotherhood, and others, believe that the gift itself is to be eliminated, that it is anathema to Jeus, which is ludicrous, of course."

I nodded, not fully understanding, but tucking the information away. "And they killed all of these women." My finger dragged down the list, stopping at the nine-year-old.

"They were most active after the laws that banished blood witches because they felt they weren't restrictive enough. The last few centuries they've been mostly a secretive organization, hiding in the shadows and striking at those who, like yourself, were living in exile in the various worlds accessible by portals, like yours. Often, those witches had little to protect them because here their access to the education they would need to wield their powers effectively had been limited."

I looked at the list again, then frowned. "The last few centuries?"

He leaned forward and looked at the list. "The last of your family taken and killed was nearly two thousand ago, here. Agatha."

"That date is only fifty years ago."

Cambious chuckled. "Ah, yes. Right. I forget you don't know the basics. Spítia and the other civilizations in my world are several millennia older than yours. It is currently the thirteenth month of the year 4189 on my side of the portal. Our calendar reset when the Great War was finally over, and new boundaries were drawn for each of the noble families. That was in the year 0, but it was several thousand years after we originally established a calendar."

Once again, the immensity of all there was to learn was over-whelming. My head was spinning, and I wasn't sure I even knew what to ask next. "Tell me about you," I finally said.

"Me?" He seemed amused. "There isn't much to tell, I'm afraid. I am the guardian of this portal, it's my job to make sure that no one uses it if they aren't family."

"Family?"

He nodded. "The land on both sides belongs to your family. Only family is supposed to use the gate without permission. We don't usually have a problem, because the land on the other side is a long distance from any city and not the most convenient to get to. There are almost no roads, and with the forest on the east and the marshlands to the south, most people are going to aim for a portal that's easier access."

"And you guard this portal in the middle of nowhere. All the time?"

He shrugged. "I don't need a lot of sleep, but my brother and I trade shifts. He's young though, he doesn't even know your family. We're…bonded I guess is a good word. Our families, I mean. The story goes that your great-grandfather on your mother's side saved my father's life. Our kind aren't particularly well loved, even in our native lands. My father swore a blood oath and bound our families together. We guard your gate, but there are others, and at certain times of the year, when the veil is thin, portals can be forced open by powerful magic, but they close quickly."

Most of that was hard to follow. It was easy to forget that Cambious didn't actually look like the man sitting next to me. No, he had horns and skin darker than night, and who knew what else that I hadn't caught on that first meeting.

"I meant you," I said after a minute. "Tell me about you."

Cambious narrowed his eyes at me. "Are you sure you're ready for that information?"

"In for a penny," I responded. "At this point, nothing is going to surprise me."

His eyebrow lifted. "Okay, but remember you asked." Cambious shifted in his seat but met my eyes with his. "My parents are a rarity. Most often Incubi and Succubi don't intermarry. Their offspring is usually mixed race. My parents are an exception. I have one brother and one sister, plus a large number of half-siblings. I was born a succubus named Cambia, but I knew from an early age that I was male. I had magical surgery about fifty years ago, once I found a compatible male who wanted to transition to female." He paused. "Still with me?"

As with just about everything since I had met Finneas, his words only created more questions. "Magical surgery? Fifty years ago?"

He nodded. "We age a bit differently than humans. So, yes, fifty years ago. We went together. I got her man bits, she got my female bits, some chanting, a sacrifice to Dianos, and a hefty payment later I was an incubus, and she was…whatever the female is for her race."

I blinked a little bit. "And what is her race?"

He bit his lip as he thought about it. "I think here you call them satyrs? The hooves and legs of a goat, but the torso and up is humanlike?"

"So, you're telling me you have a goat's...organ?" I asked, blushing from my toes up.

He grinned. "It was a good trade."

We talked for hours, well past when I should have been in bed. When I couldn't stop yawning, I reluctantly stood. "I have to get some sleep. Tomorrow is going to be a long day."

"I want you to be careful out there. As long as you are on this property, you are protected, but the Brotherhood could still have operatives here."

I nodded and headed for the stairs. I was sure that a return to something that I knew, something that was familiar would help me put all of this into perspective. What I didn't want was all of this intruding into that normal. I didn't say any of that though as I bid Cambious good night and shut my bedroom door.

CHAPTER 9
ENTER THE DAY JOB

The morning of November third dawned clear and a little bit on the cold side. I showered and dressed in the best of the clothes I had left to me, spent the time to blow dry my hair and I even applied the most basic makeup, because first impressions are important. I was going to need to find a hairdresser before long who could wrangle my unruly curls into something tamer.

Breakfast was a cup of coffee and a piece of toast, and I took the time to clean up the books on the table before I left the house in search of the train station. I wasn't prepared for the standing-room-only train, but I staked out a spot by one of the doors, put my headphones on, and turned on some music, then spent most of the forty-minute ride into the city scrolling through the email accounts I had been ignoring. We were maybe three stops from the one where I had been told I should get out and start the three-block walk when I felt eyes on me.

I looked up from my phone, scanning the crowded car that was only just beginning to thin out as we stopped at stations within San Francisco proper. I froze when I saw him, a bald man near the doors that connected to the next car, his dark eyes staring at me with naked hatred.

He didn't blink, just stared at me. I almost missed my stop because I was staring back. I waited almost too late to jump through the doors onto the platform, hoping it would be enough to keep him from following me.

Moving as fast as my less-than-fit body would allow, I raced up the escalator and to the fare gates, then up the next escalator and out onto the street. It took me a few moments to get my bearings, but once I took in the street signs and the landmarks Bonnie had told me to look for, I set out at a brisk pace, glancing behind me frequently to ensure I wasn't being followed.

I was so worried about the man on the train I didn't think about there being others, at least not until a hand grabbed my elbow and tried to pull me into an alley between buildings. I yelled and pulled away, only to find myself sandwiched between two men who each grabbed an arm. "Settle down, *Thanátou*," one of them growled at me. "Do not make us kill others by drawing attention to us."

That was not the thing to say to me to get me to comply. Instead, I began thrashing, pulling my arms away from them, and taking off at a run...not that I could run all that fast or all that far, but I sure as hell was not making it easy for them if I could help it.

"Hey!" Just as one of the men curled a fist in the back of my shirt, a man stepped up beside me and shoved my attacker away. "Ma'am, is this man trying to hurt you?"

I was panting, turning to put the man between me and the Brotherhood thugs. "They're trying to kill me," I said around my ragged breaths.

The man raised a radio to his lips and talked into it, telling whoever was on the other end of the line to get the police to their address. It was then that I realized he was wearing a security uniform. Before my savior could do anything more, both of my attackers disappeared, either into the crowd or into the ether, who knows which.

"I'm okay," I said, thanking the man.

"The police are on their way to get your statement. We'll wait with you."

I shook my head, pulling a shaking hand through my hair and looking around to figure out where I was. "I need to get to work. It's my first day."

"Frank, police should be here in a minute," a voice said behind me. "Did they get away?"

"Vanished," Frank replied, gesturing off up the street. "Ma'am, let's step inside in case they think about trying again."

I let Frank and his fellow security officer hurry me along into a lobby that I immediately recognized with my company's name over the desk. At least I had found the building. "I'm Thána Archer. I'm supposed to start work here today."

The officer who wasn't Frank slipped back behind the security desk. "Who were you meeting?"

"Bonnie Farva."

Frank offered me a seat and I sank into the chair, suddenly cold all over and shaking. Someone handed me a cup of coffee and after a minute, I realized someone was talking to me. I looked up, surprised to find the lobby was full of people. Frank was talking to two police officers and a woman in her forties was looking at me with concern on her face.

"I'm sorry," I said, shaking my head. The steam from the coffee was comforting and I lifted it closer to my face without drinking from it. "I didn't hear what you said."

She smiled softly and sat in the chair beside mine. "It's okay. I'm Bonnie. Frank said you were mugged?"

It was so much more than a mugging, but I couldn't tell her that. "Two guys. I'm not sure what they wanted; they were dragging me somewhere."

"We've had an increase in crime in this area," Bonnie said.

"Ma'am, if it's okay, we'd like to get your version of events," the female cop said, stepping around Frank. She was pretty, her dark braids pulled back neatly into a tight bun at the back of her head.

"I'm fine," I said reflexively. "Just a little shaken up."

We spent the next hour going over what had happened before Bonnie took me through security and out onto the factory floor. The building itself looked nothing like a factory on the outside. In fact, I would have guessed bank or financial institution before I stepped through those doors.

The rest of the day was filled with normal first day things, getting a computer and badge, introductions to more people than I could even begin to remember, and all the rest. My "office" was a small cubicle along the south wall, at the end of my production line, and waiting on my desk were personnel files on each of the people working the line, along with quality and defect reports for the last six months. It was a lot to go through.

The line's quality had been declining for months, but it wasn't clear if the issue was a matter of training, equipment, or the quality of the materials being used. Based on what I could see from just the reports, I knew that I wanted to tackle it with a three-pronged attack. I wrote up my preliminary recommendation: that we send the entire line up to training to be recertified, a full inspection of all of the equipment as well as a spot check of all of the materials being used on the line.

Once I'd finished that, I glanced up at the clock, surprised to see it had gone past six-thirty. The floor was mostly quiet, the small second shift crew busily about their tasks. I gathered my things and headed for Bonnie's office to drop off my recommendations.

"That was fast," she said after I handed it to her.

"I like to jump in with both feet," I replied. "But it's been a long day and I should head home."

"Let me get someone to take you to the train. We don't want a repeat of this morning."

"I'm sure I'll be fine." As much as a part of me wanted the comfort of having an escort, I knew that I couldn't avoid walking by myself forever. "I'll see you tomorrow. I'm planning on talking one on one with the entire line tomorrow. Personnel files can't tell me who a person is."

"Sounds good. Be safe."

The security guard at the front desk was neither Frank nor the other guy, whose name I never caught. I did my best to be aware of my surroundings and the people moving through the streets, taking some comfort in the crowded platform and trains, thinking it would make my attackers hesitate. I had no idea if that were true, but I held on to it as if it were.

I was on high alert the whole ride home and the walk to my car in the gathering dark, but there was no sign of the Brotherhood or self-steering cars, even as I pulled onto the street and then into my driveway. There was a man putting something in the trunk of that '67 Mustang next door though and he lifted a hand in greeting. "You must be the new neighbor, I'm Steve Marsh."

I smiled and crossed the yard to shake his outstretched hand. "Sort of. I'm Thána Archer. I lived here when I was a child. I'm just getting back." All of my ID was in the name Archer, and the last name on my birth certificate felt strange in my mouth when I had tried it that morning before leaving for work.

"Well, welcome. My wife will be glad to know someone is finally living here. It's been the only empty on the street for a while, but that guy who's been taking care of the place has done a great job with the yards. If you need names for contractors to help you with the paint job and that sagging porch, let me know. My brother and his friends do great work."

"Thanks, I'm not sure I'm ready for that, but I'll let you know." I waved goodbye and headed into the house, flipping on lights as I dropped my keys onto the table by the door. I was exhausted, wrung out from the chaos of the last weeks, the attempt on my life, and the first day in a new job. Part of me wanted to just have a glass of wine and go to bed, but I also hadn't eaten, so I knew that needed to come first. I found the stuff to make a peanut butter sandwich and opened the screw cap on the cheap bottle of wine I had bought the day before, pouring some into a tumbler I pulled from the cupboard.

I was sitting at the table thinking about just how classy my dinner was when it dawned on me that I hadn't had to look for the glass, and I hadn't even considered reaching for the wine glasses further up, just grabbed a plastic tumbler from the bottom shelf. It was muscle memory or something. I'd done it before…probably a million times before we'd left this house.

As I looked around me, I felt more at home than I had ever felt. I did have to do something about my bedroom though. I hadn't slept in a twin bed since my teens, and the childish decor was not suited to my style. I could move into my parents' room, but somehow that felt like a betrayal. As far as I knew, my mother wasn't dead, and she could come home and want her room back. No, I decided sitting there, I would buy a new bed and paint the walls a nice rust or sage, something that suited my more grown-up palette.

There was more excitement to the idea than I would have thought, but I had never really had a room of my own in a place that I owned, though I supposed technically my mother still owned it. I finished my sandwich and took my glass of wine upstairs with me. Looking around my childhood bedroom, I could almost see how it would look with a queen-sized bed, maybe a set of bookshelves, a bigger desk.

I figured I could start the next weekend, I just had to get through the week at work first. For now, I just wanted to sleep and get a fresh start the next day. I finished my wine and set the tumbler on my nightstand before crawling into the bed. As much as I wanted to sleep, flashes of the attack that morning kept playing through my head. Four times now I'd come close to losing my life for some idealistic crusade that I had never even heard of before Finneas Connor had stepped into my life.

Despite my exhaustion, sleep was not coming easily and after an hour or so I got up, grabbed my tumbler, and headed back downstairs to my collected pile of books. Maybe somewhere in them I would find an answer to why, exactly, a bunch of fanatics I had never met wanted to bleed me.

CHAPTER 10
NESTING

THERE WAS A TIME WHEN I DIDN'T FEEL AS THOUGH I NEEDED TO keep my head on a swivel just going about my daily business. Of course, that was before I knew who I was and before someone had tried to run me down, burn me out, slash my throat or kidnap me off the streets of San Francisco.

By the time Friday came around, with no further incidents the rest of the week, I was starting to relax. I left work a little early and headed to the local hardware store to pick up some paint, then hit up two of the local furniture stores to test out beds. After ordering a bedroom suite, I headed home.

Cambious was on the greenhouse porch as I came in with my gallons of paint and other odds and ends and he smiled as he came to help me. "You've been busy." He nodded toward the books on the table. I had spent my evenings trying to cram as much knowledge about my new reality into my head as I could. I'd even tried my hand at a few of the spells, including that one protection spell I'd found, though I wasn't sure if I'd used the right herbs, or gathered them at the right time because I wasn't sure exactly when the "dark of the moon" was supposed to be.

"There's a lot to learn," I said, putting my bag on the counter.

"I'm happy to see you working on it," Cambious said. "I

found a couple of books I thought you might be interested in. This one is a few years old, but it is the most thorough telling of the Brotherhood's history I've ever read." He pointed to a book beside my pile. It was thick, its cover a slick black with the image of that haunting fortress on it. "And the other is one of the only texts that survived the purges of Blood Witches. It is rudimentary, and not really an instruction book, but should ground you in the basics."

"Thanks." I lifted the first book and paged through it. The printing was small, but it was filled with pictures and quotes and looked like something I would learn from. "I was going to throw together some dinner, if you want to join me."

He nodded. "My brother is on guard duty tonight. I would love to join you."

"Great. Could you take the paint up to my room? That's my weekend's plan, to get that painted. I'll get started on food."

I sorted through the pantry and came out with a can of corned beef hash, double-checked that I had eggs, and set about making breakfast for dinner. When Cambious returned, he leaned on the counter watching. "I understand the Brotherhood found you on Monday." His voice was soft and deep, but it made me stiffen up.

"I'm fine," I responded, cracking an egg into the pan. "And I haven't seen them since."

"They must have left a contingent behind after the veil returned to normal. The next nearest permanent portal is in Los Angeles, the one Merry used to find you. It is not a well-known portal and belongs to a family who does not support the aims of the Brotherhood."

"So, I can expect more of these random attacks?" I asked, flipping the two eggs in my pan over.

"And each time they will get closer to their true purpose," Cambious warned. I could feel his eyes watching me, not with that same intensity that once made my stomach drop with desire, but there was concern.

"I'm not sure what you expect me to do about it," I said after a long silence watching the eggs cook. "I am being careful. I'm always aware of who is around me, but I'm not going to just give up living and hide away in this house."

"I wasn't suggesting that," Cambious replied, handing me a plate. "I've just been thinking about it. They won't want to kill you here unless they have no other choice. They'll need access to a portal to take you back, so unless they've found a way to create a new permanent portal, they're going to either try to use yours or transport you to another one."

"Or wait for the spring when the veil thins again," I added.

He smiled. "You have been learning."

I handed him a plate and opened the drawer for forks. "I figured I needed to." I sighed and took my plate to the table. "I am remembering more, but it's not coming fast enough."

"Go easy," Cambious warned as he sat opposite me. "You cannot learn a lifetime's worth of spell work and history in a few weeks' time."

"Now you tell me." I rolled my eyes and settled in to eat. "There is something…" It had been bothering me that all I had to learn from was what my mother left me from her side of the family and there was little about my father to be found. "You said that your family was bound to mine, to my mother's family."

He nodded. His eyes seemed to intensify as he watched me. "I can't find any information about my father or his family. What do you know about them?"

Cambious put his fork down and leveled his eyes at me. "I can tell you that your father loved your mother and you girls with every fiber of his being. He walked away from a fortune to marry your mother. His mother forbid it and threatened to disown him if he married your mother."

"Why?"

Cambious shrugged. "That is not my story to tell. Perhaps you will have a chance to ask her yourself."

"That's not an answer." I sighed in frustration and rubbed a hand over my face. "I have maybe five clear memories of him, and the strongest of them is when he died. I have no doubt he loved me. I feel that love in that memory. He gave his life to save mine. But I know almost nothing else about him."

"What is it you think you should know?" Cambious asked, returning to his food.

I sighed again. "I don't know. What was he like? What did he do for a living? When did they come here to California? Obviously, it was before I was born."

"Okay, I would say that your father was mostly a happy guy, who loved his family. He and your mother met at university and got married shortly before she graduated. They came here when they found out she was pregnant with you. He would travel back and forth for a while when you were a baby, working as a sort of inter-dimensional postman, delivering messages and packages and such between families that have exiles here."

"So, they came here because of me?" I asked without looking up. "Did they know I'd be...what I am?"

"It is never for certain. The gift is exceedingly rare, but there was precedent on your mother's side for one of her children to be born to the gift, and there was dormant history on your father's side, so the chances increased. Your mother was terrified that an increase in activity among the Brotherhood would make you a target, if only for your family names."

"And she obviously wasn't wrong."

"No, unfortunately, she was not."

"And my father...he had magic too, didn't he? I mean, he fought the guy who tried to kill me when I was six."

At that Cambious grinned. "Ah, he was brilliant! Could have chosen any specialty really, or so my father says. He was gifted. He chose to be a garden witch for the most part, with a particular focus on growing magical ingredients that could be used in regular foods, not just potions and incantations. Most of the powders, spices, and such in the pantry are from his stock." He gestured at the greenhouse porch. "But the fruits out there are all your mother's. She could make fruit trees grow anywhere."

"You seem to have known them well," I observed, suddenly curious about Cambious and how old he had to be. To my eyes, he didn't look much older than me, but between his comment a few days before about having his surgery fifty years ago, and how much time he must have spent with my parents, I had to wonder.

He nodded. "After my transition, I came up to the cabin to recover. I started to relieve my father well before your parents came here. Once they did, I spent a good amount of time with them both." We were quiet for a few minutes, then Cambious gestured at my pile of books. "Tell me, have you experimented at all?"

It was my turn to shrug noncommittally. "Not seriously? I mean, Monday night when I couldn't sleep, I tried this one...but I have no way of knowing if it worked."

"Which one?" Cambious asked, one eyebrow raised.

I fished out the book from the pile and found the spell again, then handed the book over. "And you haven't seen any of the Brotherhood since you did this?"

I rolled my eyes, not willing to be convinced it was that simple. "Mind you, I'm not sure I even got the right plants. I was tired and couldn't sleep."

"It was the right night for it," Cambious said, handing me back the book. "And I know you have all of those plants out on the porch, so if you identified them correctly, you might have managed it. I know you've used it before, after your father died. Your mother thought it might help you feel safer."

"Obviously, it didn't work," I countered. "They still kept finding us."

"Ah, but it isn't a particularly strong or lasting spell. Its purpose is to confound your enemies for a short time in order to make your escape."

"Not a whole lot of good then, is it?"

"It's given you a peaceful week, has it not?" Cambious countered. "But perhaps a better place to begin is with something more basic, something of infinite usage."

"I take it you have a suggestion?"

"I do indeed. There should have been a set of ward stones in the box you were given. Have you figured out how to use them?"

I reached for the trunk on the chair near me, rummaging until I came up with the small bag that had the stones. I dumped them onto the table. There were twelve in all, smaller than most dice, carved of what I took to be obsidian. Their edges and corners had been worn over time.

"They were your mother's when she was a girl," Cambious said.

"I'm not sure what I'm supposed to do with them," I admitted, brushing my hand over them. Automatically, I started sorting them into pairs, each of them feeling slightly different, and yet instinctively I knew which ones went with which.

"At their most basic, they keep out the things you don't want getting in. There are larger, stronger versions of those warding stones at all four corners of this property, which is why the Brotherhood cannot see into this house or cross the property line, not without knocking the wards out first."

"So, like a magical door lock?" I remembered Merry using them at the door to the motel.

"More or less. You can use as few as four stones to secure say a window, or all twelve to secure a camp location or ritual site. There are a number of different ways to activate them, but you should start with the most basic." He stabbed a finger at the small book that had been mine as a child. "You should have that incantation in there. I know your mother was teaching you how to use them before you left here."

"Do you know where she is?" I asked, a sudden melancholy filling me. I had spent so many years angry at her, or her abandonment of me at least, that this increasing sense of longing that had been building inside me all week was disconcerting.

"I'm sorry, I don't. Not for sure. She came through the portal without you about five years after she left here, said she was taking your sister somewhere to be safe, and I know that she visited family in Thelos, and Finneas Connor in Greju, but then she just disappeared. As far as I know, no one has seen her since."

Five years after we left the house, so a few years after she had left me with no memory outside that police station in Rochester, New York. I could only wonder what she and Daria had done after they left me there. I yawned and shook my head. Everything was so exhausting. And I had so much more to learn.

CHAPTER 11
GHOSTS OF THE PAST

I spent my weekend painting my bedroom and working with the ward stones. The first incantation scribbled in my childhood handwriting used only four stones, two pairs, and when properly constructed, the resulting ward could secure a window or small door.

Whenever I wasn't painting, I was attempting to make that incantation work. I don't know why I expected it to be easy, but it wasn't. It was Sunday afternoon before I got more than the four stones stacked in pairs, and then it was little more than a flash of something before the stones toppled.

I was reaching for the stones when I heard my mother's voice softly chiding me. "You're trying too hard. Relax. Let the magic flow through you."

I looked up, nearly certain I'd find her leaning on the door frame as she had in my memory. I'd had this same fight with the cubes before. "I don't know how," I whined in my memory.

"You do, Thána. You can do this."

In my memory, I heard myself speak the words of the incantation and I followed my own lead, touching first one stack of the stones, then the second. *"Prostatéfste kai apothéste aftó to chóro."* To my surprise, the stones seemed to glow for a moment, then between them stretched a field, like the one Merry had constructed in my hotel room in LA. I sat back, satisfied.

After a moment, I reached for the book again, seeking the incantation to disassemble the field. *"Elefthérosi."* The field collapsed and the stones on the left tumbled over. I ran through the process several times until I was sure I could put them up at will before I pocketed the stones and went to start cleaning up from the day's painting.

I was surprised when the room spun as I gained my feet and fatigue pulled at my limbs. I felt drained. I staggered to the bed and sat down hard, shaking my head. In the book, my younger self had written the words, "It's harder than you think." I was beginning to understand that.

After a few minutes, I was able to get up and get moving again. I went back to the white trim I had been painting before my break, putting a few finishing touches on the door frame before I called it a night. Cambious had told me that relearning the basics might mean rebuilding a tolerance to the toll magic takes on a user. I wasn't sure I had believed him. Hell, I was still on the fence about the whole idea of magic at all, but so far, Cambious hadn't been wrong about anything.

The potion seemed to have worked, which wasn't to say I wasn't still having random dreams about sex and Cambious, but I wasn't overwhelmed with the lust for him like I was at the beginning. And, as Cambious had pointed out, my "hide me from my enemies" spell seemed to have worked as well, at least for the time being. And now, I'd made the ward stones work, at least on a small scale. Maybe in a few days I'd be ready to try one of the more complicated configurations of the stones. There were several written in my childhood journal/spellbook, and I vaguely recalled seeing more in one of the other books.

My mind was still on that as I cleaned up my painting supplies, taking the pan and brushes downstairs to wash. As I stepped off the stairs and turned for the kitchen, I stopped cold. A man was there, between me and the kitchen. He turned and my heart stopped. His eyes sparkled and his smile was wide as he saw me.

"Dad?" I choked out the word, knowing that was who I was seeing, and knowing that it couldn't be real.

He nodded once, still smiling, but his eyes were sad. His mouth moved, but no sound came. His hand reached out and I stepped forward, trying to reach him, but in the split second between picking up my foot and putting it back down, he was gone.

Emptiness sank into my stomach, and I sank with it, ending up on my ass on the wood floor right where he'd been standing. My whole being reverberated with a sudden and desperate longing for the love I was starting to remember, the family I had lost. I was still sitting there, however long later, with paint drying on my hand and tears streaming down my face when I heard Cambious on the stairs. I struggled to get up before he could find me there, but my legs wouldn't cooperate.

"Thána?"

I wiped the back of the hand holding the brush across my cheeks and tried again to stand. His hands came to steady me, and he followed me into the kitchen, close behind me. I put the pan and brush in the sink and exhaled a breath I wasn't fully aware I was holding.

"Are you...?"

I nodded, sort of messy and not at all convincing. "I saw... honestly, I don't know what I saw."

"Come sit down." Cambious guided me to a chair, and I sat gratefully. "Tell me."

I licked my lips and nodded. "Okay, so...I've been working with the ward stones, like you said. Finally got a basic ward up too. Then, it was like I'd been running in sand for hours. I came down here to clean up, and as I came off the stairs, there he was. Just standing there...like when I'd come home from school." That memory flooded me, running in all excited to show him what I'd learned that day, the way he would beam at me in pride and sweep me into his arms.

"Who?"

"You're going to think I'm crazy."

He gave me a look that was all about the crazy my life had become and shook his head gently.

"My father." I whispered it, barely daring to glance up at him as I did.

He was nodding though. "I'm not surprised."

"You're not?" I asked, my voice high and tight. "I was! He's dead, Cambious."

"And you're a blood witch who helped him pass over. If he's going to appear to anyone, it's going to be you."

I shook my head. "I don't believe in ghosts."

He shrugged his massive shoulders dismissively. "Apparently that does not stop them from being."

I took a deep breath and let it out slowly. "Okay, why now? Why here? Why not all those years ago when I was alone and really could have used a father, even one who was dead?"

Cambious took my hands and held them for a moment, then tilted my chin up so he could look into my eyes. Tears ran unchecked down my face and his finger brushed them away. "He is here because here is where he died, *Mikros*. And now is when you are also here."

"It isn't fair," I muttered, knowing I sounded like that six-year-old me in my memory with the ward stones. "I barely remember him, and mostly I remember him dying."

Cambious didn't respond, just pulled me close and folded his arms around me, paint and all. I let him comfort me for a minute before I sniffed and pulled back. I stood, feeling awkward and emotional, and only one of those two things felt normal for me. I'd always been awkward. I'd learned early to shove my emotions down into a dark hole so others wouldn't be bothered by them. Over the years it had just become who I was.

I went to the sink to wash the paint off my hands and clean

my tools, working to shove the sudden loneliness and longing for my family back into its hiding place. Cambious gave me the space and was quiet until I was nearly done.

"Your room looks great," he ventured when I was pressing water out of the brush.

"Thanks."

"I was wondering if you'd be interested in coming through the portal with me? I have food and a lovely bottle of *Erythraó* that I think you'd enjoy, judging on what I've seen of your taste in wine."

I turned, thoughts about ghosts and family momentarily forgotten. "Are you asking me on a date, Cambious?"

He grinned. "Not exactly. I just think it's time you see where you come from. I promise to have you home by bedtime."

I nodded slowly. "Just let me change."

"You look fine," Cambious countered. "There's no one around for miles. It will be just the two of us."

"Sure, okay." He stood, holding out a hand to me. I slipped my hand into his, marveling again at the size of him, then he was leading me back to the stairs and down to the closet where he opened the door and held it for me.

I hesitated at the threshold, peering into the darkness beyond. The only light I could see was the soft glow of some lanterns that held down the corners of a blanket a few yards from the door. I held my breath as I stepped through, though I couldn't tell you why, and I let it out when the ground didn't disappear beneath me. The night air was warm and smelled vaguely of something akin to jasmine. The blanket looked to be hand-woven, spread out on a grassy patch between boulders. I couldn't see much beyond the warm yellow light of the lanterns, so I turned back, wondering what the door looked like from this side.

Oddly enough, it looked like a door, stuck into a rock as tall as a house. Cambious ducked his head as he stepped through the door and I gasped as he reverted to his true form, horns and all. I had nearly forgotten. I tried to cover my surprise, but Cambious just smiled. "I also figured it was time you dealt with me in my regular guise. Sit, sit."

I backpedaled to the blanket, reminding myself that horns or not, he was still Cambious, the same guy I had grown to trust in the short time I'd been in the house...which unbelievably had been less than two whole weeks. I sank down to the blanket, shifting until I found a comfortable position. Cambious joined me, his large feet eating the distance from the door. If it were possible, he was even larger in this form than the giant of a man I had gotten to know. He reached for a basket, opening the side, and pulling out first a bottle of wine, which he passed to me.

In seconds there was some sort of music playing, something that had a vaguely familiar feeling. I looked to see him setting down what I assumed was his world's version of a radio. "Like it?"

"I'm not sure," I answered.

He smiled. "It equates to your world's baroque period. Similar instruments, though entirely our own. This piece in particular is from a Greco composer named Alexi Manoko, from approximately two hundred years ago. His use of string instruments is quite inspired."

I handed him back the bottle to open. "I'll take your word for it. I'm more of a Coldplay and Maroon 5 sort of girl."

"And the wine?"

I shrugged. "I pretty much can tell it's wine," I said with a chuckle.

"Well, we will have to work on your ability to read the language of our fair land. It's a red, not too far afield from your pinot noir, though it is a blend. Shall I pour?"

I gestured for him to continue, and he fished a corkscrew and two glasses out of the basket. When he had handed me a glass and turned his attention to the rest of our meal, I took the opportunity to try to learn more about the world I found myself in. Unfortunately, there wasn't much to be seen in the dark. "What time is it here? I remember that first day, it was midafternoon, but it was dark on this side of the door."

"It is approximately two in the morning," Cambious responded, setting out containers of various kinds of food. There was a collection of what seemed to be vegetables, a meat of some kind, something mashed with what looked like cheese on top, and a pie that smelled delicious. "Our days are a bit shorter than yours, our years a bit longer. Which means there is exactly one day each year when we are more or less in sync. The rest of the time we are constantly ahead of or behind you."

I tucked the knowledge into my brain folder for all things not a part of my life prior to the arrival of Finneas Connor and took the fork and plate that Cambious offered me. I served myself some of each of the dishes, saving the pie for once I'd tasted the rest. I was surprised somehow that the meat and mashed vegetable dishes were piping hot as if just served off the stove. Honestly, I'm not sure how anything surprised me at that point, but it did.

As if guessing my thought process, Cambious chuckled. "Magic," he said, as if that alone would answer all of my questions. To be fair, it probably did.

I tasted the meat dish first. It was pale in color, except where the spices tinted it vaguely orange-red. "Chicken?" I asked as I lifted a forkful to my mouth.

"Similar to," Cambious responded, dishing up his own plate.

The taste was similar too, so I guessed it was some sort of bird. The spices brought out the natural flavor of the meat, without disguising it. Next, I tried the mashed...whatever. Had we been in my own kitchen, I would have guessed potato, but the taste was more turnip than potato. "This is really good," I said around my mouthful. I swallowed around my horror at talking with my mouth full, then reached for the wine. The flavor of the wine exploded across my tongue, and I brought the glass back to my lips to drink more. "This is amazing."

It was clear my praise made Cambious happy, his dark skin

all aglow with pleasure. "I hoped you would like it. Wine isn't always my forte. I've been working at improving my wine vocabulary." He rolled his eyes a little to the right. "Also, one of my many, many half-siblings owns the winery where this particular vintage was created. She gifted it to me when I told her why I wanted it."

I was suitably impressed, even if I didn't say so right away. We ate in companionable silence for a while, and I didn't even begin to feel the need to say anything, which for me was odd at least.

CHAPTER 12
NEW FRIENDS

ALL TOLD, WE SPENT ALMOST TWO HOURS THERE ON THAT BLANKET, eating, finishing off that bottle of wine, and sinking back into our last conversation about the history of a homeland I had never known, but found myself sitting in.

"There," Cambious said, pointing over my shoulder. "Can you see those lights?"

In the distance, a series of golden and white lights danced on the horizon, maybe fifty miles away, more if we were on a mountain. "Yeah. What is it?"

"That is Thelos. Your mother was born there. Merry lives on the outskirts."

"Merry lives there?" I stood, turning to squint in that direction…which was ludicrous. It wasn't like I was going to actually see the crazy old woman.

"Not just her. You have some aunts and uncles there too. Even one of your father's cousins. His family wanted nothing to do with him when he sided with your father."

I turned to study him in the half-light provided by the lanterns. "You seem to know an awful lot about my family."

"Well, our families have been joined for over a hundred years."

"A hundred…I thought you said your father and my…grand-father?" I glanced at the glass of wine in my hand, trying to decide if it was strong enough to absolve my inability to remember the exact details. "How old **are** you?"

Cambious seemed amused by my confusion. "Older than you might imagine…and my father was just a teen himself at the time."

I shook my head, too compromised from the wine to give it too much more thought. Even as I sipped at the remnants in my glass, I was thinking that I needed to consider that I had to go to work in the morning. "So, how do you suggest I go about not getting killed or kidnapped by Brotherhood thugs while I attempt to live my life this week?" I asked as Cambious raised the bottle and topped off my glass with the last of the wine.

"Don't go to work?" Cambious suggested. I couldn't tell whether he was being serious or not.

"That is **not** an option, Cambious," I countered. "Even if I own the house and the land, there are still bills to pay."

"And yet, the house still stands today, even though there hasn't been a member of your family in residence in over twenty years," Cambious responded, his hand dropping onto my shoulder.

"There is food, and water and electricity…" I said, shaking my head.

"Perhaps you require a vacation," Cambious offered. "Time to reconnect to a family you have never known."

I shook my head, starting to feel overwhelmed by it all. "I think what I need, my friend, is to get home and shower, sleep… get ready for my Monday."

"If that is what my lady wishes…" Cambious said with a grand bow and gesture toward the door.

"It is."

He crossed to the door and held it open for me. "Until the next time…"

I smirked and rose up on my tiptoes in an attempt to reach

his cheek. I only reached as far as the side of his neck, but I kissed it anyway. "Until next time indeed." I crossed back into my house, the house I had been left by my mother, warm and filled with good feelings. I had enjoyed the dinner and the time spent in the company of someone that my known history should have proved to be impossible. I stripped on my way into the bathroom, tipsy enough to not care about the trail of paint-spattered clothing I left behind me.

My shower was quick, just enough to wash the specks of paint from my skin and hair. A quick check that my alarm was set, and I fell into bed, more content than I could remember being. That, of course, didn't last long. I found myself trapped in bloody dreams, my clothing drenched in it, my skin sticky as it dried. I couldn't tell where the blood was coming from, and I couldn't see in the dark. I woke breathlessly nearly an hour before the alarm.

I was shaking as I sat up. Like the dreams I'd had as a child, there was no detail to them, no definition. And yet, they were just as terrifying. Pushing the hair out of my face, I put my feet on the floor and stood. There was no point trying to go back to sleep, it would just make getting up again worse. Instead, I got dressed and rescued my discarded clothing from the hallway floor, depositing it in my hamper before I headed downstairs to make coffee.

Once the coffee was started, I diverted into the downstairs bathroom to tame my hair, which had started to curl up when I went to bed without blow drying it out. The coffee machine beeped just as I finished straight ironing it into something that resembled my normal straight style, even if it was puffier than usual. A cup of coffee later and I was sitting at the kitchen table amidst my collection of books filled with arcane knowledge.

I opened the book on the Brotherhood that Cambious had brought me. The history of the Brotherhood was fascinating if disturbing. The book posited that the movement had begun as simply a stricter reading of religious texts by a small group of monks dedicated to Jeus, who I gathered was similar to Zeus mixed with Jesus, except of course that this faith had its roots thousands of years before either.

Before the Brotherhood, people with gifts like mine were called, *kapnastís*, which meant "disease eater" and they were revered and sought after to help heal the kinds of diseases that the medicine of the day could do nothing for. In the religious literature, there was a story about a gathering of *kapnastís* in the dawn of mankind who came together after collecting drops of blood from all the many scattered peoples of the world to give the blood as a gift to Hathus, to calm the cataclysm of earthquakes, volcanic eruptions, and other catastrophes as Hathus tried to expel mankind from his land.

In some versions of the myth, the *kapnastís* ingested the blood, then expelled it through their menses into the earth at a place called *Hathus Koúna*, the Cradle of Hathus. They squatted there for five days and nights, giving this gift to the god of the Underworld and when it was done, the land quieted and the volcanoes ceased their flowing. The story told of a time when the next payment would be due, and it was there that the Brotherhood seemed to cut away from the traditional understanding of what would come.

It started with small disagreements with the established understanding and grew over time until a man named Humile Racklish showed up on the scene. It was Racklish, as he rose through the ranks of the order, who poisoned his brothers with the idea that a blood witch did not cure but kill. There is some evidence that Racklish, as a child, saw his mother die at the hands of a *kapnastís* who had been called in too late to save her. Instead, she had taken away the woman's pain and eased her into the next life, and Racklish had decided that this woman had killed her.

It was a fine line, I supposed. Had the woman been left alone, she would still have died. Whoever that blood witch was, she had probably spared her days of suffering or more. Racklish went on to rise to the rank of *Evlogim Patoras*, essentially in charge of his own chapter of the monks. Under him, they moved further and further away from the original scriptures, turning to other works that supported their reading.

My coffee had gotten cold as I read, and when I realized it, I got up to refill it, but noticed the time and set the coffee down and tucked the book into my briefcase. I headed out the door and to the train station. Finding parking was challenging, especially with the construction of a new garage eating up most of the surface lots. I finally ended up on the fourth floor of the existing garage and parked, scrambling to get to the platform.

Of course, my distraction caused me to miss the train I'd been aiming to get on, so I settled in to wait the ten minutes for the next one. My mind rambled over what I'd read, the eerie parallels to some of the history I knew of the religions in the world around me. I figured it had something to do with human nature. I was still pondering that when someone said, "Good morning."

Startled, I turned to see a woman beside me, zipping up her coat. Her smile was bright, and her eyes sparkled. "Hello," I responded, thrown a little bit. I hadn't adjusted to riding public transportation, but I was fairly certain most folks just put on their headphones and minded their own business.

"Haven't seen you before. New job?" she asked amiably.

"Yeah, normally I take the train before this one. Missed it this morning."

"Well, I hope it won't make you late for work." She held out her hand. "I'm Hannah."

I shook her hand, still a little confused. "Thána," I responded.

"We're a friendly bunch on this line," Hannah said, waving as two older ladies walked past us to another spot down the platform. Hannah herself seemed to be older than me, but not by a lot. She was at least four inches shorter than me. Several others were calling out hellos as they got in line behind Hannah. "Everyone, this is Thána. Thána, this is Amber, Purav, and Josie."

I nodded hello, my eyes sweeping over the group. Amber

was younger than me, dressed in blue scrubs with a fluffy winter jacket on over them. Beside her, Purav was tall and thin with graying black hair and dark eyes. He reminded me of one of my techs back in El Paso. Josie brought up the rear, with tired eyes and what looked like a bag heavy with books. I couldn't guess her age, but she looked like someone who had been around the block a couple of times.

They bantered, trying to draw me into the conversation, but I've never been good at small talk. Eventually, they managed to get me to tell them how long I'd been in the area, that I worked in the city, and that I wasn't a fan of public transportation. Purav gave me extensive detail about how much easier it was than driving into the city, except for when there were mechanical issues, or someone jumped onto the tracks. I learned that morning that "medical emergency" was the code for a suicide on the tracks, and that it would snarl up the commute for many hours.

"Your best bet then is to get together with other people coming this way and take an Uber." His accent was subtle, very Americanized, and his voice was a beautiful, soft tenor that I found soothing.

"I'll keep that in mind," I said with a small smile. Conversation stopped as the train pulled in, too loud to try to overcome with our voices. We boarded and to my surprise, there were available seats. I pulled my book out of my briefcase as I sat, determined to get a few chapters read before getting to my stop.

"Whatcha reading?" Hannah asked, sitting next to me.

"It's the history of a cult known as the Brotherhood of God," I responded, flipping open to my marker.

"I've never heard of them," Hannah said.

"They aren't from around here." I put the book in my lap and looked at her. She looked genuinely interested, which I wasn't used to. "Some of my ancestors got tangled up with them, and so I wanted to learn more."

"Cults are spooky." She made a face. "I had a cousin once

101

that got mixed up with the Moonies. Mmmhm." She shook her head. "I'll think for myself, thanks."

I had to chuckle. "Yeah, me too. Still, the history of how they get started is fascinating."

She turned to her phone after that, and I picked my book back up. Now and then I let my eyes sweep the faces around me, looking for any hostile eyes and bald heads. As each of my new friends got off the train, they said goodbye, to both me and Hannah, until Hannah and I were the only ones of the group still on the train. I put my book back in my briefcase and stood as we approached my stop.

"Oh, this is my stop too," Hannah said, standing with me. "Which way are you heading?"

"Just a few blocks down from Mission," I replied, moving with the other commuters on their way to the fare gates.

"I'm heading that way too. We can walk together."

A part of me thought that was the worst idea ever, with people trying to kill me, I didn't want her to get caught in the crossfire. On the other hand, maybe they would be less likely to make a move on me if I had company. Either way, it was fairly obvious that Hannah was the kind of person who, once she decided to be your friend, you were not going to shake her very easily. About a block from where I could already see Frank the security guard out front of our building, Hannah hitched her thumb at a glass and steel skyscraper. "This is me. Nice to meet you, Thána."

"Yeah you too," I said, unsure whether I meant it or not. I never really was what you would call a people person. I preferred the company of animals and books.

Frank held the door for me and tipped his hat as I passed by. As I headed for my office, I put the world outside of work away so I could focus on the job at hand.

CHAPTER 13
RUN

IT WAS NEARLY THANKSGIVING BEFORE ANYTHING INTRUDED INTO the quiet life I wanted and was hoping I would get. I'd spent the time working, and when I was at home, I was trying to fast-track a lifetime full of knowledge about all of the things I never knew were real, like witches and ghosts and transgender incubi.

There were no new sightings of Brotherhood men seeking my life, and for that matter, no new sightings of my father's ghost either. I was grateful for both. Work was progressing, my line was already showing improved quality and I found myself actually enjoying the company of my fellow BART riders in the mornings, much to my surprise.

Like most other holidays, Thanksgiving had never been a special day for me. Mostly it reinforced the idea that I wasn't a part of the family I lived with. I was always treated well enough, but it never felt like home. I was, however, looking forward to a four-day weekend, time to spend working my way through my beginner's spellbook and practicing with the ward stones.

Or at least, that's what I had planned.

I let my team leave at noon the Wednesday before, finished up some paperwork, and headed home myself. I gave thought to stopping to pick up groceries, then remembered that it was the day before a holiday, and everyone was out in the stores losing their minds over a can of evaporated milk or a carton of eggnog. I decided to order take-out instead and headed for my car in the BART parking garage.

That was when I caught the first glimpse of them. Three of them, dressed in black suits with bald heads. They were standing around my car.

I shrank back to the cover of the stairwell, peeking through the railing. They stood nearly motionless. Behind them, near the front of my car, there was a shimmer of sorts, like light reflecting on water. My stomach twisted and I eased back down the staircase, nearly knocking Purav over. "Oh, sorry," I said in little more than a whisper.

"Is everything okay?"

I shook my head. "No." I wasn't sure exactly what to say. "It's…could I get a ride home, do you think? My…my ex sent some friends of his…and they're just…I don't want to deal with it right now."

"Yes, no problem. Are you sure you don't want to get the police?"

I shook my head. "No, I'll wait for them to get bored and leave. Come back later for my car." I wasn't sure the cops could handle them, with who knew what kind of magic power between them. Home was safe enough though, warded and all that. Cambious could come back with me. Maybe in the morning.

"Why don't you go downstairs and wait by the garage exit. I'll get my car. It's a white Prius."

I nodded, slinking past him down the stairs, my eyes scanning the first level and the exit for more of them. When Purav pulled up, I jumped in as quickly as I could. "I don't think they saw me," I said in relief as we pulled away from the curb. I gave him my address and tried to control the erratic fury of my heartbeat. "I don't know how to thank you. My ex is…well let's just say we see things very differently."

"Are you going to be okay alone?" Purav asked as we stopped in front of my house.

"I won't be alone. I have a friend staying with me." It wasn't a complete lie. Cambious was just on the other side of a door. "Thank you. I hope you have a wonderful long weekend."

He smiled and touched my hand. "Please be careful."

I nodded and climbed out of the car. He waited as I looked around for trouble, then let myself into the gate in the fence. For the first time, I could feel the wards let me in and close behind me. At least I had **that** going for me. I snorted to myself and fished my keys out of the pocket of my work pants, unlocking the door. I waved to Purav to let him know I was safe, and I watched him pull away.

And that was when I saw the two men in black suits step out of two different yards and turn toward me. Quickly, I closed the door and threw the deadbolt. My heart hammered at my ribs as I turned from the door. I had no idea how the wards would hold or how much trouble I was in.

I turned and nearly screamed as once again my father's ghost was standing in the hallway, arm outstretched to me. Once I caught my breath, I rolled my eyes. "No offense, Dad, but now really isn't a good time."

I dropped my keys on the table and my briefcase on the stairs. As I started to go up the stairs to get Cambious, my father moved, suddenly in front of me on the stairs, pointing at the door. "Yeah, I know," I said, staring up at him. "And there are more of them, at least three more. So, unless you're here to tell me what to do now, I need to go find Cambious."

"Your mother."

I stopped with my foot still on the stair, blinking at him. "Did you just…"

He blinked in and out for a moment, then seemed to solidify. "Go through the portal. Find your mother." And then he was gone.

"That's it?" I asked the empty air. Fear thrummed through

me, kicking my sarcastic annoyance into high gear. "Find your mother. Right. Just like that. Sure, why not." I stormed up the stairs and into the closet, wrenching the door open. "Cambious, I —" I stopped when the incubus on the other side of the door turned out to be someone other than Cambious. "Oh, sorry."

He smiled at me, his teeth sharp and white as they stood out in contrast to his black skin. "You must be Thána. I am Durious, Cam's brother."

"Oh." Yes, my witty self was on a roll. "I…there are Brotherhood goons outside."

"That isn't good," Durious said. "How many?"

"Two here, another three at the train station surrounding my car."

"That really isn't good."

"Tell me about it. I'm trapped in here now."

"I'll call Cambious. You should pack a bag. We can get you to your family here."

"What good will that do? Aren't there more of them over there?"

"Yes, but here at least the law is on your side and your family will know how to protect you."

Right. Because they'd done such a good job of that in the past. "Whatever. Just get Cambious here."

I closed the door and headed to my bedroom. I had no idea what I needed to pack to go through the portal. I pulled out an old duffle bag I had found at the back of my parent's closet and put it on the bed. I was pulling out clean underwear when the floor beneath me shook and seconds later a booming sound rattled the window. I circled the new queen-sized bed to pull aside the curtains. All five of the Brotherhood stood on the sidewalk outside, right hands extended, left hands clasped around their right wrists, as if physically pushing against the wards.

"Great." I shoved the underwear into my bag, chased it with a couple of T-shirts and a pair of jeans, then turned to strip out of my work pants, remembering to take my ward stones out of the pocket. I had taken to carrying them as some sort of placebo against my fear. I pulled on a clean pair of jeans and paused to shove my feet into my hiking boots. I had no idea what to expect on the other side, and I wanted to be prepared.

Which led me to shove the bag of ward stones in my pocket and cross to the chest beside my new desk. I pressed my thumb to the lock and pulled out the family book, plus the book on basic Blood Witch magic, my own spellbook, and what I believed to be my mother's spellbook. I wanted the history of the Brotherhood too, but that was in my briefcase. I decided to take the risk and raced down the stairs, grabbing my briefcase and hauling it back to my bedroom, shoving the book into the bag with the rest.

I went back to the dresser for a couple of pairs of socks. One of my foster mothers had been obsessed with keeping your feet dry and warm, and it had rubbed off. I even kept a pair in my briefcase, and there was a bag in my trunk with clean socks and underwear.

There was another quake and boom and I nearly fell on my ass, grabbing at the dresser to keep from falling, just as Cambious crashed against the door frame. "What was that?" he asked.

I hitched a thumb at the window. "Our visitors are knocking on the door."

He crossed to the window, glancing out before turning back to me. "They shouldn't have been able to breach the wards I put up to hide the neighborhood."

"Well, looks like they did."

"We need to go."

"Working on it," I said, tossing the socks in on top of the books.

"Now, Thána. They're almost through." He grabbed the bag in one hand and my arm in the other, just as I was reaching for Rusty to throw in the bag too. His hand propelled me toward the bedroom door and into the hallway.

"Won't they just follow us through?" I asked as we stepped through the door in the closet.

"They can try," Cambious responded through gritted teeth. "Durious?"

"Backup is on the way."

"Good. Thána, come here and give me your hand."

I stepped back toward him as he set his key to the lock and turned it. He murmured words in some language I didn't recognize, then took my left hand, quickly slicing across it with a knife I hadn't seen in his hand.

"Ow!" I tried to pull my hand back, but he kept a hold of it, using his finger to spread the blood across my palm.

"Now set it against the door and repeat after me. *Per meum sanguinem.*"

I pressed my hand to the middle of the door, and stumbled over the words, "*Per meum sanguinem.*"

"*Hoc ostium: et signantes litteras. Et nemo non per gradus sanguinis mei.*"

I repeated the words and a sharp pain flared in my palm, then a similar sensation to erecting wards from the stones flowed through me and a vaguely blue energy field grew out from my hand to cover the door, then the rock into which it was set.

"That should hold. And if it doesn't, Durious and friends will cut down anyone that comes through." Durious handed his brother a white handkerchief, which Cambious used to cover my wound. "We'll get you a proper bandage when we get down the to the cabin." He shouldered my bag and then pointed me past the spot where we had enjoyed our picnic. On the horizon, the sun was nearly down, making me pick my steps carefully. So far, I had yet to see this place in proper daylight.

Light flared to my right, and Cambious held a lantern up, casting a circle of light to guide us. The path was well worn, but little more than three-foot-wide, leading down from the hilltop. In the distance, I could see the lights of Thelos, and further to the right, I could just make out the dark line of some mountains. The trail turned to the left and I got the impression of tall grass and the smell of something floral.

"Watch your step through here, we haven't gotten up here to regrade the trail after the rains," Cambious said beside me. As if to prove his point, the toe of my boot hit a rock and I stumbled, recovering myself before I fell on my face.

"Someone should get on that," I said to cover my embarrassment.

"We have someone coming next week," Cambious replied good-naturedly. "We're almost there."

"Almost where?" I asked, just as the trail turned again and I spotted a darker shadow in the shape of a cabin with soft yellow light escaping around curtains in a window and smoke curling up from a chimney.

"Durious and I live here. Keeps us close to the portal." Cambious stepped around me as we got closer, opening the door, and ushering me inside. "We'll spend the night, and in the morning, we'll go the rest of the way down the mountain and take my car down to Thelos."

I stepped into a cabin that was not unlike the one my last foster family kept in the Adirondacks. There was a single room that served as living room, kitchen, and dining room, and off toward the back, a ladder led up to a loft that I assumed held a bedroom. It was cozy, though more what I imagined a bachelor pad to look like than the granny-decorated cabin I remembered. There were no placemats on the table, crocheted or otherwise, and a lack of family photos on the walls.

"Car?" I asked as Cambious's words sank in. "You have cars?"

Cambious chuckled. "Our society is thousands of years older than yours, Thána. Of course we have cars. Ours are far more efficient and no longer run on fossil fuels, but otherwise, they are not so dissimilar."

"Oh." Some part of me was disappointed that I had stepped into a magical realm only to find that their method of transportation was no less magical than ours. "Okay, so what's the plan after that? How do we find my mother?"

He frowned at me. "What?"

Right. I hadn't told him about my father's ghost and what he had said. "My father told me, just before you came to get me that I needed to find my mother."

CHAPTER 14
SUCCUBUS

"It is rare," Cambious said, sitting on the overstuffed couch tucked against the window, "for a spirit to manifest with the will to speak unless they are centuries old."

"Yeah, well, speak he did," I countered. "He told me, 'Go through the portal. Find your mother,' and then he just vanished."

"It probably drained him." Cambious put my bag on the floor.

"Well, it scared the shit out of me," I said, pacing the length of the cabin. The energy of that fear was still driving me with the need to run, even though we'd already run and ended up here. The compact kitchen stuck into the corner was far more modern than I would have expected of a remote cabin. The cabin my foster family had taken me to that summer had still had a wood-burning stove and the water came in from a pump attached to the sink.

This had a stove that didn't look all that different from mine, and the sink had a normal faucet. The small counter space was tidy, with canisters that lined the back. I fiddled with the canisters, turning them so I could see their labels. It brought my attention back to my hand and the bright red that was seeping through the cloth tied over it.

"Ah, yes. Let me get the first aid kit." Cambious lurched up and went to an antique-looking cabinet near the small kitchen table. "Come, sit down." He held out a chair for me and I sat, setting my injured hand on the table where he could reach it. His large hands put a metal box on the table and opened it. From what I could see around his hands it was a fairly standard first aid kit, until he put a small jar of dark ointment on the table. "Let me see."

I pulled back the handkerchief and he nodded before wetting some gauze with what I took to be alcohol. He used it to clean the drying blood off my hand before he lifted the jar and daintily used the nail of his pinky finger to scoop out a small amount. Gently, he rubbed the ointment into the cut. It smelled like a combination of ginger and cinnamon, and I expected it to sting, but it didn't. "Mugwort and blood choke," Cambious said, lifting a roll of gauze from the table. "Promotes healing. I have no idea which ointment base was used, however. Durious restocked our kit last."

"It's okay, I wouldn't have remembered anyway," I murmured, lifting my hand a little to make his work easier. Once he had covered my wound and taped down the gauze, he put everything back into the box. "Are we really just going to sit here? Won't they find us?"

He smiled as he stood. "They won't get through the portal, even if they manage to puncture the wards. We are safe enough for tonight. Now, how about some dinner? Durious made a delicious lasagna last night. It always tastes better the second day." I didn't answer, just watched him move to the fridge and then to the stove. His horns nearly scraped the ceiling as he moved about.

The adrenaline was beginning to fade and with it the energy of our escape. "I didn't call Bonnie," I said suddenly.

Cambious turned to look at me, confused.

"My boss," I said. "I don't know how long we'll be gone."

"If you expect us to find your mother, you can bet it will take a while," Cambious responded cautiously.

"I don't know what I'm expecting, honestly." I sighed and cradled my wounded hand as I sat back against the wall. The chairs had been built for Cambious and his brother, and my feet dangled well off the floor. "Mostly I was just thinking that I would rather not die."

"And so far, you are doing well if that is your goal."

I rolled my eyes. "Not really looking for validation, Cam." I sighed again, picking at the edges of my bandage. In less than a month, my life had gone from sedate, even boring, to running for my life into some magical realm with an incubus.

"May I ask what it is you are looking for?" Cambious asked, coming to sit in the chair at the other end of the table.

"I wish I knew," I said without thinking about it. "And it isn't that I'm not grateful, I am. Just…"

He nodded knowingly. "It is a lot for you to accept, these changes."

"Changes I'm pretty good with, actually," I countered. "Growing up in foster care, you get used to changes. It's more the kinds of changes. A month ago, I would have sworn to you that magic wasn't real, that magic creatures didn't exist, and here I am sitting in a cabin on some alternate world with an incubus having come through a magic door."

He chuckled. "I take your point."

I wasn't sure he really did, but I let it go. My hand was a dull throb, and I was starting to feel the adrenaline crash. I leaned back against the wall and closed my eyes. I could hear Cambious humming to himself as he went about getting dinner ready and it was oddly comforting. I dozed there until Cambious set a plate in front of me. It was beautifully set, with a square of lasagna and a bit of salad and even some green beans…or what I assumed were green beans. It was hard to know for sure since we were in a different world. Who knew what odd plants they grew there?

A taste proved that they were in fact green beans, which both relieved me and disappointed me a little. It wouldn't be the last thing to disappoint me there. We ate in comfortable silence, and before I had finished, I was yawning more than I was eating.

"There is a bed up in the loft," Cambious said softly, taking my dish to the sink.

"I can sleep on the couch," I said, stretching.

"No need. I don't need much sleep. I will be standing watch."

I narrowed my eyes at him, trying to gauge whether or not I needed to worry. "I thought you said we were safe here."

He smiled what I assumed was meant to be a reassuring smile and patted my shoulder with his overly large, and clawed hand. "We are safe. We will be safer if someone keeps watch. Off you go. Tomorrow is a big day."

I gave up the argument and headed for the loft. I couldn't see how either Cambious or Durious could even get up there. The ceiling was low at the center even for me, and I'm barely five foot six, and it sloped down on either side. It was a tidy bedroom though, with a huge bed under a round window. There was a softly glowing lamp on a small table beside the bed and a dresser tucked up under the sloping side near the ladder, with what looked like a handcrafted rug covering a large portion of the wooden floor.

I stripped out of my jeans and pulled back the covers. The bed was soft, and it cradled me as I settled in, pulling the blankets and an old-looking quilt up around me. Some part of me argued that I wouldn't sleep, no matter how exhausted I felt after the adrenaline had drained, but it didn't argue long.

My next aware thought was the smell of bacon cooking and murmuring voices. I sat up, stretching and reaching for my jeans. I pulled them on and stood, turning to find a beautiful sunrise painting the skies orange outside the round window. I moved slowly, cautious until I could see down into the kitchen.

Cambious was at the stove and someone with horns like Cambious and his brother was setting the table. She glanced up at me, smiling warmly. She was breathtakingly gorgeous, her mahogany skin smooth and almost glowing, her dark red hair left loose and flowing down her back. Her horns were similar to Cambious's s but closer in color to her hair and more delicate somehow. Her eyes though, those were the same amber as his.

"I think your guest is awake."

Cambious turned, lifting a fork in hello. "Ah, Thána, I trust you slept well."

"I did, thank you," I responded, climbing down the ladder, and crossing to my bag to dig out my brush. I ran it through my hair before turning to introduce myself. "I'm Thána."

She smiled, her teeth white and perfect. "I am glad to finally meet you, Thána. I am Lutia, Cambious is my son."

"Oh." I'm not sure what I was expecting, but that wasn't it. She looked far too young to be a mother to someone Cambious's age. "I wasn't expecting...well, any of this if I'm honest."

She smiled. "I came along with the rest of the family when Durious sent word last night. Thought you might do with a little feminine company. Coffee?"

"Oh, yes. Coffee is good."

"Come sit down. Cambious, be a dear and bring her a cup." She held a chair for me and took the one beside mine. "And don't worry, I brought it with me, Cambious doesn't drink coffee. If there was any here it would be at least twenty years old." She laughed as Cambious put a steaming mug in front of me. He looked a little embarrassed by her.

"Mother, I'm sure Thána isn't interested in all that. We would have managed."

I lifted the cup, letting the steam rise up to my face and breathing in the rich aroma. The first sip proved to be nearly orgasmic, better than any coffee I'd ever tried. "Oh my god, this is amazing," I said, looking up.

She clapped her hands and her face lit up. "I'm so glad you

like it. One of my daughters grows it. She has a farm over in Lahos, on the north side of the island."

"She doesn't know where Lahos is, Mom," Cambious said, returning to the table with a frying pan. He put some bacon and two eggs on my plate. "Make yourself useful and get the toast?"

Lutia patted his arm as she stood and went to the counter, coming back with thick slices of bread that had been toasted and buttered. "Tuck in, dear, don't want it getting cold."

I did as I was told, cutting into the eggs, and focusing on my food.

Cambious joined us at the table, putting food on his plate and his mother's.

"My son tells me that you want to find your mother." Lutia looked concerned.

I nodded. "I mean, I honestly don't know what else to do?" I scooped up eggs onto a piece of toast and popped it into my mouth, chewing thoughtfully. "I can't stop these people from trying to kill me. I clearly can't hide from them. And my father told me to find her."

She looked at Cambious who sighed. "If the dead have commanded you, then it is what you must do," Cambious said softly.

Lutia seemed to agree. "And so you must. Where will you begin?"

"Thelos," Cambious responded. "When I last saw Alana, she was headed to Thelos. Perhaps we can pick up her trail there."

"Ah, then you will be joining her?" Lutia asked, clearly not entirely thrilled with that idea.

"How can I not, Mother? She knows nothing of our world. She needs a guide."

"You will need a more convincing glamor then, if you are traveling into the midst of witches for more than a feeding."

Cambious raised a hand to lift a pendant out of the sweater he was wearing. He tapped a finger to the amber-colored stone and the air around him shimmered. When it stopped, he had been transformed. His skin was a dark brown, his eyes a soft brown. His horns were gone, and his dark hair was slightly curly. Had I not seen the transformation happen, I wouldn't have believed it possible.

Lutia nodded, reaching for his hand. "Most impressive."

He tapped the stone again and was instantly himself. "Don't sound so surprised. Merry's daughter made it specifically for me the last time I visited Thelos."

"Just promise me you won't go into Janu."

"I doubt Alana went to Janu," Cambious said. "Eat, Thána, we should get on the road. I need to finish packing." He rose from the table, leaving his food mostly uneaten. I watched him go, up the ladder into the loft, then turned to Lutia.

"What is Janu?" I asked, feeling very out of my depth.

"It is a city in the south where our kind are most unwelcome and when found there, we are executed," Lutia answered, rising herself. "I should see how the gate fares. It was very nice to meet you, Thána."

She left the cabin, and I was alone for the moment. "What have you gotten yourself into, Thána?" I muttered to myself.

CHAPTER 15
INTO THELOS

THE WALK FROM THE CABIN WAS QUIET, THE PATH WAS WELL WORN and along its edges bloomed a sort of heather, or what looked like heather, though its leaves were blue-green, and its flowers had shades of orange and red. The morning dew still clung to the leaves as we trudged along.

Cambious was quiet. I got the sense that it had to do with his mother and what she'd said about our journey. It was about a mile down from the cabin to a clear space where there were several vehicles parked. They weren't exactly Chryslers, but recognizable as cars. Cambious pointed to a blue one.

He put our bags in the trunk and slid into what I took for the driver's seat. I climbed into the passenger side, my eyes sweeping over the dash. There was no steering wheel, but a console of switches, gauges, and buttons. I noticed Cambious had changed his appearance again, looking the way he had in my kitchen. Still, his head brushed the roof of the car. He pressed a button, and I could feel the car come to life.

A moment later, we were headed down the mountain on a gravel road that eventually turned to something similar to black-top, though it was a faded green. "I am sorry about my mother,"

Cambious said after a while. "I was not expecting her to come with my brothers."

"It's okay, Cam," I responded softly.

"She doesn't approve of the closeness between our families." He sighed and shook his head. "If she had her way, we would abandon the gateway and return to Abagh for good, other than to feed of course."

"Feed?" I asked, fairly certain I didn't want the answer.

He nodded. "We need the psychic energy. At least once a month, we need to feed. More if we are expending a lot of energy. For example, when wearing this glamor, I am steadily using up that energy. When I am wearing the other, I use exponentially more energy. I will need to feed soon."

I swallowed around the fear building in the back of my throat. "How exactly do you feed?"

He smiled, turning us off one road and onto another. "Have you no knowledge of what an incubus is, Thána?"

I blushed, remembering the lust that overcame me when we first met. "So, you…induce someone to have sex and…what… suck their energy?"

"The energy that is built during the sex act is what feeds us." Cambious glanced at me, his eyes glittering. "We absorb it. We take nothing from our partner that isn't going to go to waste anyway. Well, most of us don't. We can, of course, but it is considered rude."

"Rude. Right." I shook my head, trying to file the information away, but stuck on the image of Cambious mid-coitus. It wasn't an unpleasant vision, not by a long shot, but it kept me from moving past it.

"This road will take us to Thelos," Cambious said, pulling me back to the moment. "It is a little over an hour away."

"Okay, then what?"

"Then we will begin our search. We know that your mother went there and that she visited with her family. We know that she left again with your sister. We don't know why or where. So, we start there."

It seemed to make sense. "What about these Brotherhood guys?" I asked after a few minutes. "If they tracked me back home, and realize I came through the portal, won't they expect me to go to family?"

Cambious inhaled deeply, then let it out slowly. "It is possible, yes."

My heart sped up a little. "And won't they start by hunting down whatever family I have then?"

"It is possible, yes."

"And if they find me?"

"We fight," Cambious replied, as if it were just that simple.

"Now, why didn't I think of that?" I muttered, sarcasm dripping off each word. "I'm serious, Cam. I've seen how they kill people like me." I shuddered, the image of poor Althea Anagnos hanging by her ankles as the blood drained from her body. It was not the way I wanted to go. Not that I wanted to go at all. What I wanted was to go back to the life I'd had before Finneas Connor showed up. Back to circuit boards and quality meetings and all the rest. Hell, I'd even go back to El Paso.

"I know," Cambious said quietly. "I promise you this, I will do everything in my power to prevent that from happening."

It felt like the kind of promise you made to a child to stop their crying. I was quiet then, withdrawing into my head, my fingers idly playing with my mother's pendant. If I closed my eyes, my head was filled with images of death and blood, some of it mine, most of it belonging to women in the long line of my family. As we neared Thelos, those images became more intense, words screaming in my head, curses thrown as they died, then in a sudden silence I saw the woman in the cell in the fortress again. Her hair had thinned, and gray was chasing the black away. She wore the marks of torture in her skin, and when she lifted her head, her eyes were sunken and hollow, her face gaunt from starvation, but as our eyes met, I knew.

"Mother." I murmured the word as the car came to a stop. "I can see her." I didn't want to move or blink, lest I lose the vision. "She's a prisoner. She's dying." I could feel Cambious touch my arm, but I didn't move. "She's in the fortress, the Kourt."

Her eyes grew wide, as if she could see me and she shook her head, one thin hand rising to wave me off. Fear filled the emptiness of her eyes and almost physically, I felt her push me away. The vision fled then, and I was left sweating and panting. I opened my eyes to find Merry kneeling beside me, the car door open. Her frail-looking hand was on my arm. "Good gracious, *paidía*. Let's get you inside."

I let Merry help me out of the car, my eyes blurry and the world around me feeling less than real. I stumbled up some stairs and then Merry was pressing me to a seat on something soft. I blinked, trying to clear my eyes, but felt as though they just wanted to close. Sleep was pulling heavy on me, and I wanted to demand to know what had happened but couldn't make my mouth open.

"She shouldn't have been able to do that." I heard Merry say.

"Look what it did to her." That was Cambious. I struggled to open my eyes, but they wouldn't budge.

A hand was on my head, petting over it. "Shh, little one, rest."

It had the weight of a command and within seconds I fell into a restless sleep filled with nightmares. Blood filled my dreams, dripping over my face and down my arms, running down my legs as I ran blindly through a forest of blue-black trees on feet that were being ripped by the rugged ground. The taste of it filled my mouth, flat copper and hot, like the taste of death.

I woke suddenly in a house that had sunk into night while I slept on a soft couch, covered with what looked to be a handmade afghan. There was light drifting from a hallway and soft voices that told me I wasn't alone. The dull ache in my left hand reminded me of the cut and I lifted it to fiddle with the bandage.

I had expected more pain, but it felt nearly healed…which should have been impossible.

I rose, pulling the afghan around me for warmth and I shuffled down the hallway, emerging into a tidy little kitchen, with a bay window where a breakfast nook was settled, pale blue cushions on the benches.

Merry and Cambious and someone I didn't know sat at the table, looking up as I came into the room. Merry looked a little less crazy than I remembered her, with her hair down and relatively calm, clad in a housedress like the ones my foster father's mother used to wear in a soft blue. Cambious stood and came to my side, escorting me to Merry's side of the table as she scooted down toward the middle. "How are you feeling?" Cambious asked as I sat.

"Weird," was the first word out of my mouth. It wasn't inaccurate, but less than informative. I sighed. "Thirsty. Anxious. I had nightmares."

Cambious went to the sink and came back with a glass of water for me. I drank about half of it before I asked, "So, what was that? What happened to me?"

"It is called *makrá vlépinta*," Merry said, her voice more serious than I had heard it before. "It is a rare gift given some blood witches in their later years, after much study and mastery."

I frowned hard enough that the spot between my eyes hurt. "Then why could I do it?"

"That is what we have been discussing," Cambious replied. "A blood witch who develops this gift can see into the distant past, the far future, even long distances away in the present. It is said that a strong witch can make herself seen by those of her own blood."

"Oh, she saw me all right," I said, draining the glass of water. "But I can barely make the ward stones work. I'm no strong witch." The words felt strange in my mouth. I don't think I'd ever actually said the word witch when talking about myself before that moment. Not out loud at least.

"Trauma can sometimes kick start a witch's gifts." I turned to the speaker, a woman somewhere between my age and Merry's, her hair cut in a thick, black bob and wearing a dark suit. She had Merry's eyes, though hers were blue to Merry's black. Her face was thin, her fingers stained with ink of a blue-purple color.

"Ah, Thána, darling, this is my daughter Zo," Merry said, her hand on Zo's shoulder. "She studies the effect of trauma on our gifts."

"Mostly the kind of trauma that blocks them, but there are documented cases where trauma of certain kinds, particularly the sudden near-death sort, can open up a set of gifts it would normally take a lifetime to learn, like *makrá vlépinta*."

I stared at my empty glass for a long time before I got up to refill it. As I came back to the table, my head filled with all of the near-death sorts of trauma of the last months, then back to the day my father died. "So, what if that near-death experience happened when I was five or six?"

I could feel them staring at me. Well, Merry and Zo anyway. Cambious knew the whole story. I would have thought Merry did as well, but for all I know my mother had kept that truth hidden, even from the family. "I don't remember all of it, but I very clearly remember the man trying to kill us, and I know that I used my...gifts then, to ease my father's pain as he died, and to take the life of the man who killed him. Is that the kind of thing you mean?"

"You should not have been able to do that at that age, so I'm going to say that yes, that is probably where it started. And the events of recent days have pushed you past your limits again."

"I wasn't under any particular stress when this happened," I countered, sitting back. "We were relatively safe. I was just sitting in the car."

"We should consider the fact that you have never been in the land of your ancestors before either. That could have been a factor," Cambious said.

"Has it happened before?" Zo asked, her intense blue eyes studying me.

"I've had dreams...there was one about Althea Anagnos, it was very real," I responded, getting up to pace. "I watched her die."

Zo nodded. "From what Cambious tells me, everything since we sent Finneas to you has been stressful for you, even coming home to the house where you were born. And there is familial precedent, several of our ancestors were extremely powerful blood witches. It is rumored, for example, that Althea could actually raise the dead."

"Hogswallop," Merry interjected. "Only necromancers can raise the dead. And then, the dead are never really themselves again. The child was near death, the doctor simply announced her demise before it took place."

"I have heard of others," Cambious said softly. "But it has never been proven."

My head was spinning with the implications, and I shook it in an attempt to clear it. "I know next to nothing. Like I said, I can barely use the stones. How am I supposed to...'? I waved my hands in the air, desperation nipping at my awareness. If my mother was a prisoner of the Brotherhood, how was I supposed to save her?

"Well, we shall just have to get you trained up a bit," Merry said cheerfully, patting my hand. "Come, the library is downstairs."

CHAPTER 16
RELEARNING

MERRY'S LIBRARY, AS IT TURNED OUT, WAS A CAVERNOUS BASEMENT at the bottom of a staircase at least two hundred steps down, or so it seemed as we trudged down them in a dank sort of darkness punctuated only with small yellow lights every twenty stairs or so. The walls were lined with bookshelves that were overflowing with ancient tomes on subjects I could only guess.

There was a large table filled with scrolls and notebooks and what looked to be a quill pen with an inkpot. Beyond that was a round fireplace over which hung a huge black cauldron. Smaller versions of the cauldron were stacked on yet another table off to the righthand side. In the two corners in the back, there were shelves lined with jars and bottles.

Now, this is what I had been expecting when I was told about witches and magical portals…and to be honest, since I met Merry. She was humming to herself as she moved over to one of the bookshelves, rubbing her hands along the pale blue of her housecoat as she scanned the shelves. "Ah, yes, this should do." She pulled out a large book and blew dust off its cover before crossing to the table. "Well, get over here. Can't learn anything standing by the stairs," she said over her shoulder as she set the book down on the table. I went to her a little hesitantly, not sure what was about to happen. She pulled a stool out from under the table and patted the seat while she opened the book.

"Most of this you will have learned from your mother when you were young. We just need to get you to remember."

"I've been trying. I found my…journal…" I wasn't ready to say "spellbook" out loud. "But other than the ward stones and that one protection thing in the family book, nothing has worked."

She patted my hand, a smile on her wrinkled face. Her eyes were bright as she pointed to the page. "This book is how I learned when I was a wee one. Most of us did at that time. It is a wonderful primer on magic."

My eyes scanned the page. It contained words and hand-drawn sketches of hands in certain positions. I found my hands making the signs under the table. "Start at the top," Merry said, "and learn the pronunciations and hand signs. I'll go get dinner started."

The first word was *dimiourgió,* and the pronunciation guide under it showed it as de-mi-or-geo. The accompanying hand sign showed two fists with arrows indicating that they should be brought together, left on top of the right. I murmured the word to myself and made my hands come together. Nothing happened, but then, as I told myself, it was just a word.

A word that I had no knowledge of. I searched the page for the translation but didn't find one. I repeated the exercise a few times before moving to the next word. *Ánoixe,* pronounced Ah-nix-a came next, with a hand gesture that seemed to imitate opening a book. I worked my way down the page, learning *irémise* (a finger to the lips), *prostatévo,* (hands crossed at the wrists), *páfsi* (left hand perpendicular to the right), *pigaíno* (both hands moving forward), *ýpnos* (right hand flat, left hand moving in to cover it), and *yperaspízo* (both hands come together as if in prayer, then pull apart and turn to face outward).

I went through the words and gestures until I could do them without looking. The bandage on my left hand was making it difficult, so I paused to pull it off. Under the gauze, the cut was nearly a scar, thin and almost not even visible. I had always healed quickly, but not usually this fast. I rubbed my thumb across it before turning my attention back to the words I was supposed to be studying. I felt a little silly sitting there like that, speaking these words and waving my hands around.

After I was sure I had the words and related gestures down, I got up and walked around the room practicing while I waited for Merry to return. I was just about to head up the long staircase when I heard the door open, so I went back to pacing and practicing.

Merry appeared moments later, slightly out of breath and wearing an apron that looked as ancient as she did. "Good, good. Now I will teach you to use them. Come, sit."

I went back to the stool and sat, and Merry came to stand behind me, her hands on my shoulders. "Close your eyes and take a deep breath, slow in, slow out. Let your attention narrow to my voice and your breath. This is how you center."

I followed her instructions, dragging my attention back each time it wandered until I felt something new. "This is where magic lives, *paidí*. Feel it, let it rise up with your words. Open."

I murmured "*Ánoixe*," and made the gesture. Around me, I heard pages ruffling and opened my eyes. The books nearest me had all opened and the doors on the shelving unit in the corner had as well. "What…"

Merry tightened her fingers on my shoulders. "Close."

I was pretty sure that word wasn't one of the ones I had just learned, but somewhere in the back of my brain I heard my mother's voice saying, "*Kontá*." I said the word and closed my hands, the opposite of the gesture for open. All around me pages ruffled, and I heard the clasp on the glass doors.

"Yes, remember. Your mother taught you these. Now, pick a book and connect with your magic, Go."

"*Pigaíno*," I said the word and pushed my hands toward the top book on the stack beside me. It flew away from me.

"Come."

"*Éla*." The word and the beckoning gesture came as if I knew them already. The book returned, landing in my hand.

"Good, protect."

"*Prostatévo*." I touched my wrists together and the air around me shimmered.

"There are stronger protective spells, but this will do in a pinch, and should repel most basic attacks. Remember though, it only lasts as long as your attention and energy remain." She patted my shoulder and I blinked, letting the magic release. "Defend is a more aggressive version and can be used to push back against an attack. Let's not try it down here. That can wait until tomorrow when we can go to the yard. Come, you should rest, and dinner should be ready."

I was sweating by the time I reached the top of the stairs and fatigue was pulling on my limbs. Merry and I appeared to be alone. "Where is Cambious?"

Merry went to the oven, pulling out a pan of something that smelled amazing. "He needed to feed, so he went to meet up with a gentleman he's enjoyed time with in the past. They have an arrangement of sorts."

"Oh." I'm not sure why, but I had assumed that Cambious, being an incubus, would tend toward a more heterosexual life-style, but what did I know about that sort of thing? My education never did cover the sexual appetites of incubi and succubi.

Merry chuckled as if she could read my thoughts. "Our good friend is pansexual, my dear. He can get what he needs from any gender." She put the pan on the counter and dished up two plates, bringing them to the table, then going back to the counter for utensils. "I hope it's good. I had to throw a bunch of stuff together, I haven't gone shopping yet."

The plate was filled with potatoes and what looked like ground beef or pork, spices, and a tomato-ey sauce, all of it covered in some sort of cheese. The first taste was filled with nutmeg and cloves and onion, along with potato and cheese. The meat was not beef or pork, but it was delicious, I thought maybe lamb or goat. My stomach rumbled as I ate, as if just the taste was enough to remind it that it was empty.

Merry rambled on about what she was going to teach me, and something about another memory spell, but I was too busy eating to pay close attention. By the time I had cleaned my plate, I was all but asleep. Merry cleared the table, then urged me up, taking me down a long hall off the kitchen. The room was small, but there were two twin beds and my duffle bag sat at the end of one.

It didn't take much to convince me to shed my jeans and crawl in, though it felt odd with Merry there watching me. She adjusted my blankets to her liking, then sat beside me, her hand brushing my hair away from my face. It had gotten long and was starting to revert to its natural state of thick, black curls. I couldn't even remember when I had seen a salon last, and it required maintenance every four to six weeks.

"Close your eyes. Rest," Merry said softly, her hand covering my eyes. "*Epistrofí mnímis, Epistrofí mnímis, Férte píso tis iméres tis paidikís ilikías.*"

I was already drifting toward sleep when she stood, and I could hear her leave the room and shuffle down the hallway. Sleep pulled me under quickly. My dreams were almost like a tour of my childhood: sitting with my mother on the greenhouse porch, working with ward stones; on my father's lap in the living room, opening and closing the front door with words and gestures; teaching my little sister some small spell I'd learned. They turned darker and colder after that, after my father's death. There was a repeat of that memory, in all its gory detail, and the aftermath. There was my mother's voice, desperation making her words tremble as she taught me how to use *prostatévo* to keep an attacker at bay, even a memory of using it once against a bully in school, which earned me a very strict lesson in when and where magic was allowed.

Near to morning, I fell into a memory I had wanted desperately for my whole life, but would come to despise, the days that led up to the moment when my mother had hidden my identity behind a wall and left me on a bench outside a police station.

We lived in an almost picturesque cottage on the eastern coast of the United States, huddled and hiding. Mother had not enrolled us in school, and she kept our interaction with the world to a minimum. Daria spiked a high fever one day and fell ill. We had been running and hiding for almost three years, ever since the number of Brotherhood assailants had grown beyond my mother's ability to protect us. Mother left me to watch Daria while she went out to get supplies for a potion to cure her.

To my knowledge, I had not used my unique power since the day my father had died, but in the gloom of a house with the shutters drawn and only a small desk lamp to chase the shadows, I didn't know how to help Daria, other than to comfort her, so I had crawled into her bed, pulling her tiny body up against mine. The fever raged, her skin so hot to the touch. Her dark hair was plastered to her head with sweat, and she shivered, whispering nonsense in a voice gone rough whisper from her cough.

I tried to soothe her, caressing her skin, and whispering that I would keep her safe. When she went still, every fiber of my being called out for me to save her. She was dying there in my arms. I pressed my mouth to hers and called the illness out of her, feeling its dank, ugly heat fill my mouth. I swallowed and called again, and again...until her skin cooled and her body settled with the tiniest of sighs as she lapsed into a restful sleep.

When my mother came home, I was in the bathroom, letting the blood drain from me as it had when I had eased my father into the next life. Her face was drawn and pale and I could taste the fear. I didn't fully understand it, but I knew she was terrified by what I had done. I apologized over and over, tears burning my face. I could not have lived with myself if I had let Daria die. I was her big sister, and it was my job to protect her. My love for her was so big that it filled me, even when I knew that I wasn't supposed to use that gift. My mother was a fighter though, and she buried her fear to help me, teaching me how to use sanitary pads and making me a potion to help speed the flow.

We couldn't leave until it was done, you see. The men who wanted to kill me employed those with specific gifts to track the smell of my blood. If we left before I was done bleeding, the men would find us. Of course, what she didn't say was that if it took too long for it to be over, they would find us there, in that little cottage.

It took almost two days. My mother gathered up all of my pads and left me alone with a fully recovered Daria while she went to dispose of them. She said it would leave a false trail, give us time to leave. We spent days in the car after that, zigzagging up and down the coast, then inland, then back to the sea in hopes of throwing them from our trail. Then, the morning before my birthday, they found us.

CHAPTER 17
MEMORY TRAP

IT WAS REALLY EARLY, NOT EVEN DAYLIGHT. MOM HAD STOPPED US at a rest stop sometime through the night to grab a few hours of sleep. We were just inside New York state, though Mom hadn't said where exactly we were heading. The memory was so vivid inside my dream I felt like I was once again a nine-year-old waking up in the backseat of the car needing to pee.

I could see the bathrooms through the front window. I probably should have woken Mom but decided I could go and be back before she woke up and I did my best to make no noise as I got out of the car and ran for the building with the bathroom. The air was nippy, the taste of autumn in the air. I did my business, trying not to sit on the metal commode knowing it would be ice cold. I washed my hands and went to the door of the bathroom, something making me slow and look around the area.

The boy looked out of place. He had to be about fourteen or fifteen, skinny and wearing clothes that didn't fit. He dashed for me, pushing me back inside. "Don't let them see you. I'll lead them away, then you run."

I was confused but nodded. He ran back out, calling out, "*Aderfia*, the girl went this way."

Several men in black, their bald heads reflecting the street lamps that lined the sidewalk, ran past me, following the boy. When I couldn't hear them anymore, I raced for the car, opening the door, and shaking my mother's shoulder as I got in.

We drove away, probably faster than it was safe to drive. I couldn't have known that my mother had already made the decision that would alter the trajectory of my life.

What follows that is less clear, blurred no doubt by the actions my mother was taking. I remember ditching the car and a bus ride, a lunch in a little diner along the way, and that night we got a motel room.

Mom consulted a big book I had seen out on the greenhouse porch back home, sorting through ingredients from the big bag she had brought with us as we left the car.

There was a small pot on the hotplate next to the sink and it bubbled as she murmured words and added ingredients from the bag. Once Daria was asleep, Mom called me to her. "We're going to do a spell, Thána. One that should help us to be safe for a long time."

I nodded solemnly. "What spell?"

Her smile was sad, and she kissed the crown of my head. "Just sit here and I will show you." My next true memory was of waking up on that bench, an officer talking to me.

I woke then, half surprised to still be in Merry's guest bedroom. Memories continued to flash through me as I got up and went in search of a bathroom. I relieved myself, then decided that if I couldn't remember when my last shower was, I should probably get cleaned up. I found towels and started some hot water flowing, then stripped out of my underwear, shirt, and bra before climbing in.

I tipped my head back under the spray, closing my eyes as memories darted through me of other showers in other places, at a dozen different ages. It was like a hyped-up, high-velocity deja vu that left me trembling when I finally rinsed myself clean and stepped out of the shower. The landslide didn't stop then, however. Everything I did came with echoes of every other time I had done the thing, from putting on my clothes to brushing my hair.

By the time I headed for the kitchen, my whole body was shaking with adrenaline amid the earthquakes and tremors of reliving thirty-two years in tiny snippets of time. I jumped when I heard Cambious speak, but only his voice penetrated my awareness, I couldn't understand his words. I stumbled back from the perceived threat, my eyes wide open even though I couldn't see my surroundings. I stumbled into a wall and laid both hands flat against it, looking for some stability. I blinked and leaned into the wall, willing the onslaught to stop.

There were warm hands on my back, and for a moment I couldn't differentiate them from every other pair of hands that had ever touched me that way. I groaned and tried to pull away, but there was nowhere to go. Voices echoed around me, and I couldn't tell which were real and which were memories.

"*Páfsi!*" The word screamed out of my lungs as I clung to the wall and my sanity. "Stop. Make it stop."

Hands grabbed my face and a deep voice spoke words that did not cause a series of overlapping memories, "*Zamyg khyal-barchlakh.*"

It took a moment, but the landslide slowed. It didn't stop, more like it lagged. Like a film all out of sync or something. I blinked against hot tears I hadn't been aware I was crying and Cambious appeared in front of me, his amber eyes filled with deep concern. "Really, Merry? Thána, can you hear me now?"

I nodded slowly, afraid each movement was going to start the assault again. "Okay, good. I'm going to take you downstairs. Can you move?"

I tried. I did, but two steps later I had to squeeze my eyes shut. Cambious muttered curses and scooped me up like a child. It had been a long time and a lot of pounds since anyone had been able to do that, let alone had tried.

I grabbed a hold of his shirt, my hands fisting tight as I put my forehead against his neck. Each jarring step down the stairs sent rivers of fear through my veins, but apparently, there had been very few times in my life I had been carried down a flight of stairs. My breathing slowly leveled out as we reached the bottom, and Cambious set my feet down on the floor. I didn't let go right away, leaning into his strength.

"Here, sit." Cambious guided me back until I could feel the stool behind me. "Are you okay?"

I nodded cautiously, daring to open my eyes. I could see the room and superimposed on it was a loop of the day before, but it was far less anxiety-invoking than the rest, probably due to the limited amount of time I'd spent there. "What is this?" I asked, my voice sounding strangely frail to my ears.

Cambious sighed as if the entire idea of it was exhausting. "Merry was a bit...overly enthusiastic with her spell work yesterday. All will to bring back your memory, no control over how fast. There was a reason your mother worked her spell the way she did, both the taking of your memory and the controlled way it would come back to you, so carefully. Memory spells can split a person into pieces. I warned her to be careful."

"But you did something that helped?" I rubbed my eyes and experimented with turning my head.

"I gave you some space, but at this point, all you can do is ride it out."

That did not sound like an answer I wanted to hear. "Ride it out?"

"We'll keep you down here, where it's relatively free of trigger memories and hopefully that should let it all unspool in a less traumatic way."

"How long is this unspooling going to take?" I asked.

"I don't know. It is not an exact science, this is magic of the mind and heart, not one of stones, herbs, and potions."

"And if I can't...ride it out?"

Cambious didn't answer that, just turned for the stairs. "I will bring you some breakfast, and something to help fortify you against this fight. Try to stay still, the more you try to do, the more the memory will fracture and slam you about."

"Right. Stay still." I watched him go. "Have you even met me?" I asked the empty air, cringing as I was offered evidence that the phrase was one I repeated often. I would have to find new expressions for my sarcasm.

In case that isn't clear enough, let me explain that I don't actually know **how** to stay still without something in my hands to play with or work on. I never have, as was evident by my cascading memories. I turned on the stool to the open book we had left on the table, but just that had me wanting to scream out again. The cacophony of similar turns and myriad books over the years was too much. I squeezed my eyes closed and held onto the table until the assault slowed, and I could try again.

Cambious hadn't been telling tales about staying still if something as simple as turning on the stool was enough to incapacitate me. I heard the door above, and Cambious's heavy tread as he came down the stairs. Almost as an afterthought, the smell of bacon and eggs wafted down the stairwell, but even that was too much and by the time Cambious reached me, I was on the floor under the table, knees to my chest and my eyes pressed down against my knees.

Not that it did anything to stem the tide, but somehow it made me feel a little better.

"Here." Cambious took my hand and put a cup in it. "Drink this."

I sniffled as I lifted my head, pulling the cup closer. "Do I want to know what is in it?"

He smiled gently. "It is a potion to shore up your defenses. The next few hours will be trying for you. Drink it all."

Dutifully, I drained the cup, making a face as the taste hit me. It was like that cough medicine my first foster mother would give me, some homemade glop that she insisted tasted like orange candy. I was fairly sure she had never actually tasted orange candy. Once I had handed the cup back, Cambious handed me a plate. "I know this might be hard, but you should eat."

I eyed the plate suspiciously. Already I could feel the memories queueing up to flood my head. I tried a bite and almost dropped the plate as every memory of eating scrambled eggs bubbled up. "I can't," I ground out through my teeth, giving him the plate back and dropping my head back to my knees.

"Let me help you." Cambious sat on the floor with the plate and lifted a forkful of eggs. "Thána, please try." I blinked at him and nodded. He put the fork in my mouth, smiling at me. The memories that came then went back to infancy, my mother or father feeding me in an endless barrage. I chewed and swallowed, keeping my eyes closed as Cambious put food into my mouth.

By the time I had nearly finished the food, the memories had resolved themselves into something resembling chronological order and I was able to cope with them a little better. "Thank you," I said to Cambious, returning my head to my knees.

"Do you need anything?"

I wanted to be snippy but didn't have the strength. "Coffee might be nice."

"Stay still, Thána. I will return."

I didn't watch him go. I kept my eyes closed, pressing them into my knees as if I could somehow stop the rapid-fire memory snippets with the pressure alone. He did bring me coffee, but I couldn't even hold the cup as every memory of every cup of coffee I had ever had in my life became bullets in the gun held to my sanity.

At some point, Cambious brought down the mattress from one of the twin beds and made me a bed of sorts, a nest of blankets and pillows I tried to use to insulate me from myself. I don't know if you've ever tried to hide from yourself, but here's a clue:

you can't. A lot of the next two days is something of a blur, spent in a half-comatose state punctuated by moments of clarity when Cambious tried to feed me or give me water to drink.

I slept only when my body was so wrung out it just couldn't function anymore, though it was more a state of involuntary unconsciousness than it was actual sleep. I woke suddenly, soaked through with sweat and cold. I reached for the glass of water Cambious had left nearby and downed it before I realized that I wasn't spinning my way through every memory of drinking water in thirty-two years.

Cautiously, I sat fully up. I had a jackhammer-wielded-by-elephants headache and felt like I had gone ten rounds with Mike Tyson, my entire body feeling bruised and beaten, but I was functioning. I was disgustingly in need of a hot shower and a good meal, but I had survived more or less intact.

I pressed myself up off the mattress, which was going to need a good airing out after my sweat-fest, moving gingerly lest I set something off again. That was when I noticed Cambious. He was sitting with his back against the nearest wall to my nest, head slumped down to his chest, his legs splayed out in front of him. The glamor was gone, and he looked nearly peaceful, even with the horns and all.

Figuring I should let him sleep, I tiptoed to the stairs and made my way up, emerging into the room off the kitchen. A vague red light was starting to stain the deep blue-black of the skies as I went to the sink to splash cold water on my face. I itched with the sweat starting to dry on my skin, but my stomach was making enough noise to raise the dead, so I grabbed an apple in a fruit bowl on the counter, taking it with me as I headed for the bathroom.

My first bite stopped me in my tracks. The outside looked like an apple, but inside the flesh was a light purple in color and the taste was something like a blueberry. My stomach let me know it didn't care how it tasted, it wanted it and it wanted it now. It was gone by the time I got to the bathroom, and I left the core on the counter while I showered.

I was running out of clean clothes, and I would have to ask Merry if she had a washing machine…or whatever this world's equivalent would be. I pulled on my clean pair of jeans and the last T-shirt from my bag and headed back toward the kitchen to see if I could figure out coffee and maybe breakfast, but Merry was already there, looking haggard and sleep-deprived.

Her eyes brightened when she saw me. "Thána! Look at you. Has the spell finished its work then?"

I wanted to be angry with her but discovered that my feelings were more akin to annoyance than anger. "You could have warned me what was going to happen," I growled as she put a cup of coffee into my hands. "But yes, I seem to be past the machine gun memory stage, if nothing else."

"I am so relieved. Of course, I never meant for…well, that. It's been a long time since I have worked such a spell. I may have set too much intention and will with too little caution."

Something tickled in the back of my memory, something my mother had taught me. "Be careful what you wish for."

Merry chuckled and returned her attention to the eggs and potatoes in her pan. "Yes indeed. Your mother's spell was overly cautious. You would have regained all of these memories eventually, but if you are to come into yourself enough to go save her, her spell needed a push."

"Congratulations," I said wryly, lifting the coffee cup to taste. "You shoved it right off a cliff."

"Oh, yes, Cambious was quite cross with me. He's scarcely left your side since he returned from feeding."

"How long?" I asked. I took the coffee, which tasted an awful lot like salvation, to the table and sat on one of the benches.

"Around fifty hours, all told," she replied.

Fifty hours. I could tell that everything wasn't completely sorted inside my head, things were jumbled and out of order, but if I focused I could remember my mother teaching me the words and gestures, I could remember the feeling of pulling that power from inside of me. I could remember the taste of the illness I had taken from Daria and using the *prostatévo* spell to defend the two of us one day when the Brotherhood had found us.

It wasn't everything, but it was a hell of a lot more than when I had started.

CHAPTER 18
ON THE RUN AGAIN

Cambious stumbled up the stairs about an hour later, looking disheveled and like the sleep had done absolutely no good. He did smile, seeing me sitting at the table with Merry, our dirty dishes pushed to the side as we worked on refreshing my skills with my set of ward stones.

"There's still some breakfast on the stove," Merry told him as I murmured the incantation she'd been teaching me, bringing the stones to life. "Good, good, now move them slowly."

I kept my focus on my hands, slowly separating the six piles of stones until they formed a circle around my coffee cup. The air between the stones shimmered a faint green and within the stones, my coffee cup disappeared.

Cambious ambled over, rubbing at his eyes. "Did you just teach her *ekleípo*?"

Merry was just about bursting with pride. "She really is quite talented. Alana was right about that."

I canceled out the spell and bit back a yawn. "She is also exhausted. I could use a nap."

"You've been through a lot," Cambious agreed. "You should rest now. I heard from a friend last night that there has been an increase in Brotherhood activity in the area. They may know that we're here."

"Great." I pushed myself up from the table. "That should ensure a good sleep."

My thoughts rambled over the whirlwind of the last hour as Merry tested my memory of the things I should have learned up to my tenth birthday, and then beyond, as my mother had been trying to cram as much knowledge and skill into her hunted daughter as she could, probably hoping it would be enough to protect me in some way. I understood we had just been starting to go over the more advanced uses of the ward stones before she decided to try a different method of protection. I had remembered the word, *ekleípo_* and asked Merry to show me while she quizzed me on the other uses of the stones.

Merry had also filled my head with the things a blood witch was expected to be capable of, well beyond the healing of otherwise incurable diseases. The details had been lost over the years, but family memory told tales of blood being used in various protective spells, to seal things closed, like the door that held our portal safe, and for those suitably advanced, that blood could become a weapon, infecting others with the disease she had cured in another. I could see into the past and the future, down the bloodline, and connect with those still living who shared my blood, as we had already learned.

The blood trackers who the Brotherhood used to find me were said to be male blood witches. They couldn't "eat" disease the way we could, simply because they lacked the physical mechanisms to expel the disease, but they had many of the other traits and abilities, which allowed them to track us.

There was more, an entire field of study had been made of the unique gifts of a blood witch. Unlike all of the other kinds of witches, and there were many kinds, the blood witch stood alone in that she was born with gifts that couldn't be learned. Lucky me. Most of that knowledge had been lost over the centuries however, the gift becoming more and more rare as we were hunted and killed off. The last blood witch in my mother's family before me had been the first in almost a hundred years.

I crawled into the bed that hadn't been ravaged to provide me comfort in the basement, hoping I could get past the learning and the fear and sleep. For a long time, my brain just spun around and around, but eventually, exhaustion won, and I slept.

My dreams were much more focused than they had been, focused on my ancestors specifically. I saw Althea again, her sham trial and execution, her fear coursing through me as if I were the one being chased through the woods, stripped, and bled out. Whooshing through centuries, I saw a young girl of maybe thirteen, dripping blood from a cut on her hand into a wooden cup, mixing it with herbs before lifting it to the lips of a woman very definitely in hard labor. Then, an older woman shaking her head sadly as she held the hand of a woman on a pile of animal furs. "If I had been called sooner, perhaps…"

"*Adelfés tou aímatós mou, érchontai.*" The speaker was a woman of my age, maybe a little older, with patches of white decorating her otherwise black hair. She stood within a circle, a small fire burning at its center and ward stones around its perimeter, though I had never seen a ward so red as this. It was difficult to see outside the wards, though I couldn't be sure if it was because of the warding or because it was night.

Around the circle, the air shimmered and slowly figures began to form, none solid, but all clearly there. Eight women, in clothes of varied style, each holding up a hand with a cup or chalice in it. One by one they moved to the fire, tipping their cup, and letting something drip into the cauldron that hung over it. I knew somehow that this was blood collected from their menses, and the blood became real as it fell from their cups. When they had all done so, they returned to their places and again held up their hands.

"*Échoume synkentrósei gia na plirósoume tin timí tou aímatos. Hathus, sas parakaloúme, párte tin prosforá mas.*"

The nine women began to move in a circle, just inside the

wards, faster and faster until the ground was shaking and then outside the wards, a dark shadow appeared. It was shaped like a man, but bigger than any man I had ever seen.

A voice deeper than Cambious's and louder than an air horn shook the circle. "*Déchomai tin prosforá sas, kóres tou aímatos. I gi eínai dikí sou edó kai chília chrónia.*"

One by one the specters of the women vanished until only the one present in the flesh remained. Taking the cauldron from the fire with her hands insulated by her skirt, she moved to the side of the circle where the shadow still hovered. With a nod, the wards fell, and she was face to face with…I had no context for what he was, but he towered over her and held out his hands. She tilted the cauldron and poured its contents into his hands.

From there, I fell into something that was not memory, mine, or an ancestor's. I was pulled to that tower cell, and my heart leaped as my mother looked back at me. I wanted to cry, to apologize for all the years I had been so angry with her. More than that, I wanted to feel her arms around me again.

I woke to Cambious's urgent whisper. "Thána, wake up."

He was crouched beside me, his glamor back in place. When I opened my eyes, he put his finger to his lips. I nodded my understanding. "We have to go. Now."

It had gotten dark, meaning I had slept much longer than I had intended to. Cambious had my duffle bag as he moved to the door of the bedroom, keeping himself low. I followed his example, stopping for my shoes where I had dropped them. Merry was waiting in the kitchen with a canvas bag which she handed to me. "Keep quiet and keep to the woods. Zo will find you."

I had to assume that this meant the Brotherhood had found us. Spontaneously, I hugged her, the closest thing to family I had had since my mother abandoned me. Cambious took my hand and guided me through the house and down a different set of stairs, which took us into a root cellar and then into a dark tunnel that moved away from the house at a slightly downward angle. After a while, Cambious let go of my hand and fumbled with something that became a handheld light, like the lanterns he'd lit our picnic with.

The tunnel seemed to go on forever, but after about a half-hour of walking, Cambious stopped us and pointed to a ladder. In silence we climbed, with him leading the way. At the top, he cautiously opened a hatch of some sort that I couldn't see around him, sticking his head up to scout the area. Then he was up and out, reaching back to take the bag, then my hand to aid me. I emerged into a dark forest, the air filled with the comforting smell of pine trees.

Cambious paused, looking around us before he pointed. "The road is this way."

I followed as he set out, having to hurry to keep up with his long steps. "Is the road going to be safe?" I asked.

"Safer than Merry's."

"Do we have a plan?" I asked as he changed directions.

"Right now, the plan is to not get caught by the Brother-hood," Cambious answered, his tone curt. "We'll figure out next steps once we're away from here."

"What about Merry? Will she be okay?"

He stopped and looked back over his shoulder, then at me. "She can handle herself, and she isn't who they're looking for."

"Yeah, but neither is my mother, and they've been keeping her for who knows how long."

"Yes, but your mother can lead them to you. Or could have, before you came here."

Something about that answer filled me with dread. Did it mean that now that I was here where they could track me, they had no need of her? Would they kill her before we could get to her? Which did nothing to help me figure out exactly how we were going to get to her. I mean, I am not exactly a fighter, and I certainly wasn't in supreme physical condition.

My chest tightened and I found breathing difficult. Cambious touched my hand. "We mustn't linger, Thána. It won't take them long to pick up your trail again if we do."

"That's reassuring," I muttered, letting him draw me onward. The night was dark around us, filled with the hulking shadows of trees, with softer gray spaces between them. After we'd walked about a mile, we came to what appeared to be a one-lane road where there was a vehicle waiting.

It was old and rundown, a dull blue marked in places with a darker color. Unlike the car we had taken to Merry's, its engine made some noise, vague knocking sounds in a rhythm that might have made my teeth hurt if we weren't in such dire straits. Zo was behind the wheel, and she gestured for us to hurry. Cambious held open the back door for me and advised me to lay across the seat. "Keep down, at least for now." He lifted a blanket off the floor and covered me before putting our two bags, and a backpack I hadn't noticed before, on the floor, then proceeding to the passenger side.

"I can get you into the city," Zo said, "but you'll have to make your own way from there."

"We should be fine. Get us to Stroya's."

"Are you sure?" Zo asked, her voice showing clear concern.

"We'll be fine," Cambious responded. "The bartender owes me a favor."

We drove in silence then, and slowly I began to hear the sounds of civilization. Traffic moved past us, and light punctuated even through the blanket. I could hear people talking, laughing. "It's probably safe for you to sit up," Cambious said, reaching back to tug on the blanket. I sat up, turning to look out the window. If I hadn't known we weren't back home, I'm not sure a first glance at the city outside my window would have told me differently.

There were storefronts and restaurants, what looked like office buildings, and here and there smaller standalone shops with signs with images of herbs and stones, cauldrons, and more. Zo pulled up in front of a bar with a neon sign in the window saying "Stroya's."

"You two be careful."

"Thank you, Zo," I said, touching her shoulder while Cambious opened my door and reached in for the bags. I climbed out with the canvas bag that Merry had given me and lifted a hand in farewell as Zo drove off. "What is this place?"

"This is just a bar," Cambious said, pointing to an alley between it and the next building. "We're going there. Which is also just a bar, but one for those of us who are not human."

He led me into the alley to a short staircase leading down to a door. "Stick close to me and don't talk to anyone you don't have to. Oh, and no glamors allowed in here, so...don't stare." He opened the door and escorted me in. There was a small room with a security guard on a stool. The guard appeared human, though a bit short. He nodded to Cambious and waved a hand at the door beside him. When it opened, I was nearly blown back by the sound of merriment and music and glass clinking.

"Are you going to stand there all night?" the guard asked me, startling me out of my hesitation.

Cambious led me in. It wasn't a huge place, but it wasn't the corner bar either. There were tables scattered around the room, most of them occupied, and stools along the bar, which seemed to be carved out of a dark wood, one long slab that had to be at least ten feet, and the edge was filled with carved figures, ornate and beautiful, at least where I could see it through the bodies.

Oh, and those bodies. I recognized some as incubi because they looked like Cambious, and I assumed that the women who looked similar were succubi, but the others...everywhere I looked I saw strange things I had once thought of as myth, if I'd thought of them at all. Cambious lifted a hand in greeting as a woman came toward him, all smiles and happiness.

She was pretty, in a sparkling silver blouse over a dark skirt...and the hairiest legs I'd ever seen. I brought my gaze back up quickly, taking in the wide face and soft brown hair, out of which grew an almost dainty set of horns.

"Ah, Celica, how have you been, my dear?"

"Cambious, you look well."

They hugged briefly and I felt her eyes sweep over me. "Oh, you know she won't make Stroya happy."

"Stroya can suck it," Cambious responded. "We won't be here long. I came to call in a favor."

"Then I shan't keep you." She kissed his cheek and moved away.

"Celica, she's the satyr I traded with," Cambious said with a grin as we moved to the bar. "Come on. I see Toman."

He slid onto a stool, putting my duffle bag in his lap. I took the stool beside him, trying to keep from drawing attention. To my left was a mountain of fur that was vaguely shaped like a man, but at least eight feet tall. I wasn't sure I even wanted to know what he was. Beyond him was another satyr and beyond him was a tall, impossibly slender, androgynous being who seemed more or less human, other than his curved and pointy ears and the pale blue of his skin.

Behind the bar, the person I assumed was Toman approached us. "Bringing a witch into my place, really Cam?"

"It couldn't be helped, Toman," Cambious said.

Toman put napkins in front of us, followed by glasses into which he poured a dark red wine. I caught myself staring at his hands, which weren't so much hands as they were talons. I glanced up at him, blinking a little. His face was decidedly bird-like, his nose and mouth protruding out in similarity to a beak. His red hair was filled with feathers of a deep wine red and black. And he had wings. Like, actual wings.

Cambious touched my thigh to draw my attention away. "I'm here to collect that favor you owe me," Cambious said to Toman. "We need a vehicle and a few minutes with Sibyl."

CHAPTER 19
SIBYL

"You don't want much then," Toman said darkly. "If Stroya finds out I let you in to see Sibyl, he'll have a fit." He blinked, drawing my attention back to his face, which was when I realized that he had two sets of eyes. Two were set very close to his nose/beak, and the other two were slightly higher and set wider.

"So, don't tell him," Cambious replied, lifting his glass of wine to sip. "Do I need to remind you what you owe me? This will not come close, and yet, if you arrange it, I will call us even."

Toman's face darkened and he clucked at Cambious. "Give me a few minutes. Gavin, cover the bar, I have something I need to do."

As he moved away, I could see that like his hands, his feet were talons that clicked against the floor when he walked. Cambious turned to me with his glass in hand. I frowned at him and took a sip of my own wine. It was rich and lush and fruity on my tongue. "What exactly does he owe you for?" I asked softly.

Cambious shook his head. "That is between him and I. Suffice it to say that this favor does little to restore the balance."

"And who is Sibyl?"

He smiled tightly. "You will see soon. I warn you, however, she is…not exactly sane."

Something tickled the back of my brain, something from high school English class and the section on Greek myth. "Is she…I mean, the Sibyl I know about was an oracle in ancient Greece."

He nodded and sipped his wine. "As are all Sibyls. Unfortunately, having access to all that knowledge tends to drive them mad."

I shook my head because that made about as much sense as the fact that I was sitting in a bar next to an incubus and a…Big Foot.

"Let me ask the questions though," Cambious said, putting his empty glass down on the bar. "She'll only answer three, and if you distract her, we might not find out what we need to know."

"And what is it you think she can tell us?"

"How to get your mother out of the Kourt, I hope. Ah, Toman." He gestured toward a door where Toman was waving to us.

I followed him through the door and down a long, ill-lit corridor where Toman paused to unlock another door and open it. "You have fifteen minutes. Any longer than that and Stroya will know. Your vehicle will be waiting out the back when you are done."

Cambious held out his hand. "Thank you, my friend. I shall not ask any more of you from this night on."

"Damn well better not," Toman muttered as he walked away.

"Remember, stay quiet." Cambious headed down the dark staircase and I followed, clutching the bag Merry had given me and realizing suddenly I hadn't even looked inside it to know what was there. There was a soft yellow glow as we neared the bottom of the stairs, and the air was increasingly warmer. At the bottom, we turned the corner into a small room dominated by a huge fireplace with a large fire burning, the air filled with the strong scent of the wood burning and something more fragrant, something that sent my mind whirring.

In front of the fireplace was a rocking chair and in that chair was a woman. Or what I assumed was a woman. She was tiny and frail-looking, all wrinkled skin stretched over bone. Her feet didn't reach the floor and her eyes were hazy and milk-white, likely blind. A plain white nightgown hung off her gaunt frame and gray and white hair hung in streaks from her balding head.

Unerringly, she turned her face toward us as we came to a stop. "Who comes?" she asked, her voice shaky and low.

"Pilgrims seeking guidance," Cambious responded. "May we approach?"

"What gift have you brought me, pilgrim?"

Cambious gestured at the bag in my hands. I opened it and reached inside, coming out with an old-looking bottle with no label. I handed it to Cambious who in turn held it out to the woman. "We bring a fine brandy aged a hundred years in the dark ranges of the Amerin mountains, in a cave where the ghosts of ages past fill the casks."

She gestured for him to come closer. He put the bottle in her hands. "It is a fine gift, pilgrim, but I have no need of such spirits. The ghosts of ages past fill me daily." Her face turned to me. "This woman is a blood witch."

Cambious stepped toward me protectively. "She is, but not mine to give."

The old woman smiled. "I would have a gift of her. I will answer your questions three, but once I have you will leave her with me. I would have her heal me."

I wasn't sure there was anything wrong with her other than advanced age and the blindness that came with it. Not to mention, I had no idea how my gift worked. Every time I had used it, it had been instinct. "It's okay, Cambious," I murmured. "I can try."

He looked into my eyes, judging my resolve before he nodded. "Very well then."

"Come, pilgrim, and give me your hand." As Cambious knelt in front of her, she lifted an odd-looking tube from the small table beside her and put it to her lips, inhaling deeply and holding her breath for an impossible length of time. When she exhaled, a purple mist escaped her mouth and she put the tube down, taking Cambious's offered hand.

"You have three questions. Ask them well."

"We seek the blood witch's mother who is held prisoner by the Brotherhood of God at the Mauno Kourt. What must be done to free her?"

The room was still, the only sound that of the crackling fire and when the woman lifted her head, her voice had taken on an odd inflection, stronger than it had been and deep. "Seek your way on rocky ground, find the one that must be found. He smells your blood and knows your way; his freedom is the price you'll pay."

Her head nodded back toward her chest and for a moment I thought she was asleep. "Your first question is answered. Ask your second."

Cambious licked his lips, considering his options before he asked, "The Brotherhood seeks the blood witch and will kill her if they find her. How can I keep her safe?"

Again, she lifted her head, her voice strong as she responded, "Safety is forgone and lost, and in the Kourt, you pay the cost. Look to the gods, look to the sky, her blood will spill while death is nigh."

Cambious looked over his shoulder at me, actual fear in his eyes. "One question remains, pilgrim. What will you know?"

He inhaled and let it out slowly. "Can we stop the Brotherhood?"

"Father of Brothers speaks hate, and others follow. He will burn in the fires of Apollo. Still, they will rise another day, hate born of hate finds a way."

She dropped her head to her chest again and Cambious stood, backing up. When she lifted her head, she was once again the frail old lady. "Your questions asked, your questions answered. Now leave me with the witch."

Cambious drew me back a few steps. "Be careful, Thána. I'm not sure what she will ask of you, but I promise it will not be pleasant."

I nodded, not trusting myself to speak. If I was honest, I was terrified of what she was going to ask me, not to mention terrified of what I thought her answers meant. If we couldn't destroy the Brotherhood, would I ever be safe? And what of my blood being spilled? I didn't like how any of that sounded. When Cambious could no longer be heard on the stairs, she beckoned me closer.

"I'm not sure what I can do to help you," I said cautiously, taking one knee in front of her. "My gifts are…unpredictable."

"Your gifts are strong, and I ask only that you give me a taste of them. On the mantle is a blade, bring it."

I was even less sure of what she was asking, but I got up and went to the fireplace. The blade looked to be made of black glass, shiny and sharp. I brought it back to her and went back to my knee. "Cut your arm and give it to me."

I stared at her until her eyes narrowed and her face grew hard. "You have a price to pay, *mágissa*, do not think to escape it." Her tone softened and her hand patted mine. "I won't take much, but my bones are cold."

Swallowing hard, I lifted the blade and after a couple of aborted attempts, managed to make a shallow cut about 4 inches above my left wrist. Blood beaded along the edge, but it wasn't enough. With a shaky hand, I drew the blade over it again and her hand pressed down on mine, making me slice deep enough that I gasped and had to fight the urge to drop the knife and cover the wound. Her hands pulled my wrist up toward her mouth and I had to stand to ease the odd turn on my shoulder. Leathery lips closed around the wound and a strange sucking sensation followed.

I was starting to feel faint when she finally released me and I stumbled back toward the fireplace, catching myself on the mantle. I did cover the wound now, though it was bleeding enough that I knew it would take more than my bare hand to staunch the flow. She started laughing, my blood painting her lips, and, in the firelight, shadows danced across her face, making her seem...younger somehow.

She was still laughing as I raced for the stairs, bursting through the door, and falling into Cambious.

"Are you okay?" Cambious asked, his hand going to where mine covered my bleeding arm.

"Let's just get out of here," I responded. He gestured down the hallway in the opposite direction of the bar. As we stepped out into the night, he tapped the talisman on his chest and his whole being shimmered as the glamor returned. As promised, there was a car waiting, a boxy-looking thing that didn't look big enough to even hold Cambious. It was dark grey, with a short front end and an even shorter back end with no back seat.

"He could have gotten us something made in this century," Cambious griped.

"Does it matter, as long as it runs?" I asked, moving to the passenger side, and using my wounded hand to open the door. I felt blood rushing as I flexed the muscles and must have paled because Cambious was suddenly at my side, supporting me as my knees gave out.

"Thána!"

He got the door fully open and sat me on the seat. "Let me see it." He pried my hand away and made a sound between a gasp and a growl. "Had I known that was what she wanted..." He pulled something out of my duffle bag and folded it, pressing it over the wound, then pressing my hand back over it. "Here, hold this. Press down tight."

Cambious helped me get my feet into the car and closed my door, then went around the back, dropping the bags and the bottle of brandy in the trunk before he squeezed himself into the driver's seat and started the engine. "There's a pharmacy up the street. We can get some bandages at least, if their healer is on duty, we might get lucky."

I was woozy when the car stopped, but Cambious helped me up and held me while the world spun around me. The shop in front of us looked similar to the Walgreens where I went to buy aspirin and Band-Aids, though its neon signs said "Healer on Staff" instead of something about a drive-through pharmacy window. Cambious got us in the door, with me still pressing down on what I could now see was one of my T-shirts. The place was well lit and nearly empty, but that would be expected at whatever hour of the night it was. Cambious helped me through several aisles until we came to what looked like any clinic in a pharmacy back home.

He got me sat down and went to the window beside a door. I couldn't hear him talking, but then I was busy trying very hard not to pass out. A few minutes, or possibly longer, later, the door opened and a guy who reminded me of that grandpa at my first foster family's Christmas dinner came out of the door, took one look at me, and told Cambious to bring me back right away.

Cambious helped me up, but my knees had become less solid than Jell-O which hadn't set completely and he ended up scooping me up and carrying me through the door. I realized as he set me down on an exam table that I had lost the T-shirt and I tried to get up to go find it.

I was pressed down, and Grandpa pulled my blood-soaked hand away from my arm, exposing the wound. "How did this happen?"

"I dropped the knife," I said, my words slurring.

"I'm sure," Grandpa responded. "For starters, let's get that blood flow under control. How much has she lost?"

Cambious shook his head. "I'm not sure."

Grandpa turned away and when he came back, he had a stick of some sort, the end of it glowing. "This is going to sting." He pried the wound open and put the glowy stick into it, tracing along the full length internally. Sting was not the word I would have used to describe that particular sensation. I screamed, my back arching up off the table. Cambious pressed me back down, but I still tried to squirm away. "Hold her still."

Once again, Grandpa turned away, and this time he came back with gauze that looked damp. He used it to clean the blood from my arm and wiped it over the wound. "There, now I can see what's going on."

I couldn't see what he was doing as he worked and twice, I swooned enough that I'm not certain I didn't actually lose consciousness. Then, Cambious was picking me up off the table and thanking the Grandpa witch doctor with a warning to him to be sure to clean up well if he didn't want unwelcome company. My arm was bandaged, and I was starting to feel a little more with it as we reached the car.

"I need your help here, Thána," Cambious said. "Can you stand?"

I nodded and he slowly lowered my feet to the ground and opened the car door for me. "We need to move, if the blood tracker is anywhere in Thelos he will have picked up our trail with the amount of blood you left in there."

Once I was in, Cambious closed my door and went back to the driver's side. "Where are we going?" I asked as we set out.

"Away from here."

CHAPTER 20
OUT OF THELOS

I WOKE TO DAYLIGHT PAINTING THE WINDSHIELD A GOLDEN COLOR. Beside me, Cambious was asleep behind the wheel. Outside the car, we seemed to be in a parking garage, and I could just make out the faint shimmer of wards outside the car. My left arm was an angry, screaming toddler who had been told he couldn't have the last cookie and I needed to pee badly enough that I wasn't sure I could get out of the seat to do it, even if there had been a bathroom nearby.

I tried to stretch, but the tiny cabin of the vehicle didn't give me much room. I could only imagine how much worse it was for Cambious. I shifted as much as I dared, seeing as I was now wearing the only jeans I had left, and to my dismay, they were stained with my blood. It wasn't a lot, but if Cambious was right and the Brotherhood was on our tail, this could lead them straight to us.

"How are you?" Cambious asked into the silence of the car, causing me to jump and nearly lose the hold I had on my bladder.

"Holy mother of—warn a person before you do that," I exclaimed, shaking my head. "I'm okay, but I need a bathroom."

"As do I. If you are capable of walking, we are someplace

where we can do that as well as replace our clothing and get something to eat. Then we should once more be moving on."

"Right. And where is it we are going?" I asked, opening my door, and moving gingerly so I didn't wet myself.

"Toward Mauno Kourt, for lack of any other direction," Cambious responded, also climbing out of the car. He dismissed the wards and moved around picking up the stones. "We won't rescue your mother from here."

I had serious doubts about rescuing her at all, but I didn't say that. Instead, I concentrated on my steps and followed Cambious to a stairwell. He had parked us on the fourth floor of the parking structure, which I found was attached to what looked suspiciously like a mall. My disillusionment with my Fairy Kingdom was nearly complete.

Fortunately for me, there were bathrooms near the entrance, so I was able to relieve myself of that particular problem fairly quickly. Our next stop was a small boutique that sold clothes that, while they weren't exactly the height of fashion back home, wouldn't have been completely out of place either. We quickly picked out a few items—some pants and several shirts—paid, and then backtracked to the bathrooms so we could both shed our bloodstained clothes and get dressed. I took a few minutes to clean up as well, taking some wet paper towels into the stall with me.

I stuffed my bloodstained shirt and pants into the bag I took the new shirt and pants out of and dressed as quickly as I could. I was starting to get anxious, though I wasn't sure of the cause. We seemed relatively safe for the moment. I picked up the paper towels from the floor where I'd dropped them, then shoved those into the bag too. Cambious had said we could use them to lay a false trail, though I wasn't sure how that was supposed to work.

Besides, Cambious had promised me food.

My stomach growled then, as if it needed to be reminded that I hadn't had food since breakfast the morning before. We moved through the mall, which was starting to get busy, dodging weary mothers with toddlers pulling them or dragging behind them. I could smell something delicious as we neared what I was no longer surprised to find looked just like a food court in just about every mall I had ever been in.

We walked around each of the restaurants so I could see what there was to choose from, finally stopping beside a place serving sandwiches and what looked like burritos. I ordered a sandwich filled with eggs and some sort of sausage, with a side of coffee and left Cambious to order and pay while I found us a seat where we could see most of the food court.

Cambious brought our food and we sat, both of us keeping our eyes moving while we ate. The bag with my bloody clothes sat at my feet still, next to the bag with our other purchases and we were both aware that it could give us away. We ate quickly and as soon as we were done, we all but ran back toward the car.

"How far are we from the Kourt?" I asked when we were on the road, the bag of bloody clothes in my lap.

"It's about a two-day drive, but first we're going in the other direction to drop these clothes. So, a little longer than that."

"Do you think just dropping bloody clothes by the roadside and driving in the other direction is going to work?"

He grinned at me. "No, but I have other plans."

I understood a little while later, as we pulled into a mammoth train station. Cambious directed me to the ladies' room with instructions to put the bag in the trash, then rejoin him at the ticket counter. A half-hour later, we were back on the road, with two train tickets to a city called Aténa to the north and west of Thelos. I tucked the tickets under my seat with the hope that the combination was enough to make the Brotherhood think we were trying to get away and not suspect that we were headed for their base of operations.

"Okay, so…what Sibyl had to say about this insane scheme of ours, have you given it any thought?" I asked when we'd both been quiet for a long time.

Cambious nodded slowly. "Some. You?"

"Seek your way on rocky ground, find the one that must be found. He smells your blood and knows your way; his freedom is the price you'll pay..." That one seemed the easiest for me to focus on. "We're going to need someone's help, and I'm guessing it's a blood tracker?"

"That is what I deduced as well," Cambious said. "Legend tells us that the Brotherhood uses male blood witches, trained to use their powers to sense their own kind. They can smell your blood. The best can sense it just by being in proximity. They are rare, however. I have never met one."

"Fabulous." I shook my head, a vague detail from a dream coming to mind. "How does the Brotherhood get them to do it?"

"They are usually stolen in their early childhood when possible and indoctrinated in the Brotherhood's beliefs. The older ones are simply tortured until they submit. They are enslaved, treated hardly better than the women they hunt."

There was a boy in the background of my dream of Althea's death. Clad only in a diaper-like garment, covered in dirt and half-starved, he had been on the platform, a collar of some kind around his neck, held in place with needles that pierced his skin. I shuddered and pushed the image away. There had also been that boy with the Brotherhood who had spared my life when I was still a child. "So, we're supposed to find this person, without alerting his...handlers, and convince him to help us?"

"I've thought about that too," Cambious said. "As I said, Sybyl can be difficult to understand, but it should become clear as we draw closer."

"Okay, so what? We find some kid and promise him he'll go free if he just helps us find my mother?" I asked without even attempting to keep the doubt from my voice. "Sounds easy. Sure, let's do that."

"Perhaps he will find us," Cambious countered

We were leaving the city of Thelos, headed south and east on a freeway that was slowly getting less congested. "So, we get to the Kourt, we find this guy, he leads us to Mom…then what?"

Cambious shrugged as much as was possible in the tight little space of the car, which only made me realize that even if we rescued this blood tracker and my mother, we had no way to get them to safety. I skipped over the middle prophecy and moved on to the last. "Father of Brothers speaks hate and others follow. He will burn in the fires of Apollo. Still, they will rise another day, hate born of hate finds a way. Which means what? Apollo, the sun god? How do we convince the sun to burn a man?"

"Ah, a point of mythological differences. Apollo is a god of eternal flame, light, heat…" Cambious offered. "I warned you that she often makes little sense. The fires of Apollo may mean any number of things."

Great. Exactly what I wanted to hear when the middle prophecy had talked about my blood spilling and death being nigh. I was starting to wonder if it wouldn't just be easier to find some tall building to jump off of. I rubbed a hand over the bandages on my arm, wishing it would ease the pain there.

"Safety is forgone and lost, and in the Kourt, you pay the cost. Look to the gods, look to the sky, her blood will spill while death is nigh."

Sibyl's words echoed in my head and spun into a mini-tornado. I wasn't ready to acknowledge them, or the fear that bloomed under them. I wasn't ready to think about killing **or** dying. In fact, I was beginning to wonder what exactly I was doing. I wasn't a cop. I wasn't military. I had no idea how to break into a fortress, let alone evade bloodthirsty killers, rescue an old woman and escape in a car built for two.

But my father's ghost had told me to find her and all of my repressed anger at her abandonment was floundering under the desperate love of a ten-year-old's desire for her family.

"You should rest," Cambious said. "We have a long drive."

The world outside the windows of the car was getting increasingly gray, with thick clouds forming on the horizon. "Looks like rain," I said softly.

"Snow more like. Thelos is in a temperate zone, but it **is** winter here."

We were quiet then for a while and I dozed off. It wasn't really sleeping, but I wasn't awake either. It was that weird spot somewhere between the two, where I was vaguely aware of the world around me, but not engaged with it. Maybe I could just stay there and stop worrying about the strange turn my life had taken.

Eventually, the road beneath our tires changed and we slowed, pulling me out of my stupor. Cambious pulled off the road and into the parking lot of some hotel. The gray skies had grown black and just as Cambious had predicted, snow was falling. One more thing I hadn't come prepared for.

"I'll get us a room." Cambious was gone before I could say anything, not that I knew what to say. He came back to the car and opened the trunk, pulling out our bags and the bottle of brandy before leading the way to a door marked with a symbol I assumed was a number.

It looked like any hotel room I had ever stayed in, with a dark brown rug and walls painted beige. Two double beds were covered in ghastly bedspreads that looked like the product of a night of hallucinogenic drugs mixed with confetti shots and paint. There was a flash of memory, of a room just like this with my mother and sister, and a lot of fear. I shook my head to clear it and turned to find the bathroom, thinking I needed to wash my face and get it together.

We still had no plan for what we were doing. I had no idea what to expect, other than the flashes I had seen inside the fortress where my mother was being held. I had no delusions that I was equipped for this. I turned the water on and reached for the pristine white washcloth folded in a fan shape on the counter. My reflection stared back at me, with black smudges under dark green eyes and hair that was rapidly reverting to its natural state of fuzzy black curls.

I washed my face with cool water and thought about just

running away, hiding somewhere that even the Brotherhood wouldn't find me, though I had no idea just where that might be. With a heavy sigh, I turned back into the room to find Cambious on the end of one bed, his glamor gone and his whole body looking heavy. His eyes were puffy and red. He was exhausted.

"You should rest," I said, pulling his attention to me.

"I need to feed," he replied. "The constant drain of the glamor is too much."

"Is it safe to…find someone here? I mean, I saw a bar at the corner, but…" Thus far we hadn't had to have this particular discussion, but I got the impression from his mother that an incubus wasn't exactly welcome in a lot of places.

"Likely not. I'll have to be discreet." He lurched back to his feet, his hand reaching for the amulet.

"Cam, you can barely stand." I pulled his hand away from the amulet. "How about you sleep for a while, and we can go to the bar together." He sat back down, and I went to one knee to help him with his boots. Which was when the solution came to me. "Or…we could…I mean, I could…"

He seemed to get the gist of what I was going for and shook his head minutely. "No, I couldn't ask that of you."

I grinned up at him. "You aren't asking. I'm offering. God knows I haven't had sex in a while, but I think I remember how it works."

CHAPTER 21
INTO THE WOODS

I SET THE HEAVY BOOTS ASIDE AND SLID MY HANDS UP CAM'S LEGS, nudging them apart so I could move between them. "You've done so much for me," I said softly. "Let me help **you** for a change."

He wanted to argue, I could see it in his eyes, but his exhaustion won the fight and he let me move closer, sliding a hand up under his shirt, urging it up and he responded with a shrug that brought it up to his neck before he pulled it off. I couldn't quite look him in the eye as my hands glided over his dark skin.

Cambious was a big man, built solid and strong. Randomly, I wondered if that was true before his transition, if he'd been big and solid muscle as a succubus. I shook off the distraction and turned my attention back to getting Cambious out of his clothes.

The jeans he wore did little to hide his arousal now that he had given in to the need. I leaned back to pull off my shirt, dropping it behind me as his big hands unzipped his jeans and he shimmied a little to get them down.

My surprise when he had bared himself almost threw me out of the moment. I had expected big, he'd implied that, but what I wasn't prepared for was the peachy-white skin. He followed my eyes and chuckled a little. "You saw she was white, obviously. There are ways to make it match, but I've never bothered."

"No need," I said, my voice huskier than normal. My body was certainly responding to having a naked man in front of me, even if he did have horns, and I stood to shed my own jeans. I shivered a little as I dropped my pants and panties on the bed, suddenly self-conscious of my soft, flabby body next to his, but if it was repellent, Cambious didn't show it, drawing me back to him with a gentle hand.

"You don't have to," Cambious said softly.

"I want to." If I let myself, I could reach back to the day we had met and the lust that had filled my head. It flushed through me. That rush, that need, and I was more than ready for what came next. I didn't know how the feeding thing worked, but my body certainly remembered how the sex thing did.

Cambious slid his large hands up my arms, then around my back to unhook my bra. His kiss was surprising somehow, soft lips on mine as he guided me to the bed. His skin was hot against mine as we lay down, his lips leaving a damp trail down between my breasts and over my belly. I wasn't thinking about my unfit body when his mouth moved further down, his hot breath sending a thrill of need straight into my sex. My orgasm took me by surprise and even more surprising was the accompanying sensation as Cambious sucked up the energy discharge that came with it.

I was still riding the tremors when he moved, spreading my legs apart to move between them, his own need obvious. I held my breath as he entered me, letting it out only after he started a slow pull back. "Thána, are you okay?" Cambious asked, his voice tender.

I nodded, opening eyes I hadn't realized I had closed. The air between us sizzled with energy that I vaguely recognized as coming from me, and as I ramped up to a second orgasm, Cambious breathed it in. It felt as if he were sucking my entire being out of my body and I fisted my hands in the bedspread beneath me, unable to do more than pant as I shook beneath him, my orgasm an extended experience that took my entire body to the brink of collapse.

I passed out, coming to only when Cambious started using a cool cloth to wipe the sweat from my skin. My limbs were heavy like I had run a marathon, or what I assumed it would feel like after running a marathon. I was still trembling as he lifted me like I was still a child and got me nestled into bed under the blankets. He kissed my forehead, and I wanted to say something, but my brain was already mid-shutdown procedure, so it came out as sort of a low moan.

"Sleep," Cambious said in my ear, and that was one command I had no trouble obeying.

The smell of coffee and bacon roused me sometime later and I sat up, forgetting I was naked, to see Cambious setting out breakfast on the room's small round table. "I figured you'd be hungry," Cambious said, keeping his back to me to give me time to find my clothes.

I dressed, or at least pulled on my panties and shirt, and moved to the table to join him, just as Cambious set a container filled with a mound of scrambled eggs and what looked and smelled like bacon in front of me. I reached for the cup of coffee first, peeling off the lid and sipping the hot liquid into me, feeling the warmth spread down my throat as I swallowed. My stomach rumbled and I picked up a small plastic fork to eat with.

Cambious sat opposite me, tucking into his own meal with less enthusiasm than I did. I watched him for a minute, then sat back with my coffee. "This isn't going to get awkward, is it?" I asked, pulling his eyes off his food to me. "I mean, I have no regrets, and you look restored, so…we're good, right?"

"If you mean that, yes," Cambious said, putting his empty plate on the table.

"Of course, I mean it. I wouldn't have offered if I thought I would regret it later. And I think it was pretty obvious how willing I was." I raised an eyebrow at him, nearly daring him to contradict me. "And I don't think I've ever slept harder, thank you very much. No dreams, just warm, fuzzy nothing until I smelled coffee."

"Well, I did drain you pretty good." Cambious seemed to be slowly letting go of whatever guilt he had been sitting with but wasn't all the way there.

"If I sleep that good after, you're welcome to drain me that good anytime you want," I said, blushing a little as I said it. "Seriously, Cam, I mean that. If you need it, tell me. You've done so much for me I can't begin to repay. This barely touches that debt."

He nodded, a half-smile turning up one corner of his mouth. "I will admit, I have never fed with a blood witch before. It was an amazing rush."

"There you go," I said, setting down my coffee to go back to my bacon. "So, what's up for us today? How far are we from the Kourt?"

"At least another day's drive. And we have to cross a border out of Spítia into Otadž."

I had a fleeting memory of those names. Spítia was my mother's homeland, with Thelos as its capital city. Otadž was a newer country, born out of a conflict that had torn the previous empire apart. When my mother was a girl, that country had split into Otadž and one named Orõn to the north. That was about all I remembered. "Is it going to be a problem?"

He shrugged. "It is hard to say. The government of Otadž is in a terrible state, and most of its military has been recalled to the capital to protect what remains. Their Premier has been rocked by scandal and the parliament is so divided that nothing has been accomplished. The Brotherhood and a few other militant sects have stepped up in places to secure towns and demand adherence to their religion and rules. I do not know if they have made it so far as to the border crossings. I have not been this far from your portal in a very long time."

"So, we could be driving right into their hands."

He nodded slowly. "Perhaps, but there are places to cross where it is less likely we will be seen as a threat. There is a small town that straddles the border, we can cross there."

"And then we just have to find a fortress, rescue my mother, stop the Brotherhood from hunting me and get home before I lose my job." Because none of it mattered if we didn't find a way to get the Brotherhood off my trail. Chances were good my job was already gone. I'd lost track of how long it had been since we fled, a situation not helped by my days in a stupor after Merry's memory trick. Two days without word from me probably would have Bonnie ready to fire me. "You know this whole thing is insane, right?"

"So you have said." Cambious stood, crossing to the small window, and parting the heavy drapes just enough to peer out. A blade of light cut across the dingy room, making me wince and pull away from it.

"I'm going to shower." I stood and drank the last of my coffee before grabbing my duffel bag and heading into the bathroom. I looked like I was on the bad end of a hangover, my eyes dull and the smudges under them bordering on bruised. I stripped out of my dirty clothes and turned on the water, pausing to peel back the bandages on my arm. The cut was mostly closed, scabbed over in several places. Whatever was in the medicine they used here needed to find its way home with me, when and if I ever got to go home.

The thought gave me pause. I'm not sure when I had started to consider the house in California as home, but somewhere in the whirlwind, it had become an anchor, a safe place. I hadn't had that since the day we had left it when I was still a child.

I showered quickly and dressed in the other set of clothing Cambious had purchased for me. I had no way to straighten my curls, so instead, I finger combed them into something I could live with, promising myself an indulgent spa day when this was over that would include returning my hair to my preferred style.

By the time I emerged from the bathroom, Cambious looked

like he was ready to get going, his glamor safely in place. Not for the first time, I wondered how many other races I had already seen but couldn't tell because of their glamors. And if this society was so far advanced, why did he have to hide who he was? I put the question aside for another day and followed Cambious out to the car.

I put my duffle in the trunk, pulling out the book on the Brotherhood and the blood witch primer to take into the car with me. As Cambious drove, I devoured the information the books could offer me, reading up on the various gifts peculiar to blood witches, before switching to the Brotherhood's history, up to about fifty years ago, when the book had been published. The Kourt was the ancestral home of a line of blood witches, built by a Duke as a place for protection and study. The Brotherhood had come in the night, like something out of a B-movie, with torches and spears, storming in to cleanse the Kourt, and slaughtering every living being in its halls.

The Kourt sat atop a small hill, with two roads that snaked around the hill to reach the stone walls. At the base of the hill, circling it, was a graveyard. Once a place of honor for those who had served the duke, or studied in his libraries, it had become the final resting place of generations of Brothers and was said to be protected by spells and enchantments, and creatures who guarded the Kourt.

"Great," I murmured, looking up from the book. We were driving through a wooded area, gently climbing. The snow blanketed the trees, but the road was clear, even as the snow continued to fall. "So, to get into the Kourt, we have to cross through a graveyard that the Brotherhood has warded with god only knows what."

"I expect it will include enslaved manticores at the least. I understand the Brotherhood considers them to be symbols of Jeus himself."

"Manticores?" My face scrunched up as I searched my memory. The word was familiar, but there was no easy recall.

"They are not unlike a lion, if a lion had wings, a tail like a scorpion, and the intelligence of a man," Cambious supplied. "They are extremely dangerous. One sting from a manticore's tail can kill a grown man in under ten minutes. Their claws are deadly. And they fly. There could be phoenixes as well. There was a news story a few years back about a phoenix who had escaped the Brotherhood. They also fly and can breathe fire. Toman is a phoenix. Their talons can be deadly as well. Oh, and a point of interest, they were said to guard the entrance of the cave of Apollo, where the sacred fire was kept."

"Okay, that's terrifying," I mumbled. "This rescue operation just gets better and better."

CHAPTER 22
THAT'S THE PLAN?

WE REACHED A SMALL TOWN CLOSE TO THE MIDDLE OF THE DAY. There was a sign as we approached, welcoming us to Sigur, home of the award-winning poet, Timurline, whoever that was. The town itself looked like something from a postcard of some rural European town that had never fully stepped into the twentieth century, let alone whatever century it was here.

The buildings were all dark timber and whitewashed stone with slate roofs that sloped down from the center nearly to the street. The whole town was one street lined with shops, though I imagined that there were houses beyond that we couldn't see from the car.

In the center of the town, there was a monument that stood a good twenty-five feet tall, of a woman with a torch in her hand. "It is said that she was the first to settle here," Cambious said, steering us into the roundabout that circled the statue and its pedestal. A sign warned us that we were crossing into Otadž as we reached the center of the giant roundabout. We passed without fanfare, and I relaxed minutely as we carried on unimpeded.

"That wasn't so bad," Cambious murmured.

"Don't jinx us," I responded. Ahead of us, more buildings

lined the road, but fewer of them seemed occupied. People were scarce and when we did see them, they were scurrying between doorways. It didn't feel particularly safe. There were no men on the streets with guns though, which was what I'd been expecting, if I'm being honest. I didn't even know if they had guns here.

We continued down the road and past the sign telling us we were leaving Sigur. Ahead of us was open road through a deep, dark forest that was blanketed with snow. It would have been beautiful if it didn't hide the men who wanted me dead. As we continued toward the fortress that held my mother, I continued my reading, wanting to fill my head with as much knowledge as I could in the hope that it would lead to a plan of some kind that didn't include my death.

A thought occurred to me, and I turned my head to look at Cambious. "So, I'm assuming that you aren't just a pretty face and pheromones, right?"

He frowned, glancing aside at me. "How do you mean?"

"Well, can you, you know, fight? Pick locks? Something like that?"

"I don't tend to go around getting into fights if I'm honest," Cambious replied. "Particularly here. I am a good deal stronger than most humans."

"Okay, that part is good." My brain was spinning out possible scenarios. I had access now to whatever knowledge my mother was able to impart to me before she left me, but it was admittedly not enough. I was ahead of my age group, to be certain, and she taught me protections most nine-year-olds would not learn for years to come, but protection spells and wards were not going to get us into a fortress. "Wait, I think I remember something about locks." I dug deep into the place where all of that knowledge seemed to reside, setting the Brotherhood book aside and going back to the blood witch primer. "My blood can fortify a lock but can unlock stuff too? Particularly if it was set by another blood witch."

"Are you certain?"

I shrugged. "No?" I thumbed through the primer, scanning for anything about locks. The problem was, this book was not written as a training tool. It didn't have instructions, just information. "It's theoretical anyway. I never tried it. It was in a book I read on the theory of blood magic. A lot of it went over my head, but I was only eight." Idly I wondered what had happened to that book. I remembered taking it with us when we fled, reading it in the car while Mom drove, but she must have taken it from me when she left me. "So, we can try that. If we get that far."

"Perhaps you will be able to sense your way, seeing as the Kourt was once home to the blood witches of the time?"

I shrugged again. "I guess we'll find out. And then we just have to get inside, find Mom, break her out, wipe out the Brotherhood...yeah, should be a walk in the park." I ran the words of the old woman through my head, trying to reason out how they could help us. "

Seek your way on rocky ground, find the one that must be found... He smells your blood and knows your way; his freedom is the price you'll pay. Safety is forgone and lost, and in the Kourt, you pay the cost. Look to the gods, look to the sky, her blood will spill while death is nigh. Father of Brothers speaks hate, and others follow. He will burn in the fires of Apollo. Still, they will rise another day, hate born of hate will find a way."

No matter how I turned it around in my head, it sounded like we would have to kill the leader of the Brotherhood to get them off my scent. Though, if it was as big an organization as it seemed, killing one man didn't feel like a solution of any kind. In fact, I had to wonder if it wouldn't just make it worse, turning the man into a martyr. I also wasn't sure I could do it. Kill a man I mean. Of course, I already had, when I was just a child, but I wasn't that person anymore.

I shook my head to clear it. "How far are we now?" I asked.

"Not far, another hour or so."

"We should eat. And make some kind of plan."

He nodded and pointed out the front windshield. "There is a cafe not far ahead of us. Or there used to be. We can stop."

True to his word, a few miles down the road, the trees gave way to a gravel parking lot and a little building with a faded sign in three languages, declaring the best pie in the precinct and we pulled in, parking beside a beat-up older car that vaguely resembled a Volkswagen Beetle. "I haven't been here in years, possibly since you still wore pigtails," Cambious said as he opened his door. "Used to be run by a little old man and his wife, they're probably gone now."

I kept forgetting Cambious was that much older than me, and I found myself wondering if that made the sex thing weird for him. I mean, it was weird enough for me with him being a creature stepped out of ancient superstition, but considering he'd known me since I was little, how strange had that have to have been. Unless incubi didn't have those sorts of taboos.

I put the question away for a time when we weren't an hour away from the stronghold of the men who wanted me dead, provided that time ever actually came.

The cafe had a long counter with stools and a handful of booths. A tired-looking woman with dark red-brown hair pulled back in a ponytail nodded to us. "*Sedi bilo gde.*"

Cambious nodded back. "*Hvala vam.*"

"How many languages do you speak?" I asked as Cambious led us to a booth near the back where we'd have the most privacy.

He seemed to think about it for a moment. "Fluently? Five, but I can manage in another six or so. Of course, those are languages here, I've found that on your side of the door, they've changed enough that I don't always understand them."

That made sense. Language evolves over time and could evolve in unexpected ways as cultures come together or splintered apart. We sat and the tired-looking woman approached with menus. I couldn't read it, or even figure out what language it was written in, but Cambious pointed out a few dishes he thought I might like and when the woman came back, he ordered for both of us.

He waited until she had walked away and pitched his voice low enough it wouldn't carry. "To find our way in, we will first have to get past the manticores."

"And any other creatures, plus wards or spells they've put up."

Cambious nodded. "Yes."

"Putting the mythological creatures to the side for the moment, what then?" I asked, glancing up to track the waitress.

"Well, that's going to depend on what we find once we get there."

"Right. Remind me how long the Brotherhood has been there?"

"A long time," Cambious replied. "I think we can assume any way in will be locked in some fashion. So, we deal with the lock. Then it gets tricky."

"I can tell you that my mother is in a cell up high, in a tower I think."

"Well, that narrows it down some. There are only four towers."

"So, we search them all?" I asked. "And how do we do that without being seen, caught, and killed?"

Cambious lifted a hand to the amulet that secured his glamor. "I was thinking we just walk in. We'll have to build you a glamor too. And steal some clothing."

"Okay, that sounds doable, provided we can do the glamor thing...I know Mom taught me some simple ones when I was little, but I can't promise I can make one work. From there we just have to avoid any confrontations and look like we belong."

"Simple," Cambious said, his tone indicating he thought the exact opposite.

We both sat back as our waitress brought our plates, simple enough sandwich-like meals with fried chips of some kind. They looked like potato chips, except for how they were kind of a pale blue in color. They tasted similar to potato chips, but for a bit of a sharp bite like old cheese.

"Okay, so let's get back to the mythological creatures that will want to kill us. Any ideas?" I asked as I swallowed my second bite.

"Perhaps. It will depend a great deal on the manticores themselves. I think we should probably take our time with them, watch their patrol patterns. Maybe we can avoid them altogether. We should make a circle around the Kourt itself before we settle down somewhere for sleep."

I nodded, not sure what he would have in mind, but figuring anything we planned now with our limited information would likely be useless later anyway. But at least we had the start of a plan. As we got close to finishing our food, the waitress brought the check, and with it a paper bag. Cambious handed her a payment card and thanked her. "I ordered food to go. There's no guarantee we will find a safe place to eat later."

When she came back with his card, we got up to leave, but I detoured to the bathroom. Who knew when we'd have an actual bathroom again? I relieved myself and stopped to wash my hands, glancing in the mirror at my reflection. My hair was nearly full curl, and frizzy with the lack of product in it. I almost didn't look like myself anymore. In fact, I looked like the women in the pictures in my book. I looked like Merry when she was younger.

Cambious had the car started and turned toward the road when I came out. We drove in relative silence for a while, until the forest thinned out yet again, and we began to see gravestones in front of us and on the side of the road. Cambious turned us to the right as the road dead-ended just before the graves began. Several rows back, a four-foot stone wall erupted from the ground, blocking our view of the rest of the graveyard, as well as the base of the hill upon which the Kourt stood.

I leaned forward to look up, my eyes tracking rocky terrain

until I could just make out the foundations of the fortress above us. With the wall between us and what we needed to see to plan our entry, not to mention our later escape, we were going to need to actually get out of the car at some point, but first Cambious was determined to drive completely around it, in order to get an idea of what our first obstacle would be.

CHAPTER 23
GLAMORS, NOT GLAMOROUS

THE FIRST GATE WE FOUND IN THE WALL WAS MANNED BY TWO guards in black military uniforms, with weapons strapped to their waists, and in their hands. Unlike the Brothers I had encountered before, they both had full heads of hair, one blonde, one brunette, cut close on top and shaved on the sides.

We didn't slow down, but as we drove past, I got an impression of the graveyard beyond that wall, a road through it that bore to the right before I lost sight of it.

The second was guarded the same, but the stonework around the gate seemed to need some work, and through the gates I spotted, or thought I did, the creature Cambious called a manticore. I shivered involuntarily as we drove past but grabbed Cambious by the arm a few minutes later. "Stop."

Cambious pulled us off the road well out of sight of the guards, a question on his face. I wasn't sure I could put into words the feeling that swelled up within me. Near the wall was a neat row of graves, with stones so old the words etched into them couldn't be read, at least not from the car. Something there wanted my attention. I opened the door, my eyes scanning around us to make sure we weren't being watched.

"Thána, what are you doing?" Cambious hissed at me, but I

shook my head, crossing the street and feeling my way toward whatever had called out to me. Nearest the wall was a stone that once had been white but was marred now by time and what looked like the damage of fire. I squatted beside it, brushing soot and dirt from the etched name, but it was still unreadable. It knew me, which I know makes no sense at all.

I could feel Cambious behind me, his concern palpable, even at that distance, but I ignored him, laying my hand flat against the stone, where the name had once been. As my palm connected I got a flash of the graveyard beyond the wall, not as it was right then, but as it had been when this witch had been laid there, and beyond that, the rocky face of the hill, a tumble of rocks, a hidden cave part way up, only visible when you were nearly upon it.

I heard Cambious open his door and stood, waving him back as I crossed the street back to him. "Go," I said once I had the car door closed. "There's a secret way in. Or there was. Whoever buried that witch left a…map, of sorts. I just felt it."

Cambious didn't respond, just continued us on down the road. Before we had made a complete circuit around the Kourt, we found a dirt road that took us back into the forest, and about fifteen minutes later, Cambious pulled us to a stop, nodding. "We can get some rest here. Work on your glamor."

I nodded. "Okay, but we can't sleep all night. We're going to need the darkness to protect us."

Cambious snorted. "For all the good it will do. Manticores have excellent night vision."

"Humor me? I got a look at that thing. I don't need to see it in the daylight again."

"I suggest you set up some wards, give us a good fifty feet inside, encompass the car. I'll get us set up for working."

I wasn't sure what he needed to set up, or where it was going to come from, but got out of the car all the same, pulling the bag of ward stones from the pocket of my jeans and eying the area around us, trying to figure out the boundaries of a fifty-foot circle. I decided to keep the car as the boundary to our east, setting the first set of stones about five feet from my door. I paced out the circle without activating the stones, making sure I had an even placement, so we were equally protected from all sides.

Once I had the spacing figured, I retraced my steps, marking the spot in the dirt, pine needles, or leaves so I would know where to return the stones, then brought them back to the car, arranging them on the hood in their respective pairs. I sorted through the various incantations I had learned to use with them and settled on the one that would make us disappear, as well as keep anyone from hurting us. I felt Cambious watching as I activated the pairs before holding my hand above the obsidian cubes, murmuring, *"Ekleípo."*

Green light flared and formed a dome around the circle of stones. Cambious joined me, his pride palpable. "Very good, Thána. We now must move them in tandem." He reached for a pair, and I reached for its opposite. Very carefully we moved toward the edges of the circle I'd marked out, and I could feel the dome stretching with us. We returned to the hood for the next pairs and the next, until with the last the dome stretched over our heads and all around us in a circle.

While I'd been working, Cambious had started a small fire and spread a blanket down beside it. I noticed it was the same blanket as he'd used the night we had dinner together beside the portal. He must have put it in his bag before we left his cabin. My duffle bag was on the blanket, my books stacked beside it.

"I guess it's time to learn how to glamor?" I asked as I sat.

"Unless you would prefer to sleep first?"

I shook my head. "No, let's do this." I pulled the stack of books to me, setting my own spellbook aside. Glamors would have been beyond my skill level then, even if they would have come in handy. I chose the family book first, kind of remembering seeing something about glamors in its pages.

"The thing to remember about glamors is that they are an

energy drain," Cambious said softly as I turned the pages. "They are easier to maintain if you have something to anchor them, such as my amulet." His hand lifted to caress the talisman gently. "And they are easier if you do not shift too much of yourself. I think for this it should suffice to change your appearance to be more masculine and shorten your hair. If you've noticed, the brotherhood either shaves their head or wears it cropped close. There was a monastic order as well that didn't ever cut their hair, but they are all but gone."

I nodded, tucking the information into a corner of my brain while I sought out the page I was looking for. "Okay, here it is." I set the book on the blanket in front of me, my eyes scanning over the page in an attempt to commit the information to memory. There were a number of incantations and their translations on the page. I chose the simplest to try first. "*Krýpse me apó tous echthroús mou.*"

Nothing happened, at least nothing I could see.

"Breathe deep and center," Cambious said. "Cover your face with your hands."

I did as he suggested and tried again. This time I felt something akin to bubbles under my skin, like pouring peroxide on an open wound. Something in my face shifted, blurred even and when I lowered my hands, Cambious was smiling.

"Good."

I got up and crossed to the car to see my reflection. I was still me…sort of. My hair was lighter in color and my lips fuller, my nose longer. Anyone who knew me well would see past the disguise, but someone I'd never met wouldn't be able to pick me out of a lineup.

I crossed back to the blanket and sat again, pulling the book closer. I could feel the pull of the glamor on my energy, and instinctively murmured, "*Elefthérosi.*"

"You are getting better at this," Cambious said.

"Don't go praising me yet. That didn't do much to make me look like a man."

"It's a start. Here," he pointed to an incantation halfway down the page, "add that to the first."

I nodded and read over the words a few times before I lifted my hands up toward my face, hovering just centimeters away as I reached inside of me and murmured, "*Krýpse me apó tous echthroús mou. Anatrépste to fýlo.*"

Again, I felt my skin bubble and shift, even the bones in my face felt like they were shifting. This time when I got up to look, my face was wider, my forehead thicker and my black hair was neatly shaved on the sides of my head, the top just shy of an inch long. This was a bigger drain, and I wasn't sure I could hold it for as long as we would need. "This is work," I said as I returned to Cambious.

He nodded. "Let's tweak the look first, then we'll find you an anchor item."

My hand lifted to the place under my shirt where my mother's necklace lay warm against my skin. "I know what we can use. But how do we tweak it?"

"All you have changed is your face. You need to make the rest of you more masculine as well. Stand up and cross your arms, put your hands on your shoulders and repeat after me." I did as he said, breathing into my center as I awaited the words. "*Evreís ómous. Epípedos thórakas. Stenós gofoí.*"

As the words left my mouth, I felt the changes happening. It wasn't painful, exactly, but it wasn't very pleasant either. My shoulders seemed to shift outward and upward, my breasts reduced to what they had been before puberty and my hips pulled in, making my natural curves disappear. I was panting by the time it was done.

"Good. Very good. How does it feel?"

"Damn weird," I said. "I'm not sure I can hold it."

"You must, or we will need to start again." He stood and took a step toward me. "Take out your anchor item and hold it in your dominant hand."

I moved carefully, as if movement would destroy the illusion altogether, pulling the necklace free of my shirt. I held it in my right hand and looked for my next instruction. "Essentially what we are doing is saving this exact look into the anchor, much as you would a file on a computer," Cambious said. "Cover the pendant with your other hand. Feel its weight and shape. Ask it to keep the spell safe...in your mind, in your body. No need to speak it out loud.

"Feel the dimensions of your image, memorize how it feels, take the measure of it and when you are ready, the word is *Apothikéfsete.*"

I felt silly asking an inanimate object for something, but I did it, closing my eyes and feeling like it shifted in my hand, a feeling as if it had opened to receive what I would give it. It took me a while to feel like I knew this new me well enough to commit it to the pendant, but finally, I said the word and felt a sort of pull, as if the pendant was dragging the information into itself.

"Very good. You are learning quickly," Cambious said. "You can release it now."

"*Elefthérosi.*" There was a flush of power draining from me and I swayed a little on my feet. Cambious caught my elbow to steady me.

"You should rest before we continue. I'll get our food."

I sat on the blanket, and he went back to the car, returning with the bag from the cafe. We ate in comfortable silence while I read through the rest of the page on glamors. As I finished my sandwich, I fingered the pendant. "*Anáklisi.*" The changes rippled through me. "*Elefthérosi.*" And I was back to myself again, this time without the feeling like I was going to pass out.

Here in the forest, we couldn't see the skies, but the woods around us were getting darker as night settled in. While I practiced with the glamor, Cambious cleaned up what was left of our food. I was glad our little protective dome helped to trap some of the heat from the small fire. The night was definitely colder than I was prepared for.

"You should get some sleep," Cambious said as he approached.

"What about you?" I asked, yawning as I dismissed my glamor and stretched. I suddenly realized that Cambious too had let his glamor dissipate.

"I'm fine. I need less sleep than you, remember?"

I shook my head. "Not what I meant. Do you need me to—?"

Cambious seemed to catch my meaning before I said it. "No, I am okay."

I frowned at him and stood. "Look, I know it's weird, okay? I get that. But we're going into the lion's den in a few hours, and I need you at your full capacity. What happens if your glamor slips because you're too drained to keep it? Or you don't have the strength to do whatever it is we need to do?"

"Thána, I—no, you're right. It would be a disaster."

"Assuming that it isn't already a completely bad idea," I murmured. "Here by the fire, or…"

"Well, it's been a long time since I've done it in a car," Cambious said, humor in his eyes. "I'm not sure that would work so well."

I chuckled and started to undress. "Here it is then. Just, don't let me sleep too long after. We need the dark."

CHAPTER 24
THAT WAS TOO EASY

I WOKE SHIVERING A FEW HOURS LATER, MY BODY PLEASANTLY SORE, the kind of sore that only comes after really vigorous sex. I was wrapped in the blanket and settled onto the passenger seat of the car. I sat up, my hand drifting to my mother's pendant as it shifted across my skin.

Cambious sat near the fire, though I couldn't make out what he was doing. I opened the car door, but as I moved my feet to get out, I found my clothes all folded neatly on the floor beneath me. I paused to pull my shirt on, shivering again as the cold cotton slid over my head. I didn't want to drop the blanket to pull my pants on but figured out quickly I didn't have a choice.

I shook my pants out before I moved enough to get them over my feet, losing the blanket almost at the same time. I stood quickly, yanking the pants up before sitting back down to get my feet off the cold ground.

"Your shoes are on the floor on the driver's side," Cambious said, standing now and starting to stamp out the fire.

I nodded, though I knew he couldn't see me, and reached around the steering wheel for my shoes, with my socks tucked inside. I got them on and stood, glancing around me. "We ready?" I asked as the domed space got even darker without the fire.

"As much as we can be," Cambious responded with less enthusiasm than I'd wanted to hear.

"Okay, then I guess we go."

I dismissed the wards and collected the stones and we both got into the car without speaking. We drove in silence to the spot I'd found the day before, slowing and pulling off the road. "This is a bad idea," I murmured as the car stopped.

"We don't have to go in."

I looked at Cambious, once again safely behind his glamor and I reached for my anchor, activating my own. "No, we do. I just haven't figured out how we...get back out again."

Cambious patted my knee. "If we can get in, we can get out again."

"I hope so."

I opened my door and got out, rubbing my hands over my arms to warm them. The night was clear, the heavens above us dotted with unfamiliar stars, not that I'd ever paid too much attention to the stars at home to know the difference. Off over the dark hulk of the Kourt, there was a silver sliver of a moon, and I realized with a start that there was more than one. I shook off my surprise and tried to focus my energy on the task at hand. Or at least the first one, get over the wall.

"What about the car?" I asked.

"Wait here, I'll ditch it somewhere, just don't be seen."

I crossed the road and made my way back to the grave I'd found before. Its pull wasn't as strong now that I'd gotten its message, but I found it easily enough, kneeling beside the stone and laying my hand on it again. My mind filled with the location of the entrance, the hidden climb up to it, then the cautions and warnings about the men who had taken the Kourt. Whoever had buried this message had done so after the Kourt's fall to the Brotherhood, but before the wall had been built. I'd been hoping for more though, like maybe a map of where this hidden entrance would take us, and where to go from there, or maybe an idea of the spells and wards the Brotherhood may have placed on the grounds. On those counts, however, the stone was silent.

Instead, I tried to use my time waiting for Cambious to try to determine what awaited us beyond the wall. I moved closer, and stilled, listening for any sounds that might give away the monsters that wandered the graveyard, or the humans who kept them there. I set my hand to the wall, hoping for another message, but the wall had been built by the Brotherhood and it only whispered of violence and death. The night was quiet, no sounds of footsteps or heavy breathing or flapping wings, at least not until Cambious reappeared.

He nodded and offered his hands to boost me up. I scanned the area as I moved, checking for any sign of the beast I'd glimpsed the day before. Nothing moved beyond the wall as I straddled it and reached down to offer Cambious a hand he didn't need. He merely put both hands on the top of the wall and pushed himself up and over before he helped me down.

First hurdle jumped. We squatted in the shadow of the wall, listening, and watching. My heart was slamming so hard against my ribs I was sure they could hear it all the way back in Thelos. "There," Cambious whispered after a long time, pointing off to our left.

I could just make out the sense of movement in the distance but couldn't see the beast. "We need to get to that rock," I whispered, my voice barely audible as my breath plumed the air. I pointed to the right.

"Okay, stay low and follow me." Cambious moved cautiously, keeping gravestones between us and the place we thought the manticore was. We stopped often, kneeling beside some monument or bush. We both knew that if we were even seen the whole thing would be over. Once the alarm was raised, we didn't stand a chance of infiltrating the Kourt and getting out alive.

Not that I liked our chances to begin with. It was highly likely this whole thing ended in death. *"Look to the gods, look to the sky, her blood will spill while death is nigh."* The words echoed through my head, and I had to shove them aside before the icy fear filled me and froze me in place.

Cambious moved again, taking us slowly closer to our target. I caught the movement to my right before my brain registered it, grabbing Cambious by the arm. I could smell it, the manticore, like an animal's cage at the zoo mixed with stale blood and vomit. It was moving closer, each step bringing it within reach of finding us.

We moved as slowly as we could, soft steps so that we made no sound, putting a tall stone monument between us and the beast. A memory hit me, and I lifted my hands to cover my face and murmured, *"Krývo."* It was one of the earliest spells my mother had taught me, along with *prostatévo_* and *ánoixe*. Cambious and I held our breath as the manticore passed. It stood nearly as tall as Cambious in his true form, its wings folded along its flanks. His head was crowned with a mane worthy of the king of beasts, but his face…his face was nearly human, but not quite. I shivered, though this time it had nothing to do with the cold.

After a small eternity, Cambious pointed and got us moving again. I was suddenly reminded of the time I had snuck into the campus of an all-boys school with Sandra Teller when I was a senior in high school, only this time the stakes were a whole lot higher.

We reached the last bit of cover we would have and stopped. I didn't know how long the spell would hide us, and there were maybe ten feet of open ground between us and the rock face. In the dark, I couldn't make out the path up that I knew was there, but I could sense something else. It had the feel of static electricity against my skin. Beside me, Cambious nodded. He felt it too. Wards. "Now what?" I asked as softly as I could.

Cambious seemed to weigh the question, lifting up to get a better look around us. "Where?" Cambious mouthed back to me.

I shook my head and moved a few steps to my right. I could just make out a ledge about six feet up. I pointed. I knew from the images I'd gotten from the stone that at one time there had been an easier way to get there, but it looked as though it was long gone. Our only choice would be for Cambious to boost me up, and then hope I had the strength to pull him up behind me.

"When I tell you, move quickly. I won't be able to hold the wards open for long without setting off alarms." Cautiously, he stood, his hands moving as he whispered the incantation *"Ftiáxe mia porta."* His glamor shimmered but held and I felt the hole he made in the wards. "Now."

I nodded and moved to the wall, keeping to a crouch until Cambious had joined me. We were horribly exposed as I put my foot to his hand, and he shoved me upward. I scrambled onto the ledge and lay flat as he scurried back to cover. I lay there panting, my eyes scanning the graveyard, clocking two, no, three of the death monsters patrolling. I held up a hand to let Cambious know to wait, then rolled onto my stomach, and held my hand down for him when the coast was as clear as it was likely to get.

Cambious repeated his incantation, then sprinted, his hand grabbing mine, and he jumped while I pulled, rolling away from the ledge as he pulled himself onto it. The ledge was barely wide enough for the two of us to lay side by side, but neither of us moved as we fought to catch our breath. I was the first one to recover, kneeling up to find our next step.

Cleverly concealed behind a wall of stone that blended in with its surroundings, I could just make out a trail of sorts, what had once been steps but was now just a steep trail that looked a bit treacherous. I moved for it, keeping low even after I was safely behind the wall of rock. It wasn't so tall that it would hide me from view completely. I didn't look to see if Cambious was behind me, just trusted that he would be.

I ended up staying on my hands and feet, crab crawling up a path strewn with smaller rocks and pebbles. I was sure the cacophony made by the stones as I sent them hurtling downward would rouse the guards, but there was no sound of alarm.

My calves were making me aware that they were not fans of this, and so was my lower back. I told them to suck it up, knowing I'd pay for it later...provided we survived. The trail leveled out a bit after around twenty feet, then curved in toward the hill, entering a cave that clearly wasn't a fully natural feature of the rock. I paused just inside the deeper dark for my eyes to adjust.

Cambious joined me, his sharper eyes scanning around us.

"That was too easy," I said barely aloud. "What next?"

He gestured deeper into the cave, and we moved slowly. I kept one hand on the wall as we moved, all but holding my breath and expecting something to jump out of the dark at us. Eventually, we found the tunnel blocked by a metal barrier of some kind. I felt my way around it until I found a lock. "Here," I whispered, putting my hand flat against it, and taking a deep breath to center myself and feel inside the lock. I still had no idea if I could make this work, but I turned to Cambious. "I need a knife or something to prick my finger."

He took something from a pocket, and I heard a folding knife snick open before he put the handle into my hand. I pricked the middle finger of my left hand with the tip of the knife, then handed it back before I pushed along the line of the finger, encouraging blood to flow. When I had a small bead of blood, I put the finger to the lock, spilling the blood inside. "*Ánoixe kleí-doma aímatos.*" It was a simple enough incantation, and I could only hope I had remembered it correctly as I **pushed** the lock with my thoughts, with my will for it to open.

It seemed to take forever, and I was beginning to think I had been wrong when I could hear the faint metal-on-metal sound of the tumblers moving. The gate moved under my hand and just like that, we were in. I stepped through the gate, feeling my steps without light and with no idea what to expect.

Cambious was close behind me. I was wishing we'd thought to bring a flashlight or something when I noticed that the dark ahead was not as black as the dark behind us. It wasn't light but seemed to be drawing us toward something. My hand touched a surface that I expected to be stone but felt more like wood. I pressed a hand against it, hoping I could feel my way through it. As I did, I felt a rush of something race up my arm and a word filled my head, "*Diávasi.*"

I straightened up, pushing my hand against the wood, and spoke, "*Diávasi.*" The wall moved, swinging silently open and dropping us into a dark hallway where the floors were the same stone as the tunnel, but the walls were clearly man-made.

We were, thankfully, alone in the hall. When we had stepped through, the door closed just as silently, and when flush with the wall, it seemed to disappear. I felt along the wall but couldn't find the seams. "Okay, we're in," I whispered. "Remind me, what comes next?"

Cambious started down the hall and I followed. We moved slowly and tried to minimalize the sound our feet made, easing up to a corner where faint light pooled. Cambious peeked around the corner. "I don't see anyone."

I moved around him and into the next corridor. Dingy yellow light dotted the length of the corridor, from ancient-looking light fixtures every ten feet or so. The walls reminded me of some medieval castle in some movie, all dark grey rocks of varying sizes. I half expected to find we were in a dungeon or something, but the irregular doors were wood, and there didn't seem to be anyone being tortured or imprisoned.

We came to another corner, where our corridor crossed with another. To our right, there was a flight of stairs. To our left, the corridor moved away into utter darkness. "Well, we have to go up eventually," I murmured, taking the lead.

The stairs ended with a doorway. I stood and listened, hoping it wouldn't open onto a room full of armed men or something. Cambious put a warm hand on my back, I suppose for reassurance, and I turned the nob, pushing the door open.

We both waited breathlessly, anticipating capture.

CHAPTER 25
PETER

WHEN AN AMBUSH DIDN'T HAPPEN, I TOOK THE LAST STEP INTO THE room. Shelves lined the walls, and boxes and crates were stacked haphazardly, leaving little aisles between them.

"Storeroom?" I asked, turning to look around us.

"Looks like," Cambious agreed, moving toward a nearby shelf full of books. "Some of these are ancient." He turned toward me, then froze, his eyes on a dark corner. He pulled me closer. "There is someone here," Cambious whispered, his lips brushing my ear so he could keep his voice almost soundless.

I could hear something, frightened breathing, and the near-silent shuffle of skin against stone.

Cambious gestured for me to go left around the stack of boxes between us and the corner, as he moved to the right. It didn't make sense...this was no guard hiding in the shadows. I had a feeling I couldn't place.

"*Ko je tamo?*" a tremulous voice asked, and a sudden light flared ahead of us. I got the brief impression of a slight figure before the light blinded me. Cambious moved swiftly and the light fell, rattling against the rock as that tender voice yelled out.

I scrambled for the dropped light and Cambious shoved the

small figure against the wall I could now see. "Cambious, stop," I said, moving closer with the light.

We could see now that the figure was just a boy, barely eleven or twelve, judging by his size. He wore little more than rags, his feet bare and covered with sores. "He's just a boy."

Dark eyes met mine, the pupils contracting in the bright beam of the flashlight. "You...you're *Thanátou*."

"I'm not here to hurt you," I said softly. Kids were not my forte, ask any one of my friends who had them, but I could see the terror in his eyes. "How do you know—" Oh, right. I slowly made the connection between his ragged clothing and my feeling. You can tell what I am?" He nodded. "Cambious, put him down."

"He can raise the alarm." Cambious cautioned, even as he set the boy on his feet.

"He can, but he won't. He knows what I am because he is a blood witch, like me," I said, smiling at the boy. "What's your name?"

"Peter." His voice shook, his eyes darting between me and Cambious.

"Peter what?"

He licked chapped lips and swallowed. "Peter Suelo."

"What are you doing hiding down here in the dark, Peter?" I asked.

"N-nothing. Why are you here?"

I glanced at Cambious, but his face was unreadable. I weighed my options. This might well be the person we were supposed to find, according to the madwoman. "Well, Peter, we're looking for someone."

Cambious grabbed my arm, but I shook my head. "I'm Thána. This is my friend Cam." I realized after I said it that I still looked like a man, but figured the kid already had me pegged as a blood witch, so it wouldn't matter. "Did the Brotherhood take you away from your family?"

He nodded, wiping his nose on his shirt sleeve. "Two men came when I was on my way home from school."

"Suelo isn't a local name," Cambious said. "Where are you from?"

"Juavez."

"That's three thousand miles from here," Cambious said aside to me. "How long have you been here?"

The kid shook his head. "I don't know. A while, maybe a year?"

His last name rattled around in my head until I remembered where I knew it from. "Suelo is Spanish for ground and Peter means rock. Rocky ground," I said softly to Cambious. "Are you trying to escape, Peter?"

His eyes dropped to my feet, but he nodded. "I want to go home. These men hurt me. They said they'd kill me."

"Not if we kill them first." Cambious's voice was darker than I could remember hearing it and here in the dark, it was kind of terrifying.

"We can help you, but first we have to find someone," I said softly. "A prisoner. She's in a tower cell."

Peter nodded. "They took us up there when they brought us here."

"Us?" Cambious asked.

Peter looked up at him, his eyes wide and filled with fear. "Me and Ashkān, and some bird-lady."

"Thána, we need to talk." Cambious drew me away from Peter. "We can't trust him."

"Do we have a choice?" I asked, glancing back. I could barely make out Peter's shape in the darkness. "The old lady said we to find rocky ground and that he would be able to smell my blood. He's a blood witch whose name means rocky ground. It doesn't get much more on the nose than this."

"That is what I'm afraid of. He could be a plant," Cambious said, his voice low and dark. "They know we're coming."

"Maybe," I conceded. "But he's had a lot of time while you

and I are over here whispering about him to call for help. Besides, can't you see how scared he is?"

"If we take him with us into the Kourt, he may betray us as soon as we are inside and cut off from escape."

"I agree, but he knows where she is." I shook my head. "You heard what the old lady said, Cambious. You're the one who told me she's always right."

There was a low rumbling growl that took me a minute to identify as coming from Cambious. "We are going to regret this."

We went back to where Peter stood, shivering in the cold night air. "If we promise to help get you home, can you help us find the tower cells?" I asked softly. Peter inched back into the shadows.

"I know where they are," he answered tentatively. "But I don't want to go back up there. They're looking for me."

I nodded slowly. "Can you give us directions?"

He squirmed uncomfortably, his eyes darting from me to Cambious and back. "What if they find me?"

"Hide better," Cambious said, his hand drawing me away. "We're wasting time, Thána."

"Hold on, just give me a second." I squatted to put myself at Peter's height. "If you come with us, we can keep you safe."

"Promise?"

I nodded. "I promise."

He launched himself at me, wrapping his arms around my body and burying his face in my shirt. I let him cling for a moment, then gently loosened his grip. "Just stay close."

Cambious took the light and shined it around us, but it didn't penetrate the darkness for more than a few feet. I took a deep breath and held it, imagining all of the things that could go wrong. "This is insane," I muttered.

"How do you want to do this?" Cambious asked. Peter moved so that he was touching me, not quite clinging, but clearly wanting to stay away from Cambious.

I was not usually a person who did things without a plan, but

I was so far out of my depth that I was pretty much making it all up as we went. I had a vague idea of the order of things that I'd like to see happen: uniforms or other clothing that would let us pass, find my mother, free her, and then get us all out without any of us dying. I didn't think about the whole notion of killing the head honcho. I still wasn't sure I had it in me to kill again.

My memories of that first kill were like most memories of a five-year-old, fuzzy in places and uncertain in others. I took his pain inside me though, I sucked it up, and with it, his life. I did it instinctively, and with a heavy dose of fear and rage. I wasn't sure I could do it a second time.

"Thána?"

I glanced up, realizing that I'd been off inside my head while they waited. "Right, let's go." I set out with a false bravado, hoping that doing would make it so, as one of my foster fathers used to say. "I guess first thing is to figure out where we are in relation to that tower? Any idea, Peter?"

Peter pointed one trembling hand in the direction opposite where we had come in. We picked our way through the maze of accumulated junk until we came to a large wooden door.

"We have to go through there, and then up to the main floor."

I nodded to Cambious, who opened the door. Peter's hand clutched my shirt, and I reached a hand down to try to comfort him, resting it on his back, just between his shoulder blades. He shuddered. Under my hand, I could feel his skin raised and welted. I glanced at Cambious and inclined my head toward Peter's back. Cambious lowered the light and flashed it at the torn blue of Peter's shirt, I could just make out what looked like scars from a whip of some kind, maybe a belt. I lifted my hand, and it came away bloody.

What kind of person tortured a child?

I didn't vocalize my question, but I know Cambious heard it anyway.

Maybe Cambious was right in that they knew we were coming, and they wanted to draw us in. Maybe this was how they captured me so that they could bleed me dry. The images of ancestors hung upside down while men in black cut into arteries filled my head and I shook it to clear it. Getting hung up on that would probably get me killed. We needed to be smarter than them. We needed to act in a way that they weren't prepared for.

There was no more light in the next room than there had been in the first and it seemed to go on forever, though it probably felt longer than it was due to the darkness and our own fear. And make no mistake, I was afraid. I was hoping it didn't show, that Peter couldn't feel it the same way I felt his, but my heart was pounding a rapid staccato against my ribs as we found a door. There was no telltale light seeping under or around it, so either it was also dark on the other side, or it was better sealed than most doors.

The hallway beyond was not quite as dark, a distant light coming from further down the hall. The walls were the same grey stone as the others we'd seen, but the floor had been covered with what looked like wood.

I stepped out, reaching back to draw Peter to me. He was trembling in fear, but he came easily enough. He pointed with one shaking hand toward the light. Cambious came behind us as we tried to walk as quietly as possible toward the light, which turned out to be just beyond a turn in the corridor. It was a vaguely yellow light shining out of a discolored sconce on the wall. In my mind's eye, I could imagine it had once held a torch...or maybe Hollywood had influenced my imagination too much.

Still, I cautiously turned the corner, glancing in both directions as the hallway formed an L shape. To my left, the hallway was dotted with heavy doors the same color as the stone walls. I couldn't see an end in that direction with the minimal light. Straight ahead was a shorter corridor, with a light at the end, illuminating the only door that way.

I turned left, easing down the hallway. The doors here were metal, with no indication of what might be behind them. Peter tugged on my shirt as we reached the fourth one, pointing to where the next light was. "Stairs."

I didn't respond, just started walking that way. We passed another four or five doors, more or less evenly spaced, all on the left side of the hall. At the light, we came to a crossroads of sorts. A corridor crossed the one we were in. Peeking around the corner, I spotted the stairs to the right. It was eerily quiet, particularly knowing that this fortress could easily hold a thousand people or more. I didn't want to jinx our luck by vocalizing my observation. "What's at the top of the stairs, Peter?" I asked in a whisper.

He shrugged a little. "Storerooms and stuff, I think."

"We're going to need to find clothing fast," Cambious observed. "I don't know what to do about the boy."

"Robes and stuff are easy enough," Peter offered. "If we go to the laundry. I worked there for a while when they first brought me here."

"Of course, you did." Cambious looked at me, his eyes betraying his doubt. "And I suppose you know how to get us there?"

Peter nodded. "Up three floors to the south hallway, it isn't far."

I let Peter take my hand and lead us up the stairs, turning us to the right. There were more stairs then, but Peter pulled us back and after a moment, I heard why. The sound of feet on stone, soft leather slapping the floor as two Brothers passed the top of the stairs. We waited a few more heartbeats after the sound of their feet passed before we headed up the steps. Peter stopped to poke his head out at the first landing before tugging on my hand and starting up the next flight.

When we had reached the top of the third flight, Peter pointed around the corner. I noticed his hand wasn't shaking nearly as much as earlier, but I had no way of knowing if it was because he had a role in our clandestine invasion or because he was closer to giving us away.

"You should let me go in. Just in case someone's there. Give me a few minutes." He darted away before I could stop him.

"I don't like this," Cambious said, leaning forward to watch Peter dash into a doorway. "We're exposed here."

"I know." I was itchy with nerves and sure we were about to be betrayed, especially the longer it took for Peter to return.

He did return though, in a brown jacket over a white shirt and dark pants, his arms filled with a bundle of black fabric. He grinned as he passed the bundle to Cambious. He adjusted the jacket. "The boys who serve upstairs dress like this."

Cambious took us down to a turn in the staircase where we had a line of sight in both directions and deposited the clothing on the floor, opening the bundle and sorting through it, tossing pieces to me before he stood and started to strip down. "Keep watch, boy."

"His name is Peter," I hissed at Cambious as I too started to strip so I could pull on the black pants and a navy-blue shirt. Peter had done pretty well at guessing our sizes, though the pants Cambious was now wearing were a little short and the suit jacket I pulled on was a little long in the sleeves. There were two deep crimson robes as well.

"Robes can get you past a lot of guards," Peter offered. "You should call me *slǔga*. It's what they call the servant boys."

Cambious balled up the clothing we had come in, tucking it under his arm and hiding it with his robe. "Okay, now what?"

"Now we find our way to the holding cells," I said, looking to Peter.

The boy paled considerably. "I don't like it there."

I squatted to put myself closer to eye level with him. "I know you don't, but someone important to me is being held here, and we need to get her out. Can you help us do that?"

CHAPTER 26
STEP ONE, GET INSIDE

I⸱T TOOK P⸱ETER A MINUTE, AND I COULD SEE HIM MARSHALING HIS fear before he nodded. "It won't be easy, but I'll try."

I smiled tightly. "Fast is good but unseen is better, you understand?"

He nodded again, glancing both ways down the hallway. "This way, we have a few hours before morning work begins, we can get through the kitchen to the back stairs." He set out and Cambious and I fell into step behind him, hoping we looked like we belonged there. I was starting to feel the strain of maintaining the glamor, but I pushed my fatigue away. There would be time enough to rest when we were safe.

The long hallway led us to another long hallway, then into a large room filled with tables. I could almost see them filled with witches of all ages, stacks of books punctuated with plates of half-eaten food from a time when it had served as both dining hall and study. Peter led us down one long side of the room, the wall lined with tapestries that depicted gruesome scenes of death and dying and war. A large archway waited ahead of us, with only the low flicker of a banked fire to see by.

The arch gave way to a neat and orderly kitchen, where a fire burned down to coals cast everything in a ruddy glow that was more color than light. A sturdy wooden table, looking as if it were old enough to have been built long before the Brotherhood, occupied the largest space, its surface worn smooth over years of food prep, its edges marked by knives and vague dark stains of heat. At one end of the table was a basket of not-quite-apples and another round fruit I couldn't quite make out in the dim light. Peter drew us past the table, one finger to his lips as he pointed to a door with his other hand. "The two cooks sleep in there," Peter explained in a whisper. "Very loyal."

Cambious grabbed fruit from the bowl, tucking it into the inside pocket of his robe, and I followed his lead. We would eventually need to eat.

We moved lightly, eyes stealing to that door over and over as we moved to a large pantry stocked with enough food to feed a small nation. There, Cambious grabbed what looked like sausages, strung along the front of shelves, and a box of something that I didn't see. The pantry led us out into a hallway that looked much the same as all of the other hallways we'd walked down, only somewhat better lit.

Peter led us off to the left, moving down the hall as if he were on a mission. We found the stairs he had promised and started up them. One floor up, he gestured at the hallway. "Armory is down there, and the library over there. On the opposite side of the floor is the door out to the parade grounds. That's where the road goes out and down the mountain and where they punish prisoners." He shuddered and shook his head.

"Where to next, Peter?" I prodded gently.

He looked up at me with wide brown eyes and swallowed hard. "We need to get past the guards on the stairs up to the tower." He pointed in the direction he'd said held the library, but Cambious put a hand on my arm before I could move in that direction.

"Maybe we should go by the armory first?" Cambious said softly. "The only weapon we have on hand is my knife."

"What kind of weapon are you thinking we need?" I asked,

though I nodded to Peter to lead the way.

"Anything is better than nothing," Cambious replied. "I've used guns before, though it's been a while."

"Okay." I had never used a gun. I couldn't remember ever seeing a gun in person, other than the handful of times I'd dealt with the police. I'd always equated guns with bad guys, and it had never occurred to me that I might one day need to use one.

As we approached the door that Peter indicated was our destination, two Brothers were approaching from the opposite direction, deep in conversation. I froze, pulling Peter closer, but the men just nodded at us and kept walking.

"I can't go in," Peter said once they were gone. "I'll wait here."

Cambious and I exchanged a look filled with trepidation, but we had already gotten this far, and if Peter was going to betray us, there wasn't much we could do. Cambious handed him the bundle of our clothes, then opened the door, and strode in as if he had every right to be there. I followed a step behind. Inside was a spacious room lined with locked cages that held every type of weapon imaginable. There was a counter and a weary-looking Brother in rumpled clothing. He straightened up when he heard us come in. "Good morning, Brothers. What can I do for you?"

"I will tell you, Brother," Cambious said with a rather convincing smile. "This young Brother requires some work with his pistol before we are sent out in the field. I was hoping to get in some target practice before breakfast."

The man behind the counter smiled and nodded. "Very good. Do have a specific weapon in mind?"

Cambious leaned casually against the counter, and I got the impression he did *something* that made the brother go a little moon-eyed. "Why don't you surprise me."

The man blushed and turned away, disappearing into the rows of lockers behind him. I slapped Cambious on the shoulder. "What are you doing?" I hissed at him.

He glanced after the man, then back at me. "Hopefully confounding him enough to get what we need without too much trouble."

The Brother was back then, two guns and a box of ammo in his hand. He put them on the counter, then turned to his computer, punching in some information, then scanning the guns and ammo before looking up. "If you would just put your hand on the scanner…"

I was shaking, sure this was the end of our little rescue operation, but Cambious just leaned in closer, his hand skimming across the other man's arm and down to his hand, caressing it lightly as he clearly exuded pheromones directly at him. I watched in disbelief as Cambious got their hand positions reversed and the scanner beeped in recognition.

Cambious pulled back with a smile and grabbed both guns and ammo. "Thank you, Brother."

We turned for the door and Cambious handed me one of the guns and the box of ammo, which I promptly hid beneath my robe as he tucked his gun into a pocket. "We need to find a place to drop our clothes," Cambious breathed as we exited back to the hallway. Peter was leaning against the opposite wall but stood up quickly as we appeared.

I set off down the hall back toward where Peter said the library was. "We don't need anyone finding them."

"Yes, but I need my hands free," Cambious argued, taking the bundle back from Peter

"There is a closet near the tower stairs," Peter offered. "I hid in there the first night I ran."

"What kind of closet?" Cambious asked.

Peter shrugged. "It had cleaning supplies and stuff. Mostly used by the servants at night."

"We'll have to come back down from the tower," I offered.

Cambious nodded. The corridor widened slightly and there were several doors spaced about fifteen feet apart. "Library," Peter said.

Idly, I wondered how much time had passed since we'd found our way inside, how close we were to being surrounded by the waking life of the Kourt. Even if Peter didn't give us away, we could be discovered at any moment.

As if my thought had brought them to us, a group of Brothers in their black pants and light blue shirts rounded a corner and headed toward us. There were five of them, younger than I, possibly in their twenties, though the tallest one had a face covered in acne, so possibly younger.

They all snapped to attention at the sight of us, stopping and stepping back against the wall. "Good morning, Brothers." They said it in unison, their eyes skipping over us, then snapping to the floor in submission.

We acknowledged them with slight nods but continued moving. I could hear them murmuring behind us about Cambious's stature and I turned, my eyes sweeping over them. They blushed and hurried away.

"We're running out of time," I said to Cambious. "The whole place will be awake, and we'll have no way out."

"What do you suggest we do?"

I shook my head. "First we have to make sure she's there. Then we can figure out..." I shook my head. I had no plan for what came next, but I knew that the more of the Brotherhood we ran into, the less hope we had for actually escaping, especially once we were carrying my mother. "Peter, where do we go?"

He pointed further down the hallway where I could see a wooden door beside the first steps of a staircase. We hurried to the closet, where Cambious secreted our bundle of clothes and the food he had pilfered from the pantry, and we paused to load our guns. Then, we straightened ourselves up, adopted our best serious faces, and we strode to the staircase.

We did our best to look like we belonged, like it was normal for us to be climbing a staircase toward cells that held the prisoners of the Brotherhood. The staircase curved and climbed, taking us closer to our destination. We were stopped by two

Brothers in military uniform who snapped to attention as we approached their desk on a wide landing. Behind them, bars blocked the way up the steps. Obviously, we needed to talk our way past them.

"We are here to question the mother of the blood witch," Cambious said, his voice deep and resonating.

"Yes, Brother." The man on the right turned to a board with pegs that held keys. "Here you are, third floor, last cell on the left." He handed Cambious the key and his companion moved to open the gate in the bars to allow us to pass. "Are you taking the *slúga* with you?"

I looked the man in the eye. "He needs to learn a lesson about obedience. Perhaps you also need a lesson?"

He paled visibly and shook his head. "No, brother, I am sorry."

I pulled Peter to me and pushed him ahead of us so that he was the first up the stairs, with Cambious and I right behind him. As we neared the first floor of cells, the smell of caged animals filled the air, and I wrinkled my nose in an effort not to sneeze.

The stairs opened to a large room segregated into cages filled with…I wasn't fully sure what they all were. I could see a manticore, but he looked to be no older than Peter, if manticores aged the same way people did. His wings drooped downward, and his face was dirty, his eyes dull as they watched us. Further down was a man-sized bird of some kind, with bright orange and red feathers, but the face similar to a woman's, her nose and mouth extended in a sort of beak that went from the orange of her skin to dark black, as if it had been burned. She reminded me of Toman, the bartender.

"Phoenix," Cambious said aside to me. Past her was a lizard-like thing, as big as Peter, slender, but long with a tail adorned with a dangerous-looking club-like end.

"Is that what I think it is?" I asked as Cambious pulled me toward the next set of stairs.

"If you think that it's a dragon, yes. Juvenile. Haven't seen one outside of the mountains in Ver Char in a lifetime. Come on."

My disillusionment with my magic kingdom lifted a little. Maybe it wasn't filled with fairies and castles, and came with malls and credit cards, but at least it had magical creatures. I glanced back and the dragon was now a child of maybe ten, his skin tinged blue along his hairline, his tail wrapped around his legs.

"Do all dragons do that?" I asked, a hand on Cambious's arm to slow him. He turned to look and smiled.

"Of course."

I started to return to climbing the stairs but noticed that Peter was no longer in front of us. He was at one of the cages, speaking in an approximation of Spanish to the manticore inside. I went to get him, my eyes carefully on the creature in the cage as it came to the bars. His eyes widened as I approached, but Peter stuck a hand through the bars and slid his fingers into the barely-there mane, scrubbing against the manticore in what I took to be a soothing gesture. "*Estan conmiago.*"

"Peter, come." I touched his shoulder gently, my eyes on the young manticore.

"*Volveramos por ti.*" Peter smiled and pulled his hand back.

"Peter, be careful." The manticore's voice was pitched higher than I'd expected, and he shuffled closer to the bars.

"I'll take care of him," I responded, pulling Peter along to the stairs. "Who is that?" I asked when we were far enough away.

"My friend, Ashkān. We were brought here together. They're training him to work in the *Zidna*, the graveyard guards. They've been having trouble with the older manticores." Peter took my hand. "We can take him with us too, can't we?"

Because we'd be so much less conspicuous carrying my mother with a manticore in our company. I sighed and squeezed his hand. "We'll do our best."

CHAPTER 27
MOM

My mind was still on the manticore and the idea that Peter had made friends with the thing as we climbed to the second prison level. The smell was not as bad here, more the dank kind of smell of caged human bodies. It was dimly lit, but I could make out lumps of human shape in each of the cages.

I couldn't make out much more and Cambious kept us moving up the stairs to the third and final level. My breath caught in my throat from far more than the climb as we reached the top, and my heart began to thump loud enough for the others to hear. My mouth was dry as Cambious handed me the key. The cages here were empty, and the air was filled with expectation as I took each torturous step down the row of them, until at last, I could see her, much as she had looked in my vision.

Her long hair was streaked with gray, dirty and matted like it hadn't seen a brush in months or longer. Her skin was drab and gray, her dress a dirty white that was ripped and torn in multiple places. As she lifted her head, I could see the tracks tears had made in the dirt on her face, the dark circles that smudged her eyes so that they appeared sunken.

"Wasting your time," she said in a voice that trembled,

though I couldn't tell whether it was in fear or anticipation or sheer exhaustion.

I fit the key into the lock and turned it, opening the door, then just standing there for a long time looking at her, trying to find the beautiful woman I remembered from my childhood. "M-om?" I asked, blinking unbidden tears.

She squinted at me and for a moment I had forgotten the glamor that hid me from prying eyes. I glanced back at Cambious to be sure we were alone, then touched the pendant, letting the glamor fade. I crossed to her and knelt beside her as she started to come up from her slouch.

"You shouldn't be here, Thána," she said, even as she pulled me into an embrace. "They will kill you."

I shook my head. "I couldn't just leave you here."

This close to her, I could smell something off about her, some disease...an infection. I could taste it on her skin as I kissed her cheeks. "We needed to make sure, but we can't leave just yet. It's too close to morning. But maybe I can..." I moved to place my mouth over hers, but her hand on my chest pushed me back.

"You mustn't. Their trackers will be able to find you, glamor or no if you start bleeding."

I nodded tightly, brushing away the tears I couldn't hold back. "No, you're right. Of course, you're right." I kissed her cheeks again. "We should go before we get caught, but we'll be back tonight, I promise."

She caught my hand as I started to stand, pressing her lips to my palm the way she had when I was small. I swallowed hard and turned to go before I could change my mind and try to force our way out.

I activated the glamor as I exited the cell, locking it behind me, but the tears were still falling when I rejoined Cambious and Peter. "How is she?" Cambious asked.

I shrugged. "Sick, starving, afraid. I told her we would come back tonight. We should find ourselves a place to hide, rest."

"The closet?" Cambious started us down the stairs, so he didn't see me shaking my head.

"Too close, don't you think?" I asked. "Won't they suspect I've come for my mother?"

"They're looking for me," Peter offered. "I could let them chase me."

"No, I don't think we're that desperate yet." We were approaching the guard station, so our conversation ended while I handed back the key.

"That was quick," one of the men commented.

"She requires more time to consider her fate," I replied. "We will return."

"His Excellency is returning from his latest mission to the capital today. Perhaps he will have better luck."

I struggled to keep my face neutral as I nodded. "Perhaps he will." I strode down the stairs quickly but stuttered back a bit when faced with a group of young men in their late teens moving swiftly through the corridor at the bottom. Cambious set a hand on my back to keep me from falling backward and turned us in the opposite direction.

We kept moving until we were back to the closet, stepping inside to catch our breath. Once we were a little more together and had collected our things, we stepped back out into the hall. We started walking swiftly out of the area, and I let the others take the lead until I had lost track of where we were in comparison to the tower, or anything else for that matter. "Peter, where are we?"

He shrugged. "I don't know. I've never been here before."

"Great." I looked up and down the hall, counting doors. "It looks like maybe a residential area. Dorms, maybe?"

"Well, all these men have to sleep somewhere."

I nodded and moved to one of the doors. I knocked lightly, then tried the knob. It turned easily and I opened the door just enough to peek inside. Two sets of bunk beds lined the room, with a wardrobe between them. Uniforms like the Brotherhood military wore hung on the end of one of the bunk beds. "Dorms. This one is clearly occupied, though no one is home."

"Probably at breakfast," Peter suggested.

"Try the rest," I said, moving to the next door.

"What are we looking for?" Cambious asked as he mirrored my movements on the opposite side of the hall.

"One that's empty," I responded. We made our way down the hall to the opposite end, but all of the rooms showed signs of having residents. "So much for that idea."

There was a window at the end of the hallway, showing that the sun was well on its way to risen. Below us, there was a small courtyard lined with trees that had lost most of their leaves. I could see the walls of the Kourt on either side, and I thought that it put us in the northwest corner of the fortress, at the L-junction that divided the original Kourt building, where we were, from the newer construction that was added when it became a school. If the information in my book was to be believed, we would find classrooms and more sleeping quarters there.

I knew we did not want to be anywhere near the classrooms come time for classes to begin, but perhaps we might find an empty room among the sleeping quarters. As we came to a junction in the corridors, I felt the same odd pull I had when I'd found the tombstone outside the wall. "This way."

I let it guide me, hoping it was a long-lost ancestor or other blood witch and not some Brotherhood trick. We turned right, then left until we found ourselves in front of a door. "Here." I whispered the word, feeling almost as if the place was sanctified or something. The knob turned easily under my hand, and I peered carefully into the room before I slipped inside.

At one time it had been a beautiful room, judging by what was left behind. The stone walls had been paneled with light-colored wood, and the floor bore the remnants of a thick carpet, though the color was lost to time and the low level of light. There were two beds with nothing left on them but old moldy mattresses and a vanity with an ornate mirror.

"We should be safe here," I said, though I couldn't say how I knew that to be true. "Peter, close the door."

Once the door was closed, Cambious and I both released our glamors and I sagged in relief. Peter started at the sight of Cambious in his natural state, his eyes wide, but to his credit, he didn't run or try to hide. Without a word, Cambious dropped his bundle of our clothing and the food on one of the beds, moving with me then to the vanity so we could push it to block the doorway. Peter scrambled out of the way, ending up in the far corner, under a tightly shuttered window.

"Why is this room left empty like this?" Cambious asked.

"They think it to be haunted," a soft, female voice said, making us jump.

Peter was pale and shaking as we turned to find a young woman or her ghost at least. Her skin was darker than mine, her black hair braided tightly along her scalp and left to cascade in tiny braids over her shoulders. She wore fitted pants, what looked to me like the pants you would wear horseback riding, with boots that came to her knees and over that a tunic with elaborate beading along the hem and cuffs.

She smiled broadly. "They are not wrong. I died here, in this room." Her hands spread out to the sides. "Ironically, it was not those bastards who did it. I died of a cancer no one could cure."

"I've never seen a spirit so...fully in this world," Cambious said.

"And I don't often show myself to...those of your kind." She made a face and looked at me. "What brings you to this awful place, Sister?"

I licked dry lips and tried to make words leave my mouth, but I was still processing the idea that I was talking to a ghost. "My mother," I finally managed to say. "She's a prisoner in the tower."

"They will kill you if they find you."

I nodded in agreement. "I know. But we've come this far."

"I have done what I can to help hide you, but aside from that, there is little I can do to aid your quest. You should rest while you can." She turned then to Peter, who looked franticly to me for help as her hand lifted to cup his cheek. "Brother of my line, you do us honor in your duty to our sister. Serve her well, and you will see your home again."

She offered one last smile, then vanished.

I fell back against the vanity and closed my eyes. I had to say the whole magic kingdom thing was beginning to live up to the stories in books, what with dragons and ghosts now.

"What...what did she mean?" Peter asked into the silence that had followed our ghost's departure.

"I assume she meant that you are, in some way related. She had the look of someone from your region," Cambious supplied. He nodded toward the beds. "You both should sleep. I will keep watch."

"You need rest too," I argued.

"There are only two beds," Cambious countered. "Two very small beds."

"I can sleep here," Peter interjected, already sliding down in the corner. "I don't mind. I usually sleep on the rock floor."

Honestly, I didn't like the idea of not giving Peter the comfort of an actual bed, but I could not think of a better solution. I moved the bundle of clothes and the sausage, with what I could see now was a box of some sort of cracker, to the vanity and took off my robe, depositing my fruit with the other food, then taking the gun from my pocket, grateful we hadn't needed to use it.

Peter's breathing had already evened out, meaning he was either already asleep, or really good at faking it. "Ah, kids. Can fall asleep anywhere," I said softly. I lay down on the mattress, covering myself with my robe and pillowing my head on my arms. I doubted I would have as easy a time falling asleep.

I watched Cambious fuss around the room, and realized belatedly that he was setting up wards, though I hadn't seen that particular configuration before. It was related to *ekleípo*, I could tell that, but it wasn't quite the same.

"It projects itself to be what the viewer expects to see, in this case, just a door no one opens. It should also muffle the sound," Cambious said as he came to sit on the opposite bed.

He looked tired and worried, even in his terrifying natural form. Except it wasn't actually terrifying to me anymore. I lifted my head and propped it on my hand. "Do you need me to…"

Cambious shook his head. "I am fine, Thána. Thank you."

"Because, if you do, I'm here," I said, pushing myself up to nearly sitting. "And I'll sleep after, we both know that."

He sighed and I felt a little guilty for it. We hadn't really discussed it, whatever **it** was. Slowly he nodded, dropping his robe onto the bed, and reaching for the zipper of his pants. "But only a little, and we must be quiet."

I sat up, easing my own zipper down and shimmying out of the pants. This time I went to him, reaching down to help him before I moved in, my eyes darting to Peter to make sure he was sleeping. For a moment I got distracted by the idea that our ghostly benefactor might also be watching, but I managed to pull myself back to the business at hand.

Cambious got me back onto my bed, and back into my pants when it was over, covering me with my robe and letting me sleep.

CHAPTER 28
STEP TWO, RESCUE MOM

I woke to my stomach growling and a desperate need to relieve myself. There was no way to tell what time it was with shutters closed and no lights to speak of in the room. I opened my eyes in the half-light, my glance skipping over Cambious, who was still asleep, to the corner where I had last seen Peter.

He wasn't there.

I sat up fast, my eyes skipping around the room until I found him. He was curled up under the vanity. Okay, so he hadn't run off. Yet.

I stretched and stood, surprised to find that Cambious had even gotten my shoes back onto my feet after I had passed out. I had again slept better than I ever had before sex with an incubus. Guess that made the whole relationship sort of mutually beneficial. I tiptoed to the first of the two doors in the room, hoping to find a bathroom, only to find a closet.

The next door, the one across from the beds, yielded better results. The bathroom was small, two stalls and two sinks, with a door to what I assumed was an adjoining room. I relieved myself, hoping that whoever was in the adjoining room was off to evening meal or something or too spooked by the supposed haunting to come investigate. A quick washing of my hands and I let myself back into the bedroom.

I went to the window and opened the levers on the shutters just enough to get a glimpse out. The sun was just starting to set if the lighting outside was to be believed.

When I turned, I found Cambious watching me. "Not dark yet, but getting there," I said softly.

"We probably shouldn't wait too long. It might be suspicious, us going up to the cells in the middle of the night."

I nodded and crossed to the vanity, coming back to the beds with our food. "Plus, Head Honcho guy was supposed to have come back from somewhere today. We don't know what he might have done to her."

"Okay, so do we have a plan?" Cambious asked.

"Sure, rescue Mom, escape and…try to take out the Brotherhood?" I said, my own doubt tilting the words into a higher register than my normal. I'd been taking this whole thing one step at a time, so no, I had no plan. Cambious took one of the sausages he'd stolen and cut it into pieces with his knife, passing me a few pieces.

"I have an idea."

We both turned to see Peter standing between the beds, rubbing his eyes. He climbed up on the end of my bed and took one of the apples. "Take me up there, say you're locking me up again. At least, that gives you a way up to the cells."

"But not the right keys," Cambious said.

"Can't you do that thing you did with the guy in the armory?" I asked, passing Peter some of the sausage.

"If either of them is into guys, maybe," Cambious answered. "There's no way to tell until we're too far in to get out easily."

I nodded. "Okay, it's a start. How are we getting back out again? Especially with Mom so sick?"

"We could steal a car," Peter offered with a little more confidence. "I mean, if you can drive."

A facility like this would certainly need to have a number of vehicles bigger than the one Cambious had hidden before our entrance. "Where?"

Peter shrugged and chewed for a moment. "I just know that *Patoras* has a car, and there are the trucks that bring people here." He nibbled on his sausage. "They brought someone today. I can smell her."

I was tempted to sniff the air, see if I could sense her the way Peter did.

"But that means the *Tragač Krevlju* has returned as well. You need to be careful."

I glanced at Cambious for a translation. "Essentially, their top blood tracker," Cambious supplied. "He'll be devoted to their cause and might even think he's doing it willingly." He looked at Peter. "How old is he?"

Peter shook his head. "A man. He sometimes was with them when I was punished, telling me I needed to know what I was." His hands shook and he put his apple down.

"Great." He wouldn't need me to bleed to find me. If I got close enough to him, he'd know, glamor or not.

"Okay, Cambious, what if we split up? You go find us some wheels, Peter and I go get Mom."

"No, I'm not leaving you alone." Cambious shook his head. "Besides, how are you going to get her down the stairs and past the guards?"

"And don't forget Ashkān," Peter said.

"And the dragon, the phoenix, and whoever they brought back with them. If she's a blood witch, they're going to bleed her to death," I added with a sigh. It was impossible. The whole thing just got more and more complicated with every step we took. "We're going to need a distraction to get back down the stairs." I looked at Peter. "Your friend, can he fight? If we get him out of his cell, can he go roaring down the stairs, maybe incapacitate the guards?"

Peter shrugged. "He was pretty beat up yesterday. They're trying to break him so they can train him like the others."

I shook my head. "I guess we play it by ear. Are we ready?"

No one moved, so I did, standing and wiping cracker crumbs from my stolen uniform and tugging at the shirt to try to pull the wrinkles out. I closed my hand around my mother's pendant and felt the glamor ripple over me. Cambious followed my lead and then we moved the vanity so that we could get out of the room.

There were more people about than there had been when we'd gone into the room, mostly what looked like upper-classmen in any private high school back home. They snapped to attention as we passed, some of them murmuring a greeting which we acknowledged with nods. We got out of that wing and maneuvered ourselves back toward the tower. Here too there were more people than before, men in uniforms and suits.

Few spared us even a glance as Cambious put one hand on the back of Peter's neck, using the contact to thrust him forward. As we neared the landing with the guard post, I began lecturing, as if I were angry at the poor kid. "You will learn, boy. I think a night or two in a cell will teach you to obey your betters."

Two different guards stood as we approached. "Problems with your *slúga*?"

"He is a willful, lazy *kravu*," Cambious said. "We are going to teach him a lesson. First, a good beating, then a few nights with no bed or food should do the trick."

One of the guards chuckled and reached for a set of keys. "Put him with the animals, the smell should help."

I could tell Cambious was flooding the area with pheromones and was starting to see a response in at least one of the men. He brushed his hand as he took the keys and handed them to me. "Go on, get started. I'll be along in a moment."

"Come on, *slúga*. Get moving."

I pushed Peter up the stairs and onto the floor where his friend the manticore and the juvenile dragon were being kept. On the wall near the cages were a paddle and a flogger. I pointed to them as I let go of Peter. "Make it sound like I'm beating you, I said softly as I looked at the keys in my hand. I went first to

Ashkān's cage. He was hunched down in the back of his cell, his dark red eyes on me as I fit the first key in the lock. "Ashkān, I'm Thána. I'm going to help you out, but you have to promise not to hurt me."

Peter hit the wall with the paddle and let out a small yell. "It's okay, Ashkān. She's a friend." Peter hit the wall a little harder and yelled again. It took me three tries to get the right key and open the cell. I left the door slightly ajar and moved toward the one with the phoenix. She raised an eyebrow at me as I started trying keys and Peter continued to make it sound like I was beating the life out of him.

I could see she was injured and the wings on her back appeared to be clipped together in what must be a painful manner. She wore what looked like khakis and a torn shirt that might have been white once, her taloned feet bare. I got her door open, and she moved toward me slowly, every step of her taloned feet clicking on the stone floor. "I suppose you think that disguise is going to let you walk out with all of us?" she asked as she exited the cell. She towered over me by at least a foot.

"Well, I figured I could try," I responded. "Can I help you with that?" I gestured at her back, and she turned, bending her knees so I could see the metal bands that held her wings together. It took me a minute to figure out how to loosen them and by the time I was done, Cambious had appeared, holding the key to my mother's cell. "Go on, I'll finish here."

Cambious nodded and sprinted up the stairs while I turned to the last occupied cell. The dragon was at the door watching us, deep blue eyes tracing every move as I came to him. "Hello," I said softly. I tried keys until I found the right one and opened the door. In his human form, he was naked, and I could see rags that might once have been his clothes, likely shredded during a transformation…or maybe I'd seen one too many Hulk movies. "Would you like to come with us?"

He nodded shyly and reached for my hand, pulling it to his face and rubbing it across his cheek. I smiled for him and turned to find our fantastical menagerie had been joined by Cambious carrying my mother with a young woman of maybe seventeen trailing behind him. She was dressed much like any teenager I had ever known: jeans torn at the knees, sneakers, and a T-shirt with some logo I didn't recognize. She was pale, with fiery red hair in two messy braids and there was a bruise blossoming across one cheek. She held herself stiffly and moved like there were more injuries hidden by clothes.

"Those two guards won't stay dazed for long," Cambious said. "I suggest we get moving. Everyone, follow me, we are going down the stairs and into the closet at the bottom. Peter, you're my lookout."

No one spoke as Cambious and Peter took the lead. I took the rear with the young dragon's hand still in mine. We congregated for a moment at the guards' landing while Peter made sure the hallway below was clear enough for us to achieve the closest hiding place. It was going to be a tight fit, but it would be easier to move around the Kourt after the bulk of the building's inhabitants had gone to bed.

Both guards seemed to be dazed, heads lolling on their shoulders as we moved past. Cambious hissed at us to hurry, and we went down the stairs to where Peter held the closet door open. It was a bit of a squeeze, the eight of us in a supply closet, but we managed. Cambious set my mother on her feet and shifted her weight onto me while he pulled out his ward stones and began working on keeping us hidden. It was a fair bet that someone would eventually realize that the prisoners had all escaped, but hopefully, they would turn their search to other parts of the fortress, and we could find our way out.

It was a lot to hope for.

I turned away from what Cambious was doing to look at Mom. She didn't look much worse than she had the day before, so I hoped that meant she'd be able to hold her own. Her face was gaunt, but her eyes sparkled when she looked at me. I kissed her cheek and turned to the rest. Quietly I pretended I knew what I was doing and that I was in charge. "Everyone, my name is Thána and this is my mother, Alana. The big guy warding us in is Cambious. I know Peter and Ashkān's names, but the rest of you are a mystery." I looked to the phoenix, and she nodded tightly.

"Sabina Nephus."

I looked at the teenager next. "Ciara Connelly." I smiled at her and turned to the dragon, who was clinging to my hand still.

He blinked at me. "What's your name?" I asked.

"Reyansh," he answered quietly. "Kalya."

"Okay, good. I guess we should get as comfortable as we can. We're going to wait for night to fall fully before we move out."

Around me, the group shifted and got sat down. I encouraged Reyansh to go sit with Sabina so I could get Mom settled in. "Rest, Mom. It's going to be a long night." Once she was sitting and leaning against the shelves I moved to where Cambious stood guard at the door. "Okay, now what?" I whispered.

"I got those men to give me some information. The garage is just off the parade grounds. We just have to get there and steal a truck." Cambious closed his eyes and drew in a deep breath, letting it out slowly. "We probably need to split up. A group this big is going to get caught."

I nodded. "Okay. You take Mom and the girl, and Sabina. I'll take the kids. We meet in the garage. Do you know how to find it?"

Cambious nodded. "You should take Sabina though. You need some protection, and she looks like she can fight."

I grinned. "I've got a manticore and a dragon, I'll be fine. Besides, you'll have your hands full with Mom. I'm counting on you to get her out."

CHAPTER 29
STEP THREE, HIDE

ABOUT AN HOUR LATER, WE HEARD A LOT OF MUFFLED COMMOTION through the door, booted feet pounding up and down the stairs, and yelling. I had settled in next to my mother, letting her lean on me. It didn't seem real, that this was the woman who had raised me and hidden me away, the woman who had been gone from my life for more than twenty years, and here I was holding her in a closet with a bunch of strangers.

We didn't talk, all of us afraid that even a whisper would give us away.

It seemed to take forever for the noise to die down and we waited a whole hour more before we began shifting around, stretching stiff muscles, and standing. "Cambious and his group will go first. Keep quiet and follow his lead," I said before hugging my mother to me. "I'll see you soon, okay?"

"Be careful, Thána. *Patoras* Javonic will do anything to get your blood."

"Is that his name?" I asked. "Well, I'm still using my blood, so he's going to have to wait. Go with Cambious, he'll keep you safe." I turned to Ciara. "Can you glamor? Even a little bit?" She nodded, glancing at Cambious, then back to me. "Okay, you should try to look like a man, you'll draw less attention."

Ciara closed her eyes and put a hand to her chest as if she was trying to reach inside herself. Slowly her shape shimmered and in her place was a thin young man with bright red hair. "Good. Remember, it's only as good as your concentration, and it won't save you if a blood tracker gets too close." Cambious had disabled the wards while I was getting Ciara ready.

I looked up at Cambious and nodded. "Get going. We'll meet you in the garage. Be careful."

Cambious took off his robe and draped it around my mother, pulling the hood up to hide her better. That left only Sabina with no disguise.

"I'll be fine," she said, as if she sensed my thought.

Cambious cracked open the door and peered out, nodding once before drawing my mother out into the hall. Ciara and Sabina followed, and the door closed, leaving me with the three children. Peter had shed his brown jacket and given it to Reyansh to cover his naked form. Ashkān sat in the back of the closet, looking tired and wary. Of the three, he was in the worst shape, and I was tempted to try to help him, but Mom was right about that blood tracker finding me if I did.

I glanced at Peter who was moving to sit with his friend and an idea started to form. "Peter, have you ever tried blood magic?" I asked, my voice just above a whisper. He shook his head, his eyes wide. I wasn't even sure my crazy idea would work, but he was a blood witch, and the old woman had wanted my blood to heal her, so it stood to reason that his blood held the same healing properties that mine did, and if the crazy old oracle could get healing from my blood, maybe Ashkān could get it from Peter's.

"I have an idea of a way to help Ashkān feel better without giving away our hiding place with the smell of my blood," I said, squatting down in front of the boys. "Can the tracker smell your blood?"

Peter shook his head. "Sort of, but not really. We smell different, the boys."

I pulled Cambious's knife from the pocket of my stolen pants and looked Peter in the eye. "Our blood can heal, I've seen it. If Ashkān drinks some of your blood, it may make him stronger, and give us a better chance of escaping."

Peter's eyes were wide and scared, and he actually shuffled away from me. "It is forbidden." He shook his head and closed his eyes. "Forbidden."

Leave it to me to find a taboo. "Maybe it is, and maybe there's a reason for that, but right now, we need to get Ashkān healed up so we can escape." It took a few long moments, but Peter finally gave in, nodding.

I looked at Ashkān. "Can you do that?"

He shuddered. "It will make me strong?"

"I hope so." I handed the knife to Peter. "Not too deep, and not someplace where the wound will hinder you." I gestured at my arm, where the old woman had cut me, and backed off to let them work out the details. Reyansh came to me and clung to my side. I suppose he needed comfort, which I'll admit is not my strength, but I put a hand on his shoulder and hoped it helped.

I heard Peter hiss and looked back to find him holding his bleeding arm up to Ashkān's mouth. For a long moment Ashkān just looked at the blood welling along the line of the cut, then he tentatively opened his mouth and leaned forward. He sucked at the blood and Peter held himself still with his arm up and his eyes wide. There was fear there, but bravery won out and when Ashkān released him, Peter clamped his other hand over the wound as his eyes found mine.

I looked around me and found a bag of cleaning cloths. I rummaged through it until I found one that would make a makeshift bandage. The blood had already stopped flowing by the time I got the bandage wound around Peter's arm and tied it off. "I heal fast," Peter offered.

Tucking that information away, I turned my attention to the manticore. We would know soon enough if my theory was correct. A male blood witch couldn't eat disease because he

would have no way to expel it, but if that was the only difference, Ashkān should be up to moving before too long. We were
going to need to move fast, and hope Peter could lead us safely
to the garage.

It wasn't the best plan, but there was no way I could glamor
them, I was running low on energy due to the extended use of
my own glamor and I wasn't sure it was something I could do
anyway. I paced the small space afforded me between the door
and where Ashkān sat. There was no noise outside the door, as if
everyone had abandoned the tower once the prisoners were all
gone.

Time was against us, and my anxiety was only ratcheted up
by the need to wait for Ashkān to be ready. After what seemed
an eternity, Ashkān rose and shook himself before nodding to
me. "I'm ready."

I exhaled slowly. "Okay, Peter you go out first. We need to
keep to the most unused corridors, but we need to get there fast,
okay?"

Peter opened the door, sticking his head out to make sure the
area was clear. He stepped out and I gestured for Ashkān to
follow before I tucked Reyansh to my side and followed. The
hallway was eerily empty, and a part of my brain was whispering to me about a trap, that they knew where we were going,
and they would ambush us there.

I shook it off and we headed out, not the way we had come,
but down a hall we had never used. It took us to a staircase that
we slipped down. Peter stopped us as we reached the bottom,
leaning out past the wall to look before he moved on. He led us
down a hall that seemed to be lined with storage rooms, with
automatic lights that came on as we moved.

The lights made me nervous, but Peter kept moving until we
found another staircase. "There's probably Brothers down there,"
Peter said, turning to look at me. "I can check."

"Stay here," I responded, peeling Reyansh from my side, and
moving down the stairs. Peter was right. I could see a small

cluster of men, armed with some kind of guns. They appeared to be guarding a door. I climbed back up to where the kids were waiting. "There are four of them, guarding a door. Peter, which way do we need to go?"

He pointed straight down the stairs. "Okay, I'll distract them, Peter, you lead the boys away and I'll join you.

"We need to go that way, then down another floor. That will be the library floor."

"Good. Get yourselves to the library. I'll find you there," I said.

Peter stopped me with a hand on mine, lifting his wounded arm and pulling the bandage off. "Smell."

I leaned down and sniffed at the cut, but I couldn't say I smelled anything other than the slight tang of blood. "Deeper," he said. "Clear your mind and breathe it in. If my blood can heal, then you should be able to track the scent of others like us."

I raised an eyebrow as I looked up at him, suddenly more confident than he had been before now. "Okay, I'll try." I closed my eyes to block out the shifting shadows as the boys moved around us restlessly. I breathed in, letting the feeling of air moving into my lungs pull my attention inward, to the core of me, as Merry had taught me. I let it out slowly and set my nose all but on Peter's arm before I breathed in as much as my lungs would allow.

There, just there. I don't think I can explain it well, but there was an earthy sort of smell, like rich soil and rain, with a vaguely metallic taste at the end. When I pulled back, Peter rewrapped the bandage around the wound. "Now, you should be able to find me, no matter where I go."

I was still marveling at the things I continued to learn about myself and what I could do as I got back to the bottom of the stairs. I wasn't sure exactly what I was going to do to distract those men, but I'd been improvising this entire operation, so I figured something would come to me. I took off my robe and gave it to Peter. "Take this."

At the bottom of the stairs, I squared my shoulders and lifted my head, putting on an authoritative air like it was a coat before I stepped off the stairs and turned straight toward them. I could tell that they were chatting about something not related to their duty, but I couldn't make out what it was. When they saw me, they fell silent and snapped to attention. "Lazy *kravus*! Our prisoners have escaped and here you stand chatting like children!" I reached inside of me and murmured a word I hoped I was remembering correctly, "*Sýnchysi.*" I felt a wave leave me, spreading confusion toward the men.

I moved past them, eying them up and down, pulling their eyes toward me, and away from the place where Peter and the others waited. "I should have you disciplined."

"Sir, we only—"

I held up a hand to cut him off. "You are to be attentive and aware at all times, are you not?"

"Yes, Brother."

"Good. I do not want to see any more of that behavior. Understood?" Between two of the men, I could see Reyansh and Peter moving swiftly into the corridor beyond where the men would be able to see. "And stand up straight, straighten up those shirts. You look like you just rolled out of bed."

All four of them fussed with their clothes and I moved back toward the stairs. "Keep vigilant, Brothers. There is a blood witch loose on the grounds."

I heard them muttering as I started to walk away. "Brother, may we ask your name?"

I turned back. "You may. However, I do not have to tell you. I outrank you, that is all you need know."

"Perhaps you are one of the fugitives using a glamor. If there is a blood witch, she would be capable of that."

I could see that the confusion I had caused was wearing off and suspicion was taking its place. "Very well. I am Brother Caspin. I came in with *Patoras* yesterday. Would you like me to ask him to join us to vouch for me?"

The one who had spoken blanched a little white. I crossed my arms and met his gaze with my own, hard and a little angry. "I applaud your suspicion, Brother. Continue your vigilance. I must return to the search."

"How hard can a group like that be to find?" I heard one of them ask as I headed for the corridor. "You'd think at least the freaks would stand out."

He wasn't wrong, thus the sneaking around. I didn't run, but I moved quickly until I came to the stairs, and I took them as fast as I dared. The corridor at the bottom was familiar. We had been here before. Now all I needed to do was find the library.

CHAPTER 30
STEP FOUR, ESCAPE?

THE CORRIDOR WHERE I FOUND MYSELF WAS BETTER LIT THAN I would have liked, and I saw at least two pairs of Brothers patrolling as I moved in the direction that I believed would take me to the library. I nodded in greeting as I passed two of them. They stopped walking and I could feel their eyes, or maybe I just imagined it, but I was sweating until I heard their footsteps resume.

The second pair found me just as I was opening the door to the library.

"Little late for study, Brother," the first one said.

"I thought everyone was hunting for our escaped prisoners." The second of them was taller and older than most of the guards I'd seen so far.

I turned and offered them a smile. "Indeed. I just left my robe here earlier. It's getting chilly out there." I was shaking and hoped it didn't show. That was when I smelled it. Another blood witch and it wasn't Peter. If I could smell him, he could smell me. I swallowed, not daring to look to see how close he was. "Carry on, Brothers. I'm back to the hunt."

I pulled the door closed behind me and moved away from it as fast as I could in the dark room. Tables and chairs and bookshelves were dark shadows against the faint light coming in the nearby windows. My heart was trying to beat my ribs out of its way as I kept moving, trying to escape the scent.

Peter emerged from the shadows between two sets of shelves, looking pale and gaunt in the odd lighting. He held a finger to his lips and beckoned me into the shadows where the others were hiding beneath my robe. "We can't stay here," I whispered. "And we can't go out there. That blood tracker is here."

"Where else can we go?" Reyansh asked, his fear evident in the way his voice shook.

I leaned out and looked out the nearest window. "Out there," I responded. I went to the window, moving books aside from the shelf in front of the window to make room for us to climb out. The latch was an old-fashioned sort of thing that wouldn't budge. I inhaled and reached inside me again, putting my hands together and opening them while I whispered "*Ánoixe.*" For a moment I was worried that it wouldn't open, but slowly the latch moved, and I put my hands to the bottom of the window, pushing it up. I leaned out to check for patrols or other Brothers, but there was nothing out there but a small yard that I hoped would give us a way out to the garage.

"Come on, boys."

Ashkān came first, pouncing up to the window ledge and then outside, then Peter. I had to help Reyansh up and out. I stepped through the window, reaching back through to put the books back, then pull the window down. "*Kontá.*" The latch closed easier than it had opened.

Inside the library, the door opened, and lights came on. I threw myself down so I wouldn't be seen. Peter grabbed my shoulder, pointing at a dark arch. I nodded and crawled with them toward it. I don't think I'd ever been as scared as I was right at that moment. I was certain it was the blood tracker who had entered the library, and I knew that he knew what I smelled like now because I knew what he smelled like.

We made the archway and in the deep dark on the other side, I stood. "Everyone okay?" No one answered, but I figured that was at least an affirmation that they all were good. I needed to get my bearings, figure out where we were and where the garage was, and how to get us there from the wrong side of the Kourt.

"Any idea where we are, Peter?" I asked, feeling along the wall in the dark. It wasn't going to take them long to figure out where we had gone.

"Never been here before."

"Great." My hand traced the stones in the wall and suddenly I felt the same thing I had when I had been drawn to that tombstone. I pressed my hand to the rock and got the immediate impression of another tunnel, one that ran through the walls and could get us to the parade grounds.

"They're out there." I heard the words clearly and pulled the boys closer as I reached in front of me to find the entrance.

Here, Adelfí. I laid a hand on the stone wall and whispered "*Diávasi,*" as I had when Cambious and I had made entry into the Kourt. I was genuinely surprised when the wall gave way, swinging inward to let us in. I hurried them inside and closed the door, feeling the rock welcome it back in place. It was even darker in the tunnel, and I had no light. Not that I would use one at that moment, not if it might give us away.

"They must have gone over the wall. Her scent ends here." The words were muffled, but I felt a rush of relief still the wild staccato of my heart.

We waited for a long moment before moving or speaking. "Everyone hold hands." I said it with almost no sound and felt Reyansh put his hand in mine. The tunnel went to our left and our right, and I had no idea which way to go. I tried to still and center and *feel* it, but all I felt was the anxiety to catch up to Cambious and my mother, running alongside the fear of being caught.

I let my indecision keep me immobile far longer than I should have, then chose to go to the right. I switched Reyansh to my left side and used my right hand to guide us by keeping it on the wall. Here the wall seemed to be brick, rather than stone. The tunnel wasn't very wide, just slightly larger than an average person, with low ceilings that would have made Cambious have to stoop over.

We inched our way in the dark, Reyansh squeezing my hand as if he was afraid I would let go of him and lose him in the dark. The tunnel turned and the wall under my hand was once again stone, not brick. It was impossible to tell how much time passed as we made our way in the absolute darkness, and I had lost all sense of direction when I felt wood under my fingers. "Stop, I think this is our exit," I said softly, reclaiming my hand from Reyansh and feeling over the wood until I found a latch. I pressed my ear to the door, trying to hear whether anyone was on the other side before I tried the latch and opened the door just a crack, pressing my face into the space and looking around.

I couldn't tell where we were, but the door seemed to let us out into a colonnade of sorts, with columns and arches that opened into an empty expanse, hidden by the lights on every third column. I eased through the door, holding the boys back until I could get around the door to get a better look. The colonnade stretched a long way down, took a left turn, then continued along the building, ultimately forming a giant U around what I took to be the parade grounds.

I beckoned the boys out and closed the door. Like the one we had entered the tunnel from, once closed no one would know the door was there. On this side, it looked just like the stones around it, and there were no seams to give it away. It was as if the door itself was warded with an invisible warding. Which I suppose, now that I think about it, wasn't outside the realm of possibility.

Across the parade grounds, I could see the lights of the opposing colonnade, and I could feel that my mother was nearby. "Where is the garage from here?" I asked Peter.

It was Ashkān who answered though. "Over there, behind."

He lifted a paw and pointed with one deadly sharp claw to the opposite side of the grounds.

"Okay, I think we'll be safest if we cut across the square, where it's darkest."

Just as I was about to lead them out of the lighted colonnade, a nearby door opened and four men in the Brotherhood's military uniforms stepped out. "They think some of them got out over the wall into the Ring, but those mangy manticores should deal with them," one of the men said.

"Hey!" a second of them had spotted us and was pointing his gun in our direction.

"Go, boys!" I pushed Reyansh and Peter toward the nearest archway, preparing to try the *Yperaspízo* spell, but before I could even bring my hands up, there was a deep, guttural growl and Ashkān launched himself at the nearest man, claws raking over his face before Ashkān pounced at the second.

He moved so fast I could barely keep track of him and in a matter of seconds all four were down and the area was splattered with blood. Not a single shot was fired. I didn't even get my own gun out of my pocket. I looked frantically around us, hoping no one had heard the commotion. "Come on, Ashkān, we need to move."

I didn't want to think about the fact that I had just watched him kill four men, I just wanted to catch up to Cambious and get everyone out in one piece. Ashkān and I raced across the square, finding Peter and Reyansh hiding in the shadows of a pillar. Ashkān was shaking, the rage still clear on his face. I squatted down in front of him and wiped some of the blood from his face with my fingers. "Are you okay?"

He nodded slowly. "They would have killed us."

"Yes, they probably would have," I agreed.

"I've never...well, I did fight back when they came for me, but I don't think anyone died."

"You were amazing," Peter offered, throwing his arms around his friend to hug him. "You saved all of us."

"Okay, let's get ourselves hidden a little better." I stood and looked to Peter for direction. He nodded toward the end of the building. As we neared it, I could see that a paved street ran out to the gates that I assumed would open up to the road that would take us to freedom. The paving led us back toward a hulking shape that I hoped was the garage.

I was pretty sure the Brotherhood would have put guards on the garage, and in fact, I was starting to wonder just how stupid this head guy was that he didn't have the entire grounds crawling with men. We should have run into a lot more than we had. Maybe they weren't as big an operation as I had believed. Maybe we stood a chance.

I pulled my gun out and kept us in the shadows, moving slowly along the building toward the light being spilled from a large open door. Shadows were moving through that light with tight, military precision.

I could see at least six of them. There were probably more. Suddenly, they snapped to attention. "Vigilance men, they were seen coming this way. Patoras thinks they will try to steal a vehicle." I could just make out the shape of the man who seemed to be in command.

He was tall, thin, and not very imposing physically. That made me think he'd risen to command levels by other means. The scary for us kind of means. Cunning, savagery, and intelligence.

There was no way we were getting through or around them. We inched back into the shadows, and I squatted down, gathering the boys in close. "We need to find another way."

"Can't you distract them like before?" Reyansh asked.

"There are too many of them, and I don't think these men would fall for it." I was wishing I knew where Cambious and my mother were when I smelled **him** again. "Shit."

"Thána, is that you?" The question came from behind us, whispered and yet carrying to my ears all the same.

I moved the boys further back along the wall to find the other half of our misfit gang. Cambious looked exhausted. Mother looked even worse. Sabina was sporting a few new bruises. Only the girl looked relatively unscathed by their adventure. The blood tracker was getting closer. I had to do something, or we would all be caught. The trouble was, there was only one thing I could think of, and it was nuts.

CHAPTER 31
CAPTURE

"Cambious, if I can clear the garage door of men, can you get everyone into a truck and out of here?" I asked in a whisper, my eyes on my mother's face. All of this had been to get her out, and if we failed to do that, we lost everything.

"I think so," Cambious responded. "What are you thinking?"

I shook my head. "Just keep them safe." I hugged my mother tight and whispered in her ear, "I'll see you soon," before I pressed my lips to hers and let my sense memory guide me, sucking the sickness and the pain out of her body and into mine.

I knew it wouldn't take long for the bleeding to start, not with that much illness burning inside of me. My body would need to get rid of it before it could start to take hold inside me. I turned and ran for the light, slowing only a little as the men realized I was there.

I smirked at the commander as I lifted my hand to my mother's pendant and released the glamor. I brought my hands up, shouting "*Yperaspízo*," sending those closest to me stumbling backward, then ran like hell for the dark on the other side of the garage. They clamored after me, shouting as I was swallowed up by the dark. I didn't look back to see if they were all coming for me, just trusted that if anyone was left over, Cambious and the others could deal with them.

The start of the bleeding nearly knocked me off my feet, soaking into my stolen pants and running down my leg. If that tracker hadn't already traced my scent, he would now. I rounded a corner blindly, knocking into a patrol that was responding to the alarm behind me. I dropped the first man simply with the force of our collision and got a couple of shots off before the gun was knocked from my hand.

I kept fighting my way forward, fighting like my life depended on it, which it did. I dug nails into places I knew would cause the most pain, stomped on feet, even bit one man as he tried to pull me backward, his arm around my neck. Remarkably, I found myself free of them and took off running again. I wasn't sure where I was going or what I was going to do when I got there, I just knew that the longer they were chasing me, the more time Cambious had to get the others out.

There was a blur of color above me as I found myself back at the parade grounds, and I recognized Sabina as she touched down. I changed my course and ran toward her, just as a big truck lumbered up to the gates. The truck rammed the gates and pushed through them, while Sabina and I ran toward them. I was running out of steam.

"I can't carry you; you have to keep going," Sabina said. "I'll slow them down a bit."

She took flight again and suddenly behind me I felt a heat that hadn't been there. Orange-red light lit up the night and a glance behind me showed flames eating across the carefully groomed grass. I pumped my arms and legs and ran with everything left in me, but the glamor had taken so much energy to maintain for as long as I did that there wasn't much left in the reserve tank.

Men were screaming, shouting commands, but I was almost to the gates.

And that was when it hit me.

I wasn't sure at the time what exactly it was, but I went down. I went down hard, crashing into the pavement and rolling until I hit the tumbled wreckage of the gate. Pain lanced through my shoulder, my face, my side. I hadn't even begun to feel it all when a man squatted down in front of me, his hand squeezing my chin. "Where are you going, *thanátou?*"

I recognized him, the smell of him, but also his face. I had seen him before…before all of this craziness started. In El Paso, even before Finneas had made his appearance. He was the one who had set the assassins on me.

His fingers pressed into my side, pulling my attention to the metal that pierced me and held me in place. The gate that had been my road to freedom now impaled me with the twisted metal left behind after the truck crashed through. I screamed as his fingers traced the metal into me, then again as his hands yanked me free of the gate.

"I let you escape once. It won't happen again."

He grabbed my shirt and hauled me to my feet, though he had to support me as I wobbled on knees that weren't entirely sure they remembered how to be knees. By the time he had shoved me into the gloved hands of two large men, I was fairly soaked in my own blood, and they had to all but carry me. We went into the Kourt, into a large hall with portraits of men in the black uniforms of the Brotherhood.

My thoughts were sluggishly trying to catch up as the memory of that rest stop, and the boy who had drawn the hunters away from me, bubbled up.

My captors dropped me onto a beautiful marble floor, white with threads of gold and black and the tracker came to stand beside me. He gave a salute as booted feet approached us. "*Patoras*, Thána Alizon."

"What a bloody mess you are." He squatted in front of me, a middle-aged man with a streak of gray in his black hair. He wore the military uniform, his boots highly polished. His face showed disgust as he turned my head to look at the scrape across my face where skin had met pavement at high velocity. "Get her cleaned up for the trial. And plug her up, I don't want that tainted blood spoiling the rest."

The way he said the word **trial** made me think it wasn't going to be so much a trial as a declaration of my guilt. The two big men pulled me back up and when my knees gave out, one of them scooped me up and threw me over his shoulder like I was already dead. I passed out somewhere along the way and only woke when I was dropped, none too gently, onto a cold exam table.

The room around me was some sort of medical clinic, the walls and floor a pristine white, and vaguely familiar machines filled the space near the head of the table. Two men, completely covered in white with only their eyes visible, approached. One had a tablet of some kind which he was tapping as the other reached for me. He poked at my shoulder and fire bit me there, spreading out into the surrounding skin.

"Gunshot, left shoulder, looks clean." He reached for my side, which was screaming at me in a language I had never heard from my own body. "Oh, this is a mess."

I screamed as his fingers pressed into the wound. "Likely from the gate, Patoras said she hit it at high speed. Probably has some internal bleeding as well. We may have to stitch it up so there's enough blood left for her bleeding." His hands moved to my thighs, pushing them apart. "She's killed someone already tonight, look at this."

I wanted to argue that I hadn't killed anyone, but I wasn't sure that was true. I know at least one of the shots from my gun hit flesh. I lost my train of thought then as they stripped me and washed me, awakening every single injury from head to toe. There was no care given to my pain as they scrubbed my skin and stitched up cuts and otherwise made me presentable, including shoving something akin to a tampon into my vagina to stop the blood.

When they were done, I was dressed in a simple white shift

that came to my knees, my hands bound behind me in a position I was sure was designed to make my shoulder shout obscenities at me. I was forced to walk on bare feet, and one very swollen ankle, out of the medical room and down a hall. My mind filled with the memory of Althea Anagnos and how they had killed her centuries before.

My blood still stained the marble in the hall as they pushed me out the same doors we had come into, only in front of the colonnade, where there had been only grass, there was now a platform, as if it had sprung out of the ground. Of course, it could have. I'd just helped a dragon, a manticore, and a phoenix escape a fortress. I was willing to believe almost anything at that point.

They pushed me up some stairs and onto the platform. The parade grounds were lit up like it was already day, and it was filled with what looked like every person that lived in the Kourt. I was surprised to see that most were little more than boys standing in the front row. This was to be part of their indoctrination.

Patoras Javonic stepped up to me, his smile of victory sickening. I wanted to spit in his face, but my mouth was dry as I contemplated the death I was about to endure.

"I held her here for two years. I beat her, burned her, starved her. She never once told me anything, but she still gave you to me." He spoke directly into my ear, his hand holding the back of my neck. "And now I will bleed you just as we have done for millennia. Your blood will keep me in power for decades." He pressed a gloved finger against my scraped-up cheek, just enough to get it to bleed a little for him, then he licked the blood clean. "Did you know that less than half an ounce of your blood once a week will keep me strong and healthy? The last one of you that we bled gave me almost fifty years. Yours will do the same."

My brain stuck on what he was saying. It wasn't just that his order wanted blood witches dead. Our blood could keep him alive well past a normal lifespan. Most of the rank and file couldn't know that. It went against everything I knew about the Brotherhood. How did they not see it? Had no one even noticed he'd been alive that long? And why didn't he bleed the men too? Peter had implied that he and that lead tracker weren't the only ones, and we'd proven that his blood was just as potent.

He shoved me forward. I pushed the thoughts aside and tried to focus on what was about to happen.

"Thána Alizon, you have been convicted of being *thánatou*. Your punishment is death by *Aimorragía*."

Two men came forward and pulled me toward the scaffold from which they would hang me to bleed out, and from that position, I could see something I hadn't in Althea's memory. There were holes in the platform through which tubing protruded, tubing that ended in large bore needles. I imagined that underneath the scaffolding, there were bottles or vats or something to collect it.

In the distance, beyond the destroyed gates, the sun was just starting to rise, staining the horizon in shades of orange, red, and pink. My hands were untied and one of the men raised a knife to cut the shift from me, but he stopped as a cry rang out from the back of the ranks of men, and the ordered lines split apart.

A giant manticore tore at the grass as he ran, roaring at anyone who came too close. Then came the fire, raining down out of the sky as Sabina dove at the men, setting several alight before she took back to the skies. She wasn't alone, at least five other manticores were diving into the chaos they had created. The screaming was deafening, punctuated by the sound of the flames and the stench of burning flesh.

I pulled away from my captors, but there wasn't much of a way to go to get free of them. I shoved at the closest one and ducked under Javonic's hand to grab at the gun of one of his guards. I brought it up, only to drop it as I got punched in the face. I staggered backward, and almost off the platform.

My body was yelling at me to stop, but at the same time there was an adrenaline rush fueling my fear and rage and I somehow managed to slip free again, aiming for the stairs. The parade grounds were a swirling cacophony of fire and blood and the screams of dying men. The big manticore charged toward me and at the last second said, "Duck."

I dropped and his huge, clawed foot raked the throat of the man who had been about to grab me. His blood covered me, and the manticore's face. "I will get you out. Climb on."

"What?" I wasn't sure I'd heard him right, but he squatted down and nodded his head toward his back. He was bigger than that horse I'd ridden as a teenager, but I climbed on.

"Get a good hold. I can't fly anymore, but I will get you to your mother."

I dug my hands into his thick mane and tried to squeeze my knees against his powerful muscles and he started to run, knocking anyone who got in our way to one side. I saw Sabina make another pass, saw her focus on the platform, felt the heat of it as it took to flame.

But then it was all I could do to just hold on as my great steed rammed through a clump of men, slashing at them as we passed. The jostling broke open stitches and blood oozed through the side of the shift. That was the last thing I remember of that moment because the adrenaline was fading and the blood loss was too much, and I passed out again.

I woke with a start as I started slipping from the manticore's back, grabbing onto his mane and pulling myself upright again. We were in the cemetery. The smell of smoke was strong and the skies behind us were orange against the deep blue of the last vestiges of night. Ahead of us, the sky was starting to lighten with the rising of the sun.

"Are you alright?" He was slowing now, and I was able to sit up a little bit.

"I think so. I mean, I've been shot, stabbed by twisted metal and I have road rash on my face, but I'm alive, so yeah. I'm good."

Of course, I wasn't sure how long that would stay true. Blood was still oozing from my side, and I was fairly sure that something inside of me was bleeding as well, but for the moment I wasn't actively dying. We stopped and for a moment I just wanted to lay back down and sleep.

"Thána!" My mother rushed toward me, looking much better than she had when I last saw her and her hands on my waist helped me slide down off my rescuer's back. She turned my face to look at my cheek, but I just tugged her into a hug.

"I'm okay. Thanks to the big guy here." I turned to him. "I don't even know your name."

He inclined his head. "I am Bijan. Ashkān is the son of my brother. You freed him. I have repaid the debt."

I shivered in the cold not-quite-morning air and looked around me for Cambious. He was sitting with his back to the wall, the glamor off and his black skin was strangely ashen. "Is he okay?" I asked, pressing a hand to my still bleeding side.

"He will be. He needs rest and to feed," my mother responded. "I'm more worried about you."

I was only upright at that moment because I had a hold of Bijan's mane. I figured I was due to collapse soon, probably needed a hospital…or at least that grandpa witch doctor at that clinic.

"We should move, survivors are coming down the hill." Ciara was suddenly beside my mother, green eyes sparkling. "You don't look so good."

I nodded my agreement, but it set the world spinning. "Not much you can do for me unless you're secretly a surgeon. I'm pretty torn up in here. Where are the boys?"

"Waiting by the truck."

"Let's load up then. What about you?" I asked Bijan as I shifted my weight and reached for Ciara's shoulder.

"I will see to my people. If you could send Ashkān to me, please."

On top of the pain, the cold was creeping up from my bare

feet, and the thin cotton of the shift did little to help. I leaned heavily on Ciara and together we moved slowly for the truck. Around us, manticores were landing, and I could see at least six of them now, plus Bijan. They were all bloody. Behind them, Sabina came, circling low before setting down beside us.

She helped Ciara get me into the truck's cab, then went to help Cambious up into the back where I could hear Peter and Ashkān saying their goodbyes. I drifted in and out as everyone else got settled in and when I looked up, my mother was in the driver's seat. "Where?" I asked

"To get you taken care of, then home."

I nodded my agreement. I'd like that. Home. It seemed a lifetime since we'd left.

CHAPTER 32
FREEDOM

I could hear my mother and Sabina talking about the wisdom of trusting anyone this close to the Kourt. I blinked and lifted my head. We were parked outside what seemed to be a hospital, Mom and Sabina standing on my side of the truck with the door partially open. It dawned on me slowly that my mother was wearing clothes that were not what she had been wearing.

I felt sluggish, probably the blood loss. The side of the shift was soaked through and there was blood on the seat.

"May not have a choice," I slurred. "Bleeding out over here."

"I'll take her and Peter in," my mother said. "You stay out here, keep an eye on Cambious and the other boy."

"Reyansh," I offered.

"Yes, Reyansh." My mother pulled the door open and slipped her hand behind my back. Gently she guided me to my feet and supported me as she called out for Peter to join her. We were halfway to the doors under the giant sign that I assumed meant "Emergency" in whatever the local language was when someone saw us and came running with a gurney.

The man lifted me easily and then we were running, and I felt dizzy before we stopped. My mother vanished and in her place were several men and women in green scrubs and hands all over my torn-up body. I remember screaming at one point, my back arching up off the bed and being held down. I managed to answer some of their questions before I passed out again.

I don't know how long I was out, but I could tell, as I started to wake up that they had drugged me to keep me under. I also felt nicely insulated from the pain. When I opened my eyes, I found my mother in the chair beside my bed, her hand on mine. Her eyes were closed, her face peaceful.

"Welcome back to the land of the living," Cambious said from my other side.

I turned to look at him, and even with the glamor in place, I could see that he had fed, and hopefully, slept. "You look better. How long was I out?"

He shook his head lightly. "Not long, they had to operate to get the bleeding under control."

I had figured that much out, though it didn't feel like I'd been operated on. "You should be up and around soon." He pointed up to an IV bag of blood that was nearly empty. "Our teenage friend was a match; she was happy to donate."

"I thought I heard voices." I looked up to find a woman in a lab coat at the door. "I'm Dr. Straub, I was the one who patched up your insides."

"Thanks for that, Doc," I said. "I feel almost as good as new."

My mother squeezed my hand, and I glanced her way.

"You should take it easy the next few days. I'll set you up with a course of antibiotics, to stave off any chance of infection, but I think as soon as that IV is done, we can cut you loose."

I waited until she left the room to shake my head. "We need your medical knowledge back home. I'd probably still be halfway to dead back there."

Mom moved to sit on the bed, brushing a hand over my forehead. "Without the magic, we aren't that much more advanced."

I gestured at Cambious. "Tell him that. We're nowhere near being able to do that kind of thing."

Mom chuckled. "Well, true. But it was more than Dr. Straub's magical training that saved you."

We were all quiet for a long moment, ignoring the fact that we had somehow managed the impossible. "What about the Brotherhood?" I asked softly.

Cambious inhaled deeply and let it out slowly. "Reports are still coming in, but between the phoenix and the manticores, I'd say we hurt them badly. There are some survivors here, or there were, I'm not sure anymore."

"The military has moved in to clean up the mess. I guess they finally decided to enforce the law." My mother's voice was bitter. I guess she had a right to be.

"The manticores?"

"As far as I know, all gone back to their homelands," Cambious said. "Apparently, we interrupted their plans for a rebellion." He chuckled, leaning back in the chair. "To hear Bijan tell the story, anyway."

"And the kids?"

"With Ciara and Sabina. We thought it best to not flaunt the idea that we have a dragon kid and a phoenix. Some of our people aren't fond of...well, folks who are different."

"Okay, so what's next?" I asked.

"Merry is on her way to take you, your mother, Ciara, and Peter back to her place. She has connections that can help us find their families and get them home. Sabina and I will see Reyansh home," Cambious said.

"So, it's just...over?"

Cambious shook his head and stood. "Remember Sybyl's words, it may be over for now, but as she said, hate will grow back. I'll give you two some time alone."

My mother held my hand as he left, smiling softly down on me. "I thought I would never see you again. And when I saw you there, I thought it was another one of his tricks."

"I'm sorry," I whispered.

"Sorry?"

"I didn't come sooner, that you were there so long."

She shook her head. "I'm the one who is sorry, Thána. I never wanted to leave you like that, but I was convinced it was the only way to get them off your scent."

"I did okay." I wasn't going to tell her how angry I'd been at her when I'd discovered that she had blocked my memory, hidden my gifts. I could see the pain in her eyes. "And I've kind of had a crash course in magic since Finneas Connor showed up in my life. Though I have to tell you, it was a bit of a disappointment to discover that the magical land on the other side of that closet door looked a lot like home."

"You were expecting what? Something like the Lord of the Rings?"

"Something like that." I shook my head. So much had changed. "So, we go home? Back to the house in California?"

"We could. But we should go get your sister first."

"Did you wipe her memory too?" I asked, feeling a little jealous that she had likely had more time with our mother than I did.

"No, though she might have been better off. And she was more than a little angry with me when I left her."

"Where is she?"

My mother sighed and stood up to pace the room. "Through another portal, in a land they call Vaneesh. We stumbled on the portal when we were up in the Amerin mountains and thinking that it would get us back to you, and get the Brotherhood off our trail, we went through. Only the world on the other side of that portal was not the one where we had left you. I was so tired of the running. You would have been about thirteen, I guess. We'd been running for almost seven years."

"So, you stayed?"

She nodded. "Yeah, for a long while." She came back to the chair and sank into it. "The Brotherhood didn't make an appearance for almost ten years. By then we were settled into this apartment I loved, and we had friends, some of them in rather high levels of the government. Those first few men just kind of disappeared. Then they stopped coming."

"But eventually you left her?"

"Eventually. She was married, with a son. I wanted to check in on you, and see if the Brotherhood's power here had waned. I told her I'd be back. She knew better though. She has your father's gift of seeing into the future. We fought and I left."

"How long ago?"

"At least two years, on that side of the portal. I think. Time is different there, and it's easy to lose track of time when you're being tortured."

I could believe that to be true. I'd only had a taste of what she'd endured. "So, we go get her. Then we go home." I yawned, but I didn't want to sleep. I wanted to spend time with this woman I had fought so hard to get to.

"Sleep, Thána. We have all the time in the world now that we're together again." Her hand brushed lightly across my face and as if her words were a spell, my eyes closed even though I wanted to keep them open.

When I woke, Cambious was back with clothing for me, and a bag filled with takeout sandwiches. "They aren't great, but you'll want them on the road. Merry and your mother are downstairs."

I was happy to see that I was no longer bound to an IV, and while I was still sporting a few bandages, I felt great. Maybe great is an overstatement, but I certainly didn't feel as though it had been less than twenty-four hours since I had been shot and stabbed in the gut with wrought iron. I put my feet to the floor and stood, a little wobbly but otherwise just fine. There wasn't even a twinge in the ankle I had sprained. "Yeah, I think I like the doctors of your world a whole lot more than the ones back home."

Cambious chuckled. "You say that now but wait until you have to find one to reattach your...never mind. Get dressed. I'll wait outside."

I pulled on the jeans he'd brought and realized that they must have been the clothes I'd left at Merry's when we ran, because they were my own, as was the shirt. The shoes were new though, because those were somewhere in the Kourt, probably on the floor of that medical ward, where they had cut my clothes off of me. They looked sturdy enough and though a little stiff, they fit well. Once I was dressed, I grabbed the bag of sandwiches and met Cambious in the hallway.

"Merry took care of the bill," Cambious said as he led me to a bank of elevators. "She still feels really guilty about dumping your brain box the way she did."

"She should." I wasn't angry anymore. In fact, I was kind of grateful. Who knew if we would have succeeded without it? "You're looking well fed." If I didn't know better, I would have said he blushed, but it's hard to tell on skin as dark as his.

"Yes, I am."

I raised an eyebrow but didn't press further. I didn't need to know who he was getting his meals with, though I was beginning to think it was Sabina, just from the way he wouldn't meet my eyes. My mother gathered me to her side almost as soon as the elevator doors opened, escorting me to the front door where Merry waited beside a beat-up old car with one red door and one blue fender while everything else was a dark green.

We didn't talk much as Merry took us from the hospital to the hotel where the others were waiting for us. Reyansh ran for me before I'd even cleared the door of the room, wrapping his arms around me, and burying his face in my shirt.

"Hey, Reyansh, I'm fine," I comforted as best I could, eventually peeling him off of me so I could sit on one of the beds. I felt great, but I seemed to be tiring easily. Reyansh climbed up to sit beside me, taking my hand in his. It was nice to see him dressed in something more than that brown jacket Peter had given him.

"You're really okay?" Peter asked, his face showing his worry. He too was wearing new clothes and he had a little more color in his face than the last time I'd seen him.

I nodded. "Good as new. Better even because we got out."

If I was honest with myself, I had never really expected we would. But here we were. Now we just had to worry about the ones that survived and seeing everyone home to their families. "What do we know about the Brotherhood?" I asked, putting an arm around Reyansh.

Sabina stood away from the corner where she'd been leaning, clad in dark red jeans and a deep orange shirt. The combination played up her natural coloring. "I did a recon flight earlier. The Kourt is basically deserted, the only activity was some military firefighters putting out the last of the fire. I guess most of the residential area was destroyed, some of the walls collapsed on that side."

"Survivors?" I asked.

She nodded. "I'd estimate a couple dozen escaped the Kourt, and there are probably a number of them who were off on missions."

"What about *Patoras* Javonic?"

"We aren't sure," Cambious said. "Sabina said he was caught in the fire, but identifying the dead is going to take a while."

Mom came to sit on the opposite bed. "We're safe enough, for now. Even if he lives through this, it is going to take them time to recover, and at least now we have the government of Otadž involved. Their new Premier has vowed to extinguish the Brotherhood."

"Well, I guess all that's left is to get these kids home."

"If we have a home left," Ciara said. I hadn't even seen her over by the bathroom door. "The Brotherhood killed my mother when they came for me. I haven't seen my dad in years. He left when we learned what I was."

Merry cupped a hand to her face. "If there is no home left, you are welcome in mine, *paidí*."

I stifled a yawn.

"Do I have to?" Reyansh asked into the silence left hanging around us.

"Have to what?" I asked.

"Go, with them. I want to stay with you."

My mother came to kneel in front of him. "A dragon belongs with his own people, there is no place for you where we're going."

I kissed the top of his head. "Mom and I have something we need to do, but when we come back, I'll have Cambious bring me to visit you, how about that?"

"Really?" He brightened considerably.

"Yes, really."

Cambious nodded to Sabina. "I think that's our cue. Come on Reyansh, I'll race you to the car."

CHAPTER 33
RECOVERY

Before we left for Merry's house, Mom and I went back to the Kourt. I needed to see for myself. The place was deserted in the late afternoon, charred remains still smoldering in places. Smoke lurked along the stone floors and clung to doorways.

Whatever was left of the Brotherhood had gone into hiding, so there was no one to lay claim to the property. We picked our way past the ruins of the platform where they were going to kill me and into the marble-floored hall.

The place where I had first met Patorus was marked with black where the fire had burned the blood I'd left behind. I turned away from it and turned down the hallway that I thought would lead me to the library.

The walls of the hallway were blackened, and the fire had burned away all of the wood doorways and tapestries. I had a vague notion that the Brotherhood had filled their library with all of the books they had forbidden others.

The library doors had burned away, and the damage inside was extensive. What hadn't been destroyed by fire was water-logged and smoke damaged. I stopped beside the window that I had led the children out through. "He saved my life once," I said into the silence.

"Who did?" my mother asked.

I turned to face her. "The tracker. Do you remember? When the Brotherhood caught up to us at a rest stop, but we got away?"

She nodded.

"They were using a young boy then as their blood tracker, but they hadn't broken him yet. He drew them away so I could get back to the car." I sighed. "I can't imagine what they did to him after, but the blood tracker who caught me was the same boy."

I wandered over to the least damaged section of the library, trailing a finger along the spines of books, eyes scanning titles. My finger tingled as I touched on a particular book, and I pulled it down. If nothing else, I'd had a crash course in trusting my instincts in recent weeks.

The book was old and permeated with smoke, its black cover faded and the pages inside it were like creamy old parchment, thick and elegant. With a provocative title like "Blood Magic," I had to believe that it was something that could help me find my way.

I tucked the book up under my arm and continued perusing titles. I ended up with a book on portal construction and a grimoire of defensive and offensive magics titled "The Dark Art of War" that promised to teach me to be a better protector.

I came out from between the shelves to find my mother holding a burn-damaged book with a forlorn look on her face. "You okay?"

She held the book up, letting the burned pages flutter. "It was one of the foremost books on blood witches and their peculiar type of magic. Probably the only copy still in existence. The rest of the shelf this was on is ashes."

I shrugged and showed her my haul. "I found some interesting books, so not a total loss." I suddenly remembered the collection of books in the storeroom Cambious and I had made our way through, where we had found Peter. "They may have more."

I let instinct guide me through the smokey ruins, down into the underground levels, and back to that storeroom.

My mother gasped as her eyes swept the shelves. She grabbed at the books, stacking them until she could hardly hold them. I took several as well, so she wouldn't try to carry even more. I gestured toward the stairs with my chin. "We should probably get moving. Sun will be down in a while, and we don't want to get caught here after dark."

Merry's car waited for us just inside the destroyed gate. I tossed my books in the back seat and climbed in beside my mother. "I am very proud of you, Thána," Mom said as she started the engine. "So very proud."

I was uncomfortable with the sentiment and muttered a thank you in barely audible tones. We headed for the graveyard, leaving the smoldering ruins of the Kourt behind us. As we neared the gate in the outer wall, Mom slowed us down.

All around us, the air shimmered with ghosts hovering over their graves, arms raised as if to thank us for returning their home to them. Tears burned at the corner of my eyes when the ghost who had kept us safe on our overnight in the Kourt stepped closer. She was more solid than most of the others, and her gratitude was obvious on her face.

I raised a hand to acknowledge them before Mom took us out onto the road and toward the hotel where we would spend one more night before heading back to Merry's.

The morning saw us all up early, dressed, and ready to hit the road. Peter was taking it in stride, though he seemed sad to be without his friend Ashkān. Ciara was quiet and sulking, though I suppose I would sulk in her position too.

I sat behind my mother, with Peter between me and Ciara, one of my stolen books in hand. It wasn't written specifically for blood witches, but it did go in depth on the theory of blood magic that could be done by other witches and had notes in a tiny, neat hand about alterations for blood witches.

Like so much else I had learned over the last few months, the more I read the more I realized I had to learn. It was a good thing I now had time to learn it, and eager teachers in my mother and Merry.

I spent most of that drive buried in the book, devouring it, and making plans to start testing some of the spells in it once we got back to Merry's. I dozed off at some point and woke to the smell of rain. The world outside our window was gray and wet, but I could tell we were almost to Merry's house.

It startled me, as our drive to the Kourt took much longer. "How long was I asleep?" I asked groggily.

Mom turned to look at me. "Quite a while, I'm afraid. You didn't even wake up when we stopped to switch drivers."

"Must have needed it. Maybe it's the near-death experience." I stretched, yawning and shifting, which woke Peter who had been lying against me. "Sorry."

He blinked at me blearily but smiled.

We made the turn onto Merry's street and into her driveway. Zo was waiting on the porch, rushing out to greet her mother and then mine. "I thought we'd never see you again."

My mother's smile was sad as she accepted the hug. "I am here now, thanks to Thána."

Zo pulled me into the hug too. "Thank you for bringing my favorite cousin home to me."

"No sweat," I replied, gently pulling free. I wasn't comfortable with displays of affection. "Um, this is Ciara and Peter. They helped too." Peter hid behind me, but Ciara nodded in greeting.

"Let's get everyone settled in," Merry said, making motions toward the house. "Zo, put on the kettle, we'll be wanting some tea."

Mom slid her arm around me as if I needed her support to go into the house. I didn't pull away, though I kind of wanted to. For all of the work to get her there, I still only barely knew her.

The next hour or so saw us making sleeping arrangements. Merry's house was bigger than I had imagined it, with enough bedrooms for everyone to have their own.

Once that was decided, I settled at the kitchen table with my book on blood magic in an effort to stay out of the way while Merry and Zo made dinner. The front door opened a few minutes later, and two women who looked a lot like Zo came in all aflutter.

"Is it true?" one of them asked as Zo went to greet them. "Is she here?"

The older of the two dropped several shopping bags as my mother joined them, grabbing my mother into a big hug. "If by she, you mean me, yes," Mom said, pulling the other woman into the hug too. "It is so good to see you! Thána, come here. I want to introduce you."

I inhaled and let it out slowly before I stood and went to meet them. "Thána, these are two of Merry's daughters. This is Zeph and this is Zelda. Merry really likes the letter Z. And this is my eldest daughter, Thána."

I smiled and nodded my head. "Pleasure to meet you both."

"Zo called and let us know you needed clothes, so of course, we just cleaned out our closets for you," Zelda said. She had Merry's eyes and a sprinkle of gray highlighting her black hair.

"And I pulled some things out of storage for the girl and the boy," Zeph added. "What were their names again?"

Right about then, Peter appeared on the stairs. "This is Peter," I said, nodding for him that it was okay. "These are cousins of mine, Peter. They brought you some clothes."

Zeph picked up one of the bags and passed it to Peter. "These might be a bit big on you, but they'll do."

"Thank you," Peter said, his voice small.

Mom drew her cousins into the living room, and I returned to my book, but as word spread, more and more relatives appeared, and I realized that I wasn't going to get any reading accomplished. I took the book back to my room, stopping outside Peter's door. He was sitting on the floor with Ciara, working with some ward stones.

Ciara looked up at me and rolled her eyes. "I couldn't deal with all of those people, so I figured I could teach Peter some magic."

"I hear you. I spent most of my adult life thinking I had no family. To suddenly be awash in them is overwhelming."

"Most of my family is gone, one way or another," Ciara said, her face sad.

"I have a lot of family," Peter said once he'd gotten the stones activated. "I miss them."

I rubbed a hand in his hair and gave him a smile. "Tomorrow we start finding them so we can get you home. We just have to survive this family reunion."

Family. It was such a foreign concept. But Merry's living room and dining room were full of it. There were cousins, aunts, and uncles. And they were all keen to know me.

With a sigh, I headed back down the stairs, slipping into the living room where Mom was telling a story about the world where she and Daria had been living.

She looked up at me, her eyes shining with love, and held out her hand. I went to her and took her hand, sinking to the couch beside her. "Thána, this handsome fella is your uncle Christophe and his lovely daughter Emily."

"Hello." My uncle Christophe was a mountain of a man, easily six foot five, with broad shoulders and a full beard that came to his chest. Emily was a slight young woman by comparison, thin and short, with red-brown hair and glasses. It felt like the whole room was staring at me, expecting me to speak. "Um, I guess you want to know about me?"

"Well, you are a bit of a mystery to us," Zeph said.

"Not so much a mystery. I'm just a mid-level corporate manager who discovered I was a witch and followed an incubus into a land where magic is real."

"Oh, there's a story or five in that." I looked at the speaker, an older woman with gray hair cut in a short bob whose name I couldn't remember.

I shook my head. "Some Brotherhood thugs attacked me, I came through the portal, and here I am."

"I hear you all but demolished the Brotherhood," Emily said. "Is it true?"

I shrugged. "Well, their leader is not likely to live for long. He was pretty badly burned. There were a fair number of them killed or injured, but they'll regroup. Or that's what Sybyl said."

I was uncomfortable being the center of attention and I shifted my weight a little as if it would help. "You should write a book about it," Christophe said. "We have several authors in the family."

I put a hand on my side where my injury was and yawned. "I'm pretty wiped out. Still healing, you know. I'm going to go lay down."

Mom stood with me, walking me toward the stairs. "Are you okay?"

I nodded. "Just tired. And overwhelmed."

She kissed my cheek. "I understand. Let me know if you need anything."

I wanted to say that I was a big girl now and had been taking care of myself for a long time, but I didn't, just left her standing at the bottom of the stairs.

I don't know how long the house was filled with people, but it went well into the night. The air was filled with voices and laughter and punctuated with singing from time to time.

Idly, as I lay there, I wondered about the house in California, and my father's ghost who had told me to find my mother. I still wasn't sure how the ghost thing worked, but I couldn't help but wonder if he knew somehow that I had found her.

California felt like a lifetime ago as I lay there, staring at the wall. I had no idea when or if we would go back. Mom wanted to go to Daria, but she had mentioned that the portal was quite a hike from where she could park a car, so she wanted me to recover more before we made the trek.

Who knew what would follow that? Would we end up staying there? Would we come back here? There were no solid answers. Just the looming questions and familial obligations.

A NOTE FROM THE AUTHOR:

This book has been a labor of love, which I know is cliché as all get out, but this character has become a friend, and she has a lot of me in her DNA.

I love that this genre, and the world of publishing as it is today, allow me to play with characters like these and create worlds like this for us to frolic through. These characters are diverse by design, without apology. All genders, all orientations, and all races are represented (or even made up) and magic brings them together.

I hope you enjoyed this journey and will come along for the sequels.

Thank you!

Natalie J. Case

GLOSSARY OF TERMS

A

Adelfí: Sister
Aderfia: Brothers
Ánoixe: Open
Ánoixe kleídoma aímatos: Open this lock by my blood
Apokalýpto: Reveal

C

Kravu: Cow

D

Dimiourgió: Break

E

Ekleípo: Disappear (used with ward stones)
Éla: Come

Elefthérosi: Release
Evlogim Patoras: Second Father

F

Ftiáxe mia porta: Open a door

I

Irémise: Quiet

K

Kapnastís: Disease eater
Kleidóste sto aíma mou: Lock to my blood
Kontá: Close
Krývo: Hide

M

Mágissa: witch
Makrá vlépinta: Ability of a blood witch to see past/future
Mikros: Little one

P

Páfsi: Pause
Paidí: Child
Pigaíno: Go
Prostatévo: Protect

S

Slúga: Servant
Sýnchysi: Confusion

T

Teíchos: Wall
Thanátou: Death bringer, angel of death
Thráfsi: Break

X

Xekleídoma: Unlock

Y

Yperaspízo: Defend
Ýpnos: Sleep

ABOUT THE AUTHOR

 An avid reader since kindergarten, Natalie had read her way through the children's and young adult section of the library by nine years old, and during the summer spent most of her days scouring the library for something new to read. When the Librarian handed her The Hobbit the summer before she turned ten, thinking it would be enough to keep the girl out of the library for a few days at least, a whole new world opened up. Natalie devoured the tome and returned it to the library the very next day, wanting to know that there was more like it.

With a love of vampires and other paranormal types, Natalie infuses her fiction with magic and mythological beings, and explores the sometimes vanishing line between good and evil. Natalie makes her home in Walnut Creek, California with her two cats, Morrigan and Freya, and occasionally a stray cat she calls Artemis.

———

To learn more about Natalie J. Case and discover more Next Chapter authors, visit our website at www.nextchapter.pub.

Thanátou
ISBN: 978-4-82414-494-2

Published by
Next Chapter
2-5-6 SANNO
SANNO BRIDGE
143-0023 Ota-Ku, Tokyo
+818035793528

4th August 2022